INSPECTOR SINGH INVESTIGATES

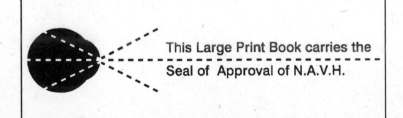

INSPECTOR SINGH
INVESTIGATES

A MOST PECULIAR MALAYSIAN MURDER

SHAMINI FLINT

THORNDIKE PRESS
A part of Gale, Cengage Learning

GALE
CENGAGE Learning

Detroit • New York • San Francisco • New Haven, Conn • Waterville, Maine • London

GALE
CENGAGE Learning·

Thorndike Press® Large Print Basic.
The text of this Large Print edition is unabridged.
Other aspects of the book may vary from the original edition.
Set in 16 pt. Plantin.

LIBRARY OF CONGRESS CATALOGING-IN-PUBLICATION DATA

Flint, Shamini, 1969–
    Inspector Singh investigates : a most peculiar Malaysian murder / by Shamini Flint.
        p. cm. — (Thorndike Press large print basic)
    ISBN-13: 978-1-4104-3156-1
    ISBN-10: 1-4104-3156-8
    1. Police—Singapore—Fiction. 2. Singaporeans—Malaysia—Kuala Lumpur—Fiction. 3. Murder—Investigation—Malaysia—Kuala Lumpur—Fiction. 4. Kuala Lumpur (Malaysia)—Fiction. 5. Large type books. I. Title.
PR6106.L56I57 2010b
813'.6—dc22   2010029277

Published in 2010 by arrangement with St. Martin's Press.

Printed in the United States of America
1 2 3 4 5 6 7 14 13 12 11 10

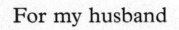

For my husband

'It is a far, far better thing that I do, than I have ever done; it is a far, far better rest that I go to than I have ever known.'

(A Tale of Two Cities, Charles Dickens)

'Merdeka! Merdeka! Merdeka!'

(Proclamation of independence by Tunku Abdul Rahman, first Prime Minister of Malaya on 31 August 1957)

ONE

The accused, Chelsea Liew, was in court. She sat on a wooden bench in a wooden box, handcuffed to a police woman.

The prosecutor, a large, shiny Malay man, marking time until his own elevation to the Bench, watched the court official read out the charge in a slow, ponderous voice, 'That you, Chelsea Liew, on or about the eighteenth day of July, committed murder by causing the death of Alan Lee.'

The judge said, 'How does the accused plead? Guilty or *not* guilty?'

The shrivelled old man with large, yellow, herbivorous teeth and a thick head of implausibly black hair managed to inject a wealth of disbelief into the possibility of a not guilty plea. Many of the judges in Malaysia were drawn from the civil service, which meant they had previously been public prosecutors themselves. Their instincts were conservative and their sympathies rarely with the accused in criminal trials.

Chelsea's lawyer, a tall, thin Indian man with a large Adam's apple bobbing above his white, winged collar, struggled for diplomatic words that would not involve criticising any party for whom the judge had sympathy — basically, everyone except his client. 'My lord, the evidence is circumstantial. The police and prosecution have rushed to judgement because this is a high profile case. The charges should be dismissed outright.'

Teeth were exposed in a parody of a smile. The judge, hunched over his elevated table, black gown bunched about his shoulders, looked more like a vulture than a member of the Bench. He said, 'Guilty or not guilty?'

The lawyer recognised a lost cause. He stole a quick nervous glance at the woman in the dock. At last the accused muttered, 'Not guilty.' Her lawyer sighed with relief.

The judge rapped his gavel. 'Accused to be remanded in custody until trial dates fixed.'

Her defence lawyer made one last attempt to assist his client. 'My lord, this is an unusual case involving a mother of three. Although bail is not usually granted where the charge is murder . . .'

He was interrupted. 'Application for bail denied!'

The judge stood and the lawyers, members of the public in the gallery and court staff rose hastily to their feet. No one was permitted to sit in the august presence of the law. Even, thought the lawyer angrily, if it was personified by an incompetent, semi-senile old man with a stunted sense of justice. Gown billowing, the judge walked out — his work done for the day.

Chelsea's lawyer slumped back into his chair, shoulders bowed. The prosecution team looked pleased. Only the accused did not react. Her anger and emotion had been spent long before her marriage had culminated in the murder of her husband. She stared at the ground between her feet. When a policewoman took her arm and led her out, she went without resisting.

Inspector Singh was wedged into a small plastic seat at Changi Airport. Hunched up, his belly compressed his lungs. His fleshy, sweaty knees were pressed together chastely to avoid inadvertent brushes with the people on either side. Inspector Singh had a strong dislike of physical contact with strangers. Unfortunately, his girth made it difficult for him not to encroach onto their seats. His

11

shirt was wilting and his shirt pocket, full of pens, was tearing slightly at the corner. Patches of damp were visible under his armpits and just above his belly. Only his white sneakers looked as fresh as when he had put them on before setting out for the office — blissfully unaware that he was about to be assigned to the case that he had, only that morning, been reading about in the newspapers. He remembered feeling sorry for the policeman who had the dismal task of finding the murderer of Alan Lee. He felt much sorrier now that he knew it was himself.

Inspector Singh was waiting for a flight to Kuala Lumpur. He sighed, a breathy, wheezy sound; a heavy smoker, his breathing always sounded strained. He needed a cigarette but smoking was prohibited indoors and pretty much everywhere else in Singapore. He wondered whether he dared nip outside for a fag. As much as he viewed his assignment in Malaysia with trepidation, he did not want to miss his queue number. Singh knew he would not be on the case if he was not the unofficial 'most likely to be forced into early retirement' entry in the Singapore police yearbook. He sighed again, causing his neighbour, a middle-aged white woman, to glance at him surreptitiously.

Singh knew what she was thinking. A dark man in a turban who seemed worried and preoccupied? She was hoping not to be on the same flight as him. Singh had neither the patience nor the inclination to explain to her that the six metres of cloth that he had wound around his head expertly that morning into a black, pointy turban reflected his heritage as a Sikh. It did not indicate terrorist proclivities and neither, for that matter, did anyone else's turban.

Singh felt his need for a cigarette sharpen. To hell with it. He would have to risk missing his flight. He felt in his trouser pocket for the reassuring rectangle of his cigarette packet and hauled himself with difficulty out of his seat. He wiped his forehead along the band of his turban with the back of his hand. It itched when he was hot.

He lumbered towards the exit and was brought up short by the sound of raised voices. He looked around with mild curiosity. It did not take him long to identify the source and cause of the altercation. Two men squaring-off. One white, the other Chinese. On the First Class carpet. It seemed that they had converged on the desk at the same moment and were now disputing right of way.

Singh really didn't feel like interfering. He

took a step towards the exit and then glanced back. He saw the long-suffering expressions on the faces of those queuing up to fly 'cattle' class and made up his mind. He moved silently towards the men, his sneakers muffling his approach. Not that they would have heard him anyway. They were so engrossed in shouting each other down. The white man was beefy and red-necked, his nose a mosaic of broken veins. The Chinese man was slim and fit, wearing the yuppie uniform of polo shirt and chinos, his expensive matching luggage in a heap by his side.

Singh walked up to the men standing almost toe to toe, placed a fat-fingered hand on each man's chest and shoved. They parted like the Red Sea. The white man tripped over the edge of the deep blue First Class carpet and barely avoided falling over. He said angrily, 'Who the hell do you think you are?'

The Chinese man nodded to second the question, his face contorted with rage. Singh was amused to see this united front between the erstwhile combatants.

He smiled pleasantly and said, 'Inspector Singh, Singapore Police Force.'

Both men looked disbelieving. Singh didn't blame them. He was an overweight, sweaty, hairy, unconvincing example of a policeman.

He asked, 'So what's this about?'

'He took my place in the queue!'

'No! He cut in front of me.'

The pretty woman behind the check-in counter rolled her eyes at Singh.

Singh looked at the two men, one eyebrow raised thoughtfully.

Then he turned his back abruptly on them and walked over to the Economy queue. He counted out the first ten and beckoned to them imperiously. The passengers looked doubtful but succumbed to Singh's air of authority and followed him. He gestured to the First Class check-in and they lined up quietly, one tiny woman in a *saree* saying sheepishly, 'But I only have an economy ticket.'

'Not to worry, madam,' said Singh politely.

He turned to the two men, 'You two — at the back of this line.'

'What do you mean?' blustered the Caucasian.

'You heard me, get in line here.'

'Behind all these people?'

'Yup.'

'You can't do that!' It was the Chinese man.

'I've just done it . . .'

'I'll have your badge for this!' he stammered angrily.

Singh grinned, suddenly happy. He said, 'There's a long queue for that too!'

He waddled back towards his seat, ticket stub between clammy fingers. There was no time left for a cigarette. But it had been worth it.

Forty-five minutes later he was on the plane, sitting next to an elderly Malay man wearing a white shift, open sandals and a neat, white, round turban on his head. The Malay man grinned at Singh as he sat down, baring sparse, long teeth clinging to red, receding gums. But after a brief inquiry had elicited that his companion was Singaporean, the older man lost interest and slumped back in his chair.

The plane juddered and Singh looked nervously out of the window. He could see the coastline of Peninsular Malaysia. Singapore, a small island separated from the Malaysian mainland by a thin strip of water, the Straits of Johor, and connected by two bridges, had disappeared from view.

He forced his mind back to the matter at hand — the reason for this unexpected trip to Malaysia. He had the file in his briefcase but he did not take it out. There was no privacy on board the aircraft to be reading the details. Besides, he knew the skimpy facts by heart. It was the depth of passion running beneath the surface that had occupied the newspapers in Malaysia and Singapore for the last couple of weeks and promised to make the case a nightmare. Inspector Singh's superiors had decided that the poisoned chalice would be his. From their point of view it was a splendid choice. If he managed to find a way through the thicket of politics overwhelming the case, they would claim the credit. If he failed, they would hang him out to dry, pleased to get rid of one of the last mavericks in the Singapore police. His was not an organisation that appreciated instinct over method, results over means, footwork over paperwork. He was the elephant in the room that no one talked about but everyone hoped would do the decent thing and take early retirement. As he had not done it so far, he was on a small plane, enduring a bumpy flight, to a town up in arms.

Inspector Singh was quite convinced there was absolutely no possibility of a successful resolution to the case he had just been handed. There never was when religion trumped rational behaviour and politics influenced police work. Malaysia and Singapore were both former British colonies, once part of the same country but now two suspicious and independent neighbours. For both countries, every act of state by the other was potentially a threat or an insult. The tabloid press and politicians in both countries were competing for airtime by issuing the most inflammatory statements. There was talk of 'unwarranted interference in domestic affairs' by Malaysian officials. Singapore officialdom had adopted a superior tone about 'justice being seen to be done'.

And yet, thought Inspector Singh, the historical and family ties that bound the two nations together were stronger than the disputes that divided them. But that just exacerbated every disagreement between the countries. Between Malaysia and Singapore, there was none of the polite distance and formal dispute resolution of strangers — every difference of opinion was a family feud. And there were all too many opinions being vented in newspapers and online about his new case.

The plane came in to land over undulating hills covered in neat grids of oil palm. Singh caught a glimpse of the Formula One racetrack — yet another project by the previous government to drag Malaysia onto the world stage. Mahathir, the previous prime minister, was convinced that as long as he built the biggest, the best and the most expensive of everything, Malaysia would be treated with respect by the international community. Predictably, Malaysia had instead become a byword for the funding and construction of white elephants.

Singh walked towards the trains linking the Kuala Lumpur International Airport terminal building and the arrival hall. The ceiling above was lit with hundreds of small lights intended to look like the stars at night. He had read somewhere that a computer program had been used to locate the lights randomly and so no pattern was detectable. He scowled. Programmed randomness struck him as an oxymoron. He caught the connecting train and was further irritated. It was automated — did not have a driver. Inspector Singh had spent a career exploring the fallibility of man but he preferred the risk of human error to the certainty of electronic indifference to his well-being. Moments later, he stepped out of the air-conditioned coolness of the terminal into the sweltering tropical heat.

Singh strolled to the massed ranks of Mercedes Benz and climbed into the back of the first one. The Malay driver — almost all the drivers on the authorised limousine service were Malay — had an unkempt, wispy, black beard. His car on the other hand was immaculate. A verse of the Quran was plastered on the rear window. Inspector Singh did not read Arabic but he knew the expression was 'There is no God but Allah and Muhammad is his only Prophet'. Across the glove compartment there was another sticker with the words 'You'll Never Walk Alone' emblazoned next to a logo of Liverpool Football Club.

Noticing the inspector looking at it, the driver asked, 'You Liverpool supporter?'

Inspector Singh watched continuous cricket coverage on the cable cricket channel in Singapore. But he felt mischievous and said, 'No, Manchester United.' He had forgotten that United was no longer the hate figure of the football world.

The driver nodded sympathetically. 'Very hard now for other teams. Chelsea boss got all the money.' He guffawed, exposing two rows of gold fillings that Singh could see glinting in the rearview mirror. 'Last time, what is important is who wins the game. Now what is important is who has the richest boss. *Bagi orang kaya trophy sahaja!*' Give the rich man the trophy right away!

Inspector Singh laughed and then pulled out the newspaper he had picked up on the plane and settled down to read the latest on the matter that had brought him to Kuala Lumpur.

Two

'There is nothing for you to do here! I don't know why you came. The Malaysian police can handle everything. You should go back now.' The speaker's moustache, a neat black brush with flecks of grey, bristled angrily as he shouted at the man across the desk from him. His eyes, under straight, thick brows, glared at the inspector from a nut-brown face.

Inspector Singh remained expressionless. He said, 'You have no choice and I have no choice. So we can do this the easy way or the hard way.' Seeing that the Malaysian Superintendent of Police was unmoved by this call to reason he added, 'After all, neither of us wants to see a miscarriage of justice.'

The officer did not respond. He sat at his desk, drumming his fingers on the table in an impatient tattoo. His desktop was devoid of anything that looked work related. Perhaps, thought Singh, the higher-ups in Malaysia merely waited around behind big, empty desks until there was an opportunity to throw their weight around with some foreign cop. He knew from his own experience in Singapore that the further up the ladder one got, the more the job was about politics and statistics than actually dealing with crime.

The Malaysian policeman was waiting for some reaction from his Singaporean counterpart. Singh wondered if he was expected to acknowledge the wisdom of the man's remarks, pick up his bags and head back to Singapore with his tail between his legs. Surely it was obvious that his superiors in Singapore had more leverage over him than the officer glowering at him across the desk? Still, if there was a waiting game to be played, Inspector Singh was a past master. He sat nonchalantly in the chair, eyeing a display of plastic flowers in a plastic vase.

The Malaysian was the first to blink. He stood up, walked over to a filing cabinet, slid open a drawer and took out a large folder.

He said, 'I do not like it but certain quarters have demanded that I cooperate. This is what we have done so far. We have the wife in custody. You can see her if you like. You can interview any other person in Malaysia but only if they agree. We cannot make anyone talk to you. I will send you my ADC. He will assist you.'

And watch my every move and report back to you, thought the inspector, but he did not say anything. This was a higher level of cooperation, however reluctant, than he had expected. Pressure must have been brought to bear at the highest levels. He nodded his thanks to the scowling man and picked up the folder.

The Malaysian leaned forward and put two splayed hands on the table. He said, 'One more thing: if you overstep your authority, I will put you in the jail cell next to the accused. And I don't think the Singapore government will send anyone to rescue you!'

Inspector Singh nodded cheerfully, assuming correctly that amusement would be the response that his opposite number would find most infuriating. He wondered when Malaysian officialdom would get over its need to indulge in theatrical bullying.

A few strides later he was out of the door. The muffled sound of footsteps caused him to turn round and he saw a young policeman hurrying after him. Singh stopped and waited.

'Sir!' A smart salute accompanied the greeting. 'I am Sergeant Shukor, aide-de-camp to Superintendent Khalid Ibrahim. He asked me to help you with this case.'

'Good. You can start by finding me a place to sit down and read this report,' ordered Inspector Singh. 'And then I'll need some tea.'

Inspector Singh lumbered after the young policeman assigned to be his minder and was shown into a small room with a desk and filing cabinet. He sat down heavily in the lone chair in the room which creaked a noisy protest. Singh swivelled around to look out of the heavily tinted glass windows behind him. On a field, a posse of young men dressed in blue shorts and white T-shirts were being put through their paces by a trainer whose booming voice could be heard faintly by the inspector. At least there was still an emphasis on fitness and not just computer skills in the police-training manual, he thought. As if to emphasise his own devotion to health, he lit a cigarette and wedged his large posterior more firmly into his chair.

He glanced at Sergeant Shukor, who was still standing smartly to attention. The young man had a tanned strong jaw, a broad flat nose and eyes that were slightly too widely spaced. If the sergeant has been a briefcase carrier his whole career, he could not have got his hands very dirty, thought the inspector. The Malaysian policeman's dark blue uniform was pressed to perfection and tight enough to grip muscular thighs and forearms. His regulation service revolver — shiny, black and dangerous — was neatly holstered.

Singh asked, 'So who is actually in charge of the Lee murder investigation?'

'Inspector Mohammad, sir.'

'Shouldn't I be talking to him before getting to work?'

The sergeant looked uncomfortable. He was remarkably transparent for a police officer. His emotions were both visible and decipherable as they flitted across his face.

Singh asked, 'What is it?'

'He was supposed to be here to meet you, sir. But he hasn't turned up.'

The inspector from Singapore grimaced. 'Not another Malaysian policeman with a bad attitude?'

'He's not exactly like that, sir.'

Singh was just about to probe deeper when there was a quiet knock on the door.

At a glance from the senior policeman, Shukor opened it.

A very tall man with thick, short, iron grey

hair and a thin, ascetic face walked in. He was dressed in an extremely smart, dark suit, wore a pale blue shirt and a darker blue tie and had cufflinks with a college crest on them. He looked like he belonged on the stage, playing a Shakespearean tragedy, or in a boardroom with lots of deferential subordinates agreeing to everything he said.

He said, 'Inspector Singh? I'm Inspector Mohammad. Thank you for coming down to help us poor Malaysians stumbling around in the dark on this case.'

His voice matched his looks — smooth and effortlessly classy. And his hostility was going to be subtle and difficult to overcome. Singh, suddenly conscious of his damp shirt and pot belly, took the cigarette out of his mouth and said, 'It's my pleasure, Inspector Mohammad.'

'Please call me Mohammad. We don't have time for formality if we're to work together.'

Inspector Singh nodded. 'I understand from the sergeant here that you're in charge of this case?'

'The murder of Alan Lee? Yes, I'm afraid so. Still, it seems a fairly open and shut case, doesn't it?'

Singh gestured to the pile of papers in front of him. 'I was just making myself familiar with the facts.'

Inspector Mohammad's lip curled. 'It's not pretty, I'm afraid. Well, I'd better leave you to it. Shukor here will get you anything you need and I'm in my office when you're done.'

He walked out, closing the door quietly behind him.

Inspector Singh whistled softly through pursed lips. He said, 'Now where did that come from?'

Sergeant Shukor did not pretend to misunderstand the question. 'He's from a very wealthy family, sir. Perak royalty, actually.'

Singh nodded his head. Nine of the thirteen states in Malaysia were former sultanates and had hereditary royalty. It meant that there were a lot of people who could claim to be royalty, or at least related to royalty, knocking about.

Shukor continued, 'He went to boarding school in England and has a doctorate from Cambridge in Criminal Psychology.'

'Then what's he doing here?'

'They say he loves the job and doesn't want to be promoted till it's all management and no police work.'

Inspector Singh could understand the reluctance to turn into a bureaucrat. He had the same instincts.

'They leave him alone, you see — because he's so well connected,' explained Shukor further.

Singh frowned. He was *not* well connected — and his higher-ups left him alone when it suited them, but not otherwise.

He set aside his curiosity about the Malaysian policeman, and said brusquely, 'Can you get me in to see the suspect?'

The young man nodded. 'Yes, sir. Inspector Mohammad said you would want to see her first so I have already arranged it.'

Good anticipation but he did not like the suggestion that he was predictable or predicted. 'I will see her in two hours. I will familiarise myself with the investigation first.'

The young man understood this to be a dismissal and saluted smartly. 'In that case, I will get you a cup of tea, sir.'

Inspector Singh looked around for an ashtray. There wasn't one. He dropped the fag end on the carpet and stamped it out hurriedly. The material covering the floor looked flammable. He kicked the butt under the desk. It was time to get down to work. He needed to find the quickest way out of this mess and back to Singapore. Singh untied the string that held the case file together and started to read.

The file heading was 'Chelsea Liew' and

in brackets were the words 'Singapore IC'. In that short reference was the whole reason for his being in Malaysia. Chelsea Liew was a Singapore citizen. She held a Singapore identity card. She had married a Malaysian and had lived in the Kuala Lumpur suburb of Bangsar for the last twenty years. She had three children who held Malaysian passports. But she was Singaporean. And she was accused of murdering her ex-husband. As a rule, the arrest of a Singaporean by any foreign country would not have involved the Singapore police. The embassy might have had a quick look if requested to ensure that the citizen in trouble was getting the rudiments of due process, but nothing more than that.

This case was different though. The religious overtones, custody battles, public outcry in both countries and political sensitivities between Malaysia and Singapore had resulted in a request by the Singapore government — keen to be seen to be doing something — to the Malaysian government — keen to be seen to be above the fray — that a Singaporean policeman be seconded to the investigation. So here he was, sitting in a grubby room in the Malaysian Police Bukit Aman headquarters, with a file three inches thick, feeling very sorry for himself.

Singh looked at the folder. He thought he recognised the efficiency of Sergeant Shukor in the neatly labelled piles of newspaper clippings, court transcripts and police interview notes. He was familiar with the essentials of the matter. But now he sat back in his protesting chair and let the full story unfold before him. The cup of tea Shukor had brought him sat untouched on the table.

THREE

From the day of their white wedding twenty years before, Chelsea Liew and her Malaysian husband, Alan Lee, had featured regularly in the gossip columns. Even Inspector Singh was aware of the beautiful Singaporean model swept off her feet in a whirlwind romance by the dashing Malaysian heir to a timber fortune. She had married her mogul and gone to live in a secluded bungalow with twenty-four-hour security and a car to match every dress. Singh stared at the faded newsprint of the happy couple. It was the Singapore equivalent of a royal wedding. Details of the matching placemats, the politicians in attendance and the estimated cost of the celebratory dinner for a thousand guests were dissected in depth in the newspapers. The wedding dress, especially made for her by a Parisian designer, had been imitated by almost every bride in Singapore that year.

The fairy tale of a poor but beautiful girl who had gone on to marry one of the most eligible bachelors in Malaysia had captured the public imagination. And through all the publicity, speculation and envy, the bride had looked serene and the groom proud.

Chelsea had given up her modelling career upon marriage. It was rumoured that she had wanted to continue working but her husband had put his foot down. They didn't need the money. There was no need for her to make an exhibition of herself. Singh vaguely remembered his own wife, she of the firm opinions and grim forebodings, had warned that no good ever came of a woman giving up her independence for a man. The inspector had been vaguely irritated by this. She, Mrs Singh, had promptly abandoned her job as a teacher on marrying him and never hinted at a desire to go back, not even when it became apparent that no children would be forthcoming from the marriage. Although to be fair, thought Singh, his wife had not given up her independence on their wedding day — she had merely confiscated his. Anyway, her bleak outlook for the couple had caused Singh to secretly wish the rich man and his trophy bride well. Perhaps this fairy-tale marriage would have a happy ending.

But it was his wife who was proved right. The gossip and innuendo had started almost immediately the honeymoon was over. Chelsea Liew was reported to have put on weight. Her husband was seen out on the town. She had an unexplained black eye. Instead of the radiant pictures of her smiling into the camera, magazines started to carry pictures of her turning away hurriedly or holding up her handbag to obscure her face. Then she had three difficult pregnancies and bore her husband three fine sons. There was a temporary respite in the steady drip of bad news. Alan Lee was reported to be ecstatic over the birth of his sons and heirs. She was briefly described as the perfect role model for mothers everywhere — devoted to her growing family.

His business dealings were also generating publicity. Alan Lee had taken over the family business upon his father's death, bypassing the elder brother, Jasper, who had rejected the timber business and become a wildlife activist — ensuring regular run-ins played out on the front pages of the Malaysian newspapers. Alan Lee was an important man in business and his patronage was sought by politicians. As Chelsea disappeared completely from the public eye, Alan Lee was often photographed with other women, described coyly as his friends or colleagues.

Finally, twenty years into the marriage, Chelsea had sued for divorce and sole custody of the children, alleging abuse and adultery. The accusations and counter-accusations were a large part of the file. The transcripts of the divorce proceedings, with both parties fighting tooth and nail for custody of the children, made vicious and ugly reading. Her medical records showed evidence of traumatic injuries consistent with beatings. Alan had insisted they were self-inflicted and the symptoms of a danger-ous, deranged woman who should not have the care of her children. She had, through her lawyers, asserted persistent adultery. He had looked sorry and insisted that he had just needed some comfort after his wife had turned on him. It did not affect his ability to be a good father.

Even the renegade brother, Jasper Lee, had testified — appearing on behalf of Chelsea. He claimed that Alan Lee, far from being a model parent, was an absent father whose business dealings were so tainted with criminality that he would be an unfit father for his children. Alan Lee's lawyers had done their best to discredit his brother on the grounds he was the frustrated black sheep of the family who, not content with breaking his father's heart by walking out on the family business, was now seeking revenge against the brother who had taken over. The youngest son of the family, Kian Min, had stepped in to contradict Jasper by testifying to Alan Lee's strong character and kind heart. This had caused some surprise. It was no secret that the youngest son had tried to persuade the father, when Jasper had walked out on the business, to give him control of Lee Timber. It had not been an unreasonable request. Alan was a playboy, pursuing beautiful women. He had not completed the engineering degree for which he had been sent to the United States and was always asking for money. The father was tempted to bypass his middle son in favour of the youngest.

But Alan, perhaps suspecting that he had pushed his luck far enough, had returned home in the nick of time, settled down with Chelsea, shown a tepid interest in the business and the rules of primogeniture had triumphed. It was implied in the newspapers that Kian Min, who still worked at the company but was barely on speaking terms with Alan, must have received quite a sweetener to perjure himself on behalf of his despised brother.

Public opinion favoured the wife when court was adjourned suddenly for two weeks. There was much speculation in the interim as to the reason for the sudden delay. Did Alan believe he was going to lose? Did he have a plan to kidnap the children and spirit them out of the country? Did she? And being Malaysia, there was the inevitable suggestion that the judge had an interest in reaching a particular outcome. After all, Alan Lee had money. And money had been known to subvert justice.

In the end, it was none of these things.

When court reconvened, Alan Lee dropped his bombshell. Sergeant Shukor had a flair for the dramatic because he had included the court transcript of proceedings and artist sketches of the main characters. Inspector Singh lit another cigarette and was soon absorbed in the courtroom drama.

The policeman intoned, *'Bangun,'* or 'All rise' in a solemn voice. The judge, a huge Indian man with a beak for a nose and scanty hair, walked through the hidden door behind the dais on which he sat. He hitched up his gown, cleared his throat loudly and sat down. The courtroom was packed. This was the first day back after the unexpected two-week adjournment. The press, including members of the Singapore press, had queued since early morning to ensure a seat. The lawyers made a show of rustling papers and diving into thick legal tomes. Journalists whispered to each other and scribbled notes furiously.

Artists sketched rapidly, trying to convey the atmosphere of the courtroom with a few quick strokes of the pen. Inspector Singh, looking at the pictures in the file, thought that they had done a good job. There were hints of dark wood panelling and a cool mustiness. The judge seemed larger than life — the court staff smaller. The couple fighting over their children sat next to their respective lawyers, an aisle and twenty years of unhappiness separating them. She was dressed conservatively. A dark suit with a white shirt, the skirt well below her knees. Her make-up was light, not sufficient to hide the shadows beneath her eyes. Her lips were pursed together tightly, as if she was physically battling to prevent her anger from spilling out.

Alan Lee, on the other hand, had spent less time thinking about his clothes. Or perhaps he was badly advised. He wore a light suit. It struck an inappropriate note in the sombre setting. His tie was almost festive. And he appeared smug — as if he alone did not doubt the outcome would be in his favour. The lawyers, drawn wearing their white shirts, winged collars and black gowns, looked like birds of prey picking over the carcass of what had once been a marriage. The journalists were pencilled in quickly and indistinctly, like a pack of scavengers hovering on the perimeter, waiting to pounce on the remnants of the celebrity couple's privacy.

The judge glared at the packed courtroom before him and waited until there was complete silence.

He asked, 'Are all parties present in the matter of Liew *v.* Lee?'

He spoke in English although Malay was the official language of the courts. When the trial had first begun, he had, as was required, opened proceedings in Malay. But senior counsel on both sides had immediately asked for permission to proceed in English and the judge had granted it with alacrity. Their excuse was not that their Malay (and that of the judge) was atrocious, but that Chelsea Liew, being Singaporean, would not be able to follow proceedings.

Singh knew that so many languages were spoken in Malaysia that quite often the wheels of justice ground to a standstill for the lack of an interpreter who could restore the Tower of Babel to a court of law.

At the judge's question, Chelsea Liew's counsel said respectfully, 'Yes, my lord.'

Alan Lee's lawyer, Mr Loh, was a feisty Chinese man who had a reputation for using every trick in the book to ensure success for his clients. Despite that, it had never been suggested that he broke the law. It was just that he used the complexity of the law to the advantage of his clients in circumstances where more honourable practitioners might have shown some latitude and more rectitude. He said now, brightly, 'Yes, my lord!'

The judge, looking vaguely irritated at this unnecessary good cheer, said, 'I assume counsel for both parties are ready to proceed with the custody hearings?'

Mr Loh said unexpectedly, 'We are making an oral application to dismiss these custody proceedings, my lord.'

There was complete silence in the court.

Chelsea Liew's lawyer leapt to his feet. He was angry and his voice radiated with it. He said, 'On what grounds? My lord, the respondent is wasting the court's time!'

The judge said, 'Mr Chandra has a point. On what grounds could I possibly dismiss proceedings? We have almost reached the conclusion of the custody hearings.'

Mr Loh said firmly, 'We are invoking Article 121(1A) of the Constitution of the Federation of Malaysia, my lord.'

There was a muttering in the court as journalists asked each other what the provision was and members of the public echoed the question. Alan Lee was smiling. Chelsea Liew sat up straight on the wooden bench, her anxiety peaking as she looked from the judge to her lawyer, her eyes demanding an explanation.

Her lawyer did his best. He said, 'Article 121(1A)? But what has that got to do with anything, my lord?' He looked at the judge almost pleadingly. 'My client has suffered enough. She is desperate to rebuild her life with her children. Mr Loh and his client are in contempt of court with their irrelevant application.'

The judge said, 'You *are* trying my patience, Mr Loh.'

Mr Loh said firmly, 'We are applying to dismiss proceedings on the grounds that this court has no jurisdiction to hear this matter. The proper forum for a custody dispute between the parties is the Syariah court.'

There was uproar in the court as the massed audience suddenly and collectively got wind of where the argument was going. The judge rapped his gavel loudly and glared around the court. The volume of noise subsided although there were still low murmurs. This genie could not be forced back into the bottle.

The judge turned back to Mr Loh and asked in a long-suffering voice, 'Why should the Moslem religious court — the Syariah court — have jurisdiction?'

Mr Loh replied in a high, clear voice that could be heard in all corners of the courtroom, 'My client, Alan Lee, has recently become a Moslem, my lord. All family law matters concerning Moslems are within the jurisdiction of the Syariah court under Article 121(1A) of the Constitution.'

Mr Chandra said indignantly, 'But Chelsea Liew is not a Moslem. Neither are her children!'

Mr Loh had the upper hand and he knew it. He said, 'I am not an expert, of course, but I understand the religion of minors under Islamic law is that of the father . . . or he can declare them to be Moslem, which he has done.'

The transcript that Inspector Singh was reading ended rather prosaically with, 'Court adjourned. Applicant, Mdm. Chelsea Liew, caused a disturbance and had to be removed.'

The newspapers were less reticent about

the 'disturbance in court' caused by Chelsea Liew. Inspector Singh found an article from the *Malay Mail,* an afternoon tabloid, which was particularly graphic. 'Madam Chelsea Liew started to scream obscenities at her ex-husband, Alan Lee. She tried to push past her lawyer, Mr Subhas Chandra, but he blocked her path. At this point she clambered over the table, leaving one shoe behind. She rushed over to Mr Lee and kicked and scratched him. He tried to protect his face but she raked him down the side of his cheek with her fingernails. Blood trickled down his face. The *Malay Mail* understands that he needed medical treatment, including stitches, from a plastic surgeon to prevent long-term damage to his physical appearance. It took the intervention of three policewomen to restrain Chelsea Liew, who was taken into custody and later released without charge. Her last words to her husband as she was dragged from the courts were "I will kill you for this!" '

FOUR

In an interview with the press outside the hospital where he received treatment for his face wounds, Mr Alan Lee said, 'It is an insult to me and my religion to suggest that I converted to Islam to get custody of my children. In these difficult times since the breakup of my marriage, I have been looking for spiritual guidance and I found it in Islam. I am proud to be Moslem and look forward to raising my children in the one true faith.'

Turning the page, Inspector Singh saw that the next document was the autopsy report on Alan Lee, killed exactly one week after the tumultuous court hearing. The autopsy had established that Alan Lee had died of injuries sustained from a bullet wound to the chest. The bullet from the revolver had penetrated a lung and then proceeded to sever the main artery leading to the heart. The deceased had succumbed to the heart wound before the lung injury but either would have been sufficient to kill him.

He had been shot on a deserted street two hundred yards from his front gate. The gun had not been traced. His wallet, Rolex watch and gold chain were left undisturbed. He was pronounced dead on arrival at the Kuala Lumpur General Hospital.

His ex-wife and the mother of his three children, Chelsea Liew, was arrested within hours and charged with his murder.

Inspector Singh wiped the newsprint off his fingers by rubbing his hands against his trousers. He felt like a voyeur, not a policeman. To look at facts like these could not leave anyone untainted. He tapped his foot, in his trademark white sneakers, against the ground. For a while, he watched the steady drip of water from the air-conditioning unit soak into the carpet.

It was hard, thought Singh, to believe that Alan Lee's sudden discovery of religion was anything except cynical. The judge had agreed to adjourn the custody hearing until the various issues of jurisdiction were determined. But he did not hide his contempt for what he saw as a cheap legal trick that brought the administration of justice into disrepute. The newspapers interviewed friends and colleagues expressing surprise that Alan Lee, of all people, should seek solace in a higher power. But the conversion to Islam, suspect as a matter of faith, was a powerful weapon as a matter of law.

Inspector Singh extricated himself from his chair with difficulty, stretched and went in search of Sergeant Shukor. He found him waiting outside the door. He stood to attention and saluted smartly as the inspector came out.

'Have you been here all this while?' asked the inspector in surprise.

'Yes, sir.'

'Crime rates must have come down a bit in Kuala Lumpur if you have time to loiter outside my door all day . . .'

Sergeant Shukor smiled. 'Not really, sir. But I have been told to stay close to you.'

Inspector Singh shrugged. 'Well then, take me to the widow!'

'I'm here to help you,' said the inspector, almost pleadingly.

There was no response from the woman sitting opposite him at the table. She was in the small interview room when they arrived, brought up from her cell. But she had not yet uttered a word nor even looked at them. She sat, as she had from the moment they entered the room, knees together, shoulders rounded, head bowed. Unmoved by the inspector's pleas and unmoving.

The inspector tried again. 'You are a Singapore citizen. The Singapore government sent me to make sure that you are treated fairly.'

He reflected when he said this that it was not an exact truth. The government was largely indifferent to the fate of this one woman. It did, however, want to look authoritative and caring in an election year. And public opinion in Singapore was incensed by what it saw as the victimisation of someone they felt they knew personally, so intense and detailed was the media coverage of the divorce and custody battles.

The policeman could see just enough of Chelsea Liew's face to understand her success as a super-model, although her recent experiences had left their mark. Her cheekbones were high, almost protruding through translucent skin. She had large almond eyes but they were red-rimmed, with deep blue shadows underneath. Her hair was scraped back firmly and tied in a ponytail. Grey hairs were visible all along the line of her forehead. Her lips, so luscious in those cosmetic adverts of the late eighties, were bloodless, dry and chapped. Her neck, thin and long, protruded from an oversized T-shirt. The inspector could see that she was at least six inches taller than him. Even seated and slumped, it was evident that the long legs in baggy prison pyjamas, feet slipped into flip-flops, were of a length to have stridden down catwalks — before marriage and murder had reduced her to silence.

He said, 'If you do not help me, I cannot help you.'

She looked up for the first time. For a second, as she had glanced up at him with those famous almond-shaped eyes, he had felt a remarkable sense of *déjà vu.* It was like looking at an old magazine cover, to once again be at the receiving end of that celebrated gaze. But now the brown eyes were filled with pain.

She spoke, the words wrenched reluctantly out of her. 'Nobody can help me now.'

'Why do you say that?' he asked, more gently than was his wont. The case-hardened policeman felt an unusual sympathy for the accused.

She gestured, a small sharp movement with one hand which encompassed the prison walls around her.

'I will only leave this place to walk to my death.'

'Did you kill your husband?'

'You would use that word for twenty years of brutality?'

'What about the children?'

'What can I do for them now?'

'Not much while you're in here.'

Quiet descended on the room again.

The inspector said, 'At least let me talk to people. Find out what happened. Please! It will cost you nothing if I fail. But if I succeed, we might get you out of here and back with your kids.'

She nodded once, a terse gesture, as if she was conferring a favour on him rather than dependent on him to find her an escape route.

Chelsea Liew rose to her feet. Inspector Singh got up too and watched her shuffle to the door. Sergeant Shukor opened it for her and she walked out. Inspector Singh had almost forgotten the sergeant was there. The waiting policewoman handcuffed her briskly and led her away.

The two men left in the room were a study in physical contrasts. One fit, strong, clean-shaven, well groomed. The other dishevelled, overweight and bearded.

Inspector Singh asked, 'What do you think? Did she do it?'

Shukor shrugged. 'She had the best motive.'

The senior policeman nodded. 'She certainly did. What does your boss think?'

'Inspector Mohammad?'

Singh nodded curtly.

'That she's one hundred per cent guilty, sir.'

The policeman was not surprised. Police work was rarely complicated. Locked-door mysteries and multiple suspects were the stuff of fiction. Usually, the person last heard threatening to kill someone who was later found dead was the murderer. He could not even blame Inspector Mohammad. He was not leaping to conclusions, just following the facts.

'What now, sir?' asked Shukor, interrupting his reverie.

'I go to my sister's house for the evening and then back to my hotel.'

'I will get the car, sir — and wait for you in the front.'

Alan Lee's brother, Jasper, sat in a small office on the second floor of an old shophouse near Chinatown. From his shuttered windows, he could see the red, pagoda-roofed entrance to Petaling Street, bustling and crowded as always. Rows and rows of stalls sold knock-off Gucci handbags, Tag Heuer watches and Mont Blanc pens. The quality was often indistinguishable from the original right down to the labelling and watermarks. Jasper Lee wore a fake Rolex he had bought down the road almost three years earlier. Hordes of tourists wandered down the narrow streets, summoned in imperative tones by the Chinese vendors; the experienced bargained hard for their fakes, the uninitiated paid top dollar and felt content to have something to show off when they got home.

Jasper was indifferent to the sounds of horns blaring and engines revving directly under his window. He had learnt to tune out the sounds. He ignored the stink of overflowing garbage-filled drains mingled with the pungent, eye-watering odour of dried anchovies piled high on the pavements in front of the dry food wholesaler on the ground floor.

In the early days, when the freedom of having walked away from the family business and his father's expectations had filled him with a sense of profound relief, he was delighted by the sights and sounds that were in such contrast to his own privileged upbringing. It was so colourful and raw compared to his stultifying existence under the watchful eye of a stern father.

Those heady, early days of autonomy were behind him. His past had caught up with him. He remembered his father's last words, shouted after him in angry Cantonese, as he had stormed out the door of the family home. 'One day you will understand that your family is what is most important.'

He had disagreed with the old man, the patriarch of the family, insisting that shared values were more important than shared blood. He was not so sure any more. His younger brother had been gunned down on a Bangsar street. His sister-in-law, for whom he felt an overwhelming sense of panic, was in prison. His mother was in a state of collapse. His three nephews were in the care of Chelsea's mother. God only knew what his youngest brother was doing. Perhaps it did come down to family in the end.

Jasper looked around him at the photos of orangutans stuck to the walls, all taken in the depths of the Borneo rainforest on one of his excursions into the wilderness. There were wizened patriarchs looking calmly at the camera, young bucks captured on film screeching their aggression at any intruder, family groups of female orang-utans and their babies. The whole sense was of a gentle, separate community — so different from the ugly reality of his own existence.

He got to his feet slowly, like an old man. There was one more thing he needed to do before making up his mind.

A heavy thunderstorm had reduced traffic to a standstill. The sky was dark although it was still early in the evening. The rain fell like large teardrops, straight down. It was a few years since Inspector Singh had been to Kuala Lumpur and he had forgotten the flash floods and gridlock that rain caused. Kuala Lumpur was just one large construction site, he thought, peering out of the window. There were looming cranes, looking spindly and unstable, in every direction. Every now and then one of them would take a direct hit from a bolt of lightning that would light up the sky to the brightness of a tropical noon. In the briefly illuminated skies, jagged half-built skyscrapers looked like twisted ruins. Concrete pillars to carry automated trains, the latest attempt to deal with traffic congestion, stood at regular intervals, like giant sentries that had been petrified by some powerful enemy.

The inspector thought that the very skies were weeping for the three boys whose father was dead and whose mother was in prison charged with his murder. It was a fanciful thought for the taciturn policeman.

The strange surroundings were affecting his natural balance. He found himself unable to forget the brown, pain-filled eyes of the widow. Chelsea Liew! A ridiculous name — par for the course with the adoption of Western names by Singaporeans aiming to give themselves a cosmopolitan air. Unfortunately, they often picked the most improbable monikers. Inspector Singh had come across young Singaporeans revelling in first names like Mayfair and Rothmans.

A sudden lull in the rain drumming down on the roof of the car interrupted his daydreaming. He realised that they had inched forward a few yards and were now sheltered by a massive six-lane flyover. Both sides of the road were jammed with motorbikes, their riders taking refuge from the rain under the looming concrete structure. The car lights glinted off their shiny, plastic raincoats. A few youths were perched along the side of the road smoking cigarettes, probably the clove cigarettes from Indonesia that had become so popular — as if the fumes from the dozens of cars crawling forward in first gear were not sufficient poison to the lungs.

The inspector, who had started the day in Singapore in a bad mood, was now extremely irritable. He contemplated the sheer impossibility of the case that had been dumped on his lap as they inched forward towards their destination. How was he to investigate the murder of Alan Lee? He had no jurisdiction. The Malaysian police did not intend to be helpful. Inspector Mohammad was going to be a handful. He was being spied on by the young man patiently driving the car he was stuck in and, as if these things on their own were not a sufficient impediment, Chelsea Liew was not cooperating. He had assumed that she would be full of suggestions as to alternative suspects — desperate to save her own neck. Instead, she seemed indifferent to his promised efforts and had given him no information to work with. Exhausted, perhaps, with what she had been through. Unable or unwilling to take on the system any more. All he had got was a grudging agreement that he should try to find the truth. And that, Inspector Singh admitted to himself, was the rub. *Was* he looking for the truth? Or was the most obvious answer, quickly seized upon by the Malaysian police, the correct one?

Finally, they drew up outside the house of Inspector Singh's sister. The sergeant indicated that he would be around the corner having dinner at one of the stalls that lined the streets in the evening. The inspector nodded and then, mentally girding himself for the encounter with his family, rang the doorbell.

His sister, a large, big-boned woman with a nose Caesar would have been proud to possess, was dressed in a cotton caftan — floral *batik* in hot pink. The material was frayed around the neck. She nodded to her brother and held the door open to indicate that he was welcome. They did not hug or kiss despite not having seen each other for over a year. It would have been completely out of character for either of them to have expressed emotion physically. Asians of their generation were not tactile. Affection was expressed, if at all, through food. To make an effort over dinner, to have a few extra dishes, to remember what someone liked best and serve it piping hot — that was the way to show family feeling.

The house was furnished in what could only be described as traditional Malaysian Sikh. It was the end lot of a row of single-storey terrace houses. The original thin strip of garden skirting the property on one side was built on as well as paved over. No blade of grass had survived the expansion. The interior was furnished with a heavy faux leather brown three-seater sofa with two matching armchairs. In the small sitting room it was oppressive. Handmade doilies, crocheted in white, hung on the back of each chair and on each arm. In an earlier era, when coconut hair oil was *de rigueur* amongst long-haired Sikh women, such protection for couches was prudent if the furniture was not to be permanently stained by oily, resting heads. In his sister's house, the doilies were merely decorative. Singh thought they were quite ugly. On the other hand they reminded him of his boyhood and were also comforting. An Indonesian oil painting of a village scene in heavy dark brush strokes hung on one wall. The purchase of cheap original art had been fashionable approximately thirty years earlier and this painting had no doubt been an 'investment' dating back from that period (no respectable Sikh family would buy art merely for its aesthetic qualities). Prior to the short-lived boom in art, houses were decorated with religious artefacts, photos and, for those with money, wallpaper featuring Alpine scenes. His sister's house was dimly lit with forty-watt bulbs — adding to the overall tone of middle-class gloominess.

Baljit had been a widow for thirty years. Her husband had died of a diet of sweet desserts and sweet tea when all three of her

children were still under five. He had left
her well provided for with a large insurance
policy as well as a house, the value of which
had increased exponentially over the years
as Bangsar changed from a small rural
development to the hub of the Malaysian
middle class. Inspector Singh rather suspected that after the initial grief at the death
of her husband she had found the whole arrangement satisfactory — money in the
bank, the complete governance of her three
children and no titular head to the household.

She asked now, 'How is Dev?'

He answered the inquiry about his wife
brusquely, 'Fine, same as usual.'

'Still too thin? Not you. You should eat
less. You know what happened to my poor
husband!'

She poured him a mug of hot strong tea,
thickened and sweetened with condensed
milk, as she said this and pushed a plate
heaped with Indian sweetmeats at him.

'What is the use of telling me to diet and
then serving me this sort of thing?' asked
the inspector tetchily.

He had only been in the company of his
older sister for ten minutes and she was annoying him with the general trait of Sikh
women of her generation — an ability to

maintain a constant stream of insulting observations coupled with suggestions for his improvement.

She changed the subject. 'Why are you here?'

'I am helping out in a Malaysian murder investigation. The chief suspect is Singaporean.'

She said with relish, 'I saw it in the newspapers. I am not surprised she killed him — converting to Islam to keep the children!'

'It is not certain that she did kill him,' pointed out the inspector.

'Don't be silly. Who else?'

'That is what I am here to find out.'

'You are wasting your time, lah!'

Later that evening in his hotel room, Inspector Singh took off his shoes, peeled his socks off and wriggled his toes. Wrinkling his nose at the whiff of athlete's foot, he wondered if his sister was right. She was insufferable but she did have a knack, with her direct, tactless observations, of hitting a core truth from time to time. The popular sentiment was that Chelsea Liew had killed her husband and for very good reason too. Even Moslems were muted in their support for the dead man. The official line, as adopted by the religious authorities, was that any conversion to Islam had to be assumed to come from the heart. However, public sentiment was highly doubtful that a Chinese businessman of dubious repute, locked in a bitter custody battle with his abused wife, would suddenly find God, except as a matter of convenience.

The body of Alan Lee was at the Kuala Lumpur General Hospital morgue. The reason that he remained in the morgue a month after his death was due to the dispute between the State Islamic Council and Alan Lee's mother, both of whom claimed the body. The disagreement was over whether Alan Lee should be buried according to Moslem or Buddhist rites. The Council insisted that Alan Lee had converted to Islam shortly before his death. They had records of his official conversion. His mother said that was not possible. She had cooked him his favourite meal the week before he died — *bak kut teh,* a pork belly soup that would have been an anathema to a Moslem for whom pigs were unclean animals, the eating of which was forbidden in the Quran.

The hospital, acting under a stay of execution granted by the civil courts to the mother, refused to release the body to the Council for burial. The Council was incensed and argued that Moslem religious practice required that a body be interred as soon as possible after death. Pointing out that the necessity for an autopsy had obviated the possibility of compliance, the court granted a stay until the matter was determined of what, if any, Alan Lee's religion had been at the time of his death.

The widow was asked if she had an opinion.

She looked coldly at her lawyer. 'Buried six feet under, buried facing Mecca, burnt to cinders . . . it does not matter. He is rotting in hell this very moment.'

Her lawyer's protruding nostril hairs quivered as he exhaled deeply. 'You will have to rein in that sort of emotion, or at least not express it, if we are to get you off.'

'But where is Mummy? I want Mummy to put me to bed!' The little boy in his Spiderman pyjamas sobbed, the heavy tears rolling down his face. He turned his face imploringly to his brother. 'Where is Mummy?' The older boy, a stoic expression on his face, looked at his grandmother. She was helpless. Unable to tell them the truth, unconvincing in her lies. She had used discipline, not affection, as her primary tool in bringing up her own children. Now faced with the desperate need of her two young grandchildren, offspring of a murdered man and an imprisoned woman, she did not know how to wrap her arms around them and drive away their fears. The older boy turned to his younger brother and put his own skinny arms around him. Two dark heads together, hair damp from their bath, the brothers sought comfort from each other.

FIVE

The small two-seater Cessna aeroplane was buffeted by the winds. It was a wild bouncy ride with the updraughts from the rolling hills. The single propeller on the nose of the aircraft spun vigorously and noisily as if it was conscious of its responsibility as the only thing between the plane and a long downward spiral into the thick jungle below. There was no coming back once swallowed by the trees. The canopy was so high and thick that nothing was visible once a plane penetrated the foliage. Just a few months earlier, an eighteen-seater private plane had crashed in Borneo. Nothing was found of the wreck or the passengers. Surviving in the jungle for any length of time was near impossible. Cuts turned to gangrene. Scratches became infected. Leeches latched on in a bloodthirsty frenzy. Clothes and shoes rotted in the intense humidity. Rainstorms washed away strength. Food was scarce. And there was always the threat of centipedes and cobras to make each step forward an adventure.

The few human habitations were small and far apart. The larger towns in Borneo all hugged the coast, keeping the jungle on one side and an escape route by sea on the other. The villages in the jungle were indigenous. Treks to the nearest big town could take weeks. Even a river ride in a canoe with the much-sought-after outboard motor took days. Only the narrow, short airstrips carved out of the jungle offered a quick way out in an emergency.

Jasper Lee, at the controls of the small plane, envied the villages their seclusion. It was his idea of heaven to be a week in any direction from cities with their brothels, cinemas and drains clogged with plastic bottles. He looked down at the rolling expanse of green canopy punctuated by a few emergents, exceptionally tall dipterocarp trees. If he went ahead with his plan, he would never again know the rich beauty of Borneo — never hear the chattering of the orang utans nor the harsh cry of a rhinoceros hornbill. He would never catch a glimpse of a clouded leopard disappearing into the trees or follow the tracks of a pygmy elephant deep into the rainforest. Jasper had forced himself to visit Borneo one last time, taking to the air in a hired plane. He had to test his resolve. Jasper wanted to remind himself of what was at stake.

Alan Lee's younger brother sat behind the desk of his dead brother and smiled. He was a slight man, impeccably dressed with expensive elegance. It was an extra-large desk, a little too big for the brother who had inherited it, with a top of wood so highly polished as to be mirror-like. Its surface was bare except for a telephone, a Macintosh Power Book with the Apple logo glowing mysteriously and a notepad with a Mont Blanc pen next to it. The room itself consisted of bare cream walls except for a couple of pieces of art by leading Malaysian artists. A frantic Ibrahim Hussein dominated one wall. There was a sofa and a couple of comfortable chairs in a corner of the big room, for more informal business discussions.

Lee Kian Min was a happy man. He had waited a long time to get his feet under the desk of his father and, later, his undeserving brother. He had worked hard and put in all the face time in the world, learning the ins and outs of the business while his older brothers had pursued orang utans and women respectively. He despised them for their weaknesses and envied them their seniority. But he had always known his time would come.

When Jasper Lee walked out on the family and almost killed the old man doing so, Kian Min was sure his moment had arrived. But in the end his father had insisted, despite misgivings, that Alan take over. Kian Min was devastated. But rather than emulating Jasper and leaving, he stayed, worked hard behind the scenes and kept the company together. When his father died, he continued to do the same. He allowed Alan to play the timber mogul while he quietly controlled the business. He learnt to be patient, to bide his time, to hide his ire when Alan would make one of his sporadic visits to the company offices. And now he had his reward. The company was his and he was going to savour every moment behind the big desk.

Inspector Singh met Sergeant Shukor at the entrance to the Ritz Carlton. He had delayed setting out on the pretext that he could not face any more time in traffic. The sergeant had taken the postponement philosophically. Now, replete with the hotel buffet breakfast, his belly straining against his shirt, Inspector Singh felt energised and ready to confront the case head on.

'Take me to the morgue,' he ordered.

'The morgue, sir?'

'Yes, I want to meet Alan Lee.'

'I have the autopsy report if you would rather look at that.'

'I've read that. I want to meet Alan Lee!'

They weaved their way towards the hospital, parking some distance away from the main building. The car park was brimming with cars, largely Protons. The Proton, Malaysia's national car, had, through a combination of subsidies and tariffs, achieved a substantial share of the Malaysian car market. It meant that a large number of patients who were too poor to buy themselves private health care could still drive to a government hospital for their subsidised treatment. It also meant that Malaysia was being rapidly paved with new roads to accommodate the burgeoning car population. It seemed, pondered the inspector, that no sooner did you give a man a car than he wanted to drive somewhere and do something. Gone were the days when life proceeded at a gentle *kampung,* or village, pace. Now Malaysians raced around in cheap cars with go-faster stripes looking for somewhere to go. Their usual destination was a concrete, bunker-style 'mega-mall'.

The two policemen walked past the array of cars distinguished with tinted glass, enlarged bumpers and sporty hubcaps. The main waiting area of the hospital was crowded with people — the cheerful visitors to the mildly ill and the distraught relatives of the dying. The morgue was difficult to find, a design feature of hospitals worldwide. An attempt, wondered the inspector idly, to hide the ultimate destination from those who were nearest to it? Contemplating the question, Singh could not help but think that, in a hospital, the proximity of death was probably best disguised — and the actual dead hidden. It was not conducive to the right frame of mind for recovery to have the morgue signposted for patients. It would be the medical equivalent of 'Abandon hope all ye who enter here'.

Inspector Singh was dragged to the present by a wiry hospital orderly dressed in baggy green hospital garb. He was struggling to pull out the steel drawer that contained Alan Lee. With the suddenness of a champagne cork, the drawer popped open. The orderly grinned at them in sweaty triumph, his teeth black and rotting. A packet of cigarettes poked from his top pocket and the faint smell of tobacco in the air suggested that a job tending to the dead was not sufficient to dissuade him from a habit that would only hasten his visit to the drawers. The graphic picture of a pair of diseased lungs on the cigarette packet, the latest in a long line of health warnings imposed by the government, seemed superfluous in the circumstances. Singapore had imposed the same health warning and Inspector Singh, repulsed by the pictures of diseased organs, now carefully transferred the cigarettes from each new packet he bought to a grubby old one with only a verbal warning. He *had* changed his behaviour, but only to take steps to avoid being graphically forewarned. The orderly was made of sterner stuff.

The policeman turned his attention to the body. It was a bloodless corpse, yellow and dry skinned with puckered lips and closed eyes. Between a few sparse, dark chest hairs, the black hole of the bullet's entry wound was clearly visible, as were the gunpowder burns around the edges.

'He must have been shot at almost point-blank range by someone standing directly in front of him,' remarked the inspector.

'How do you know that, sir?' asked the young sergeant.

'There wouldn't have been powder burns

if the bullet had travelled any distance. Also, the burns around the wound are even. That means the bullet went in straight. Otherwise, the burns would be lopsided, more towards one side or the other.'

'What else can you tell, Inspector?' asked the sergeant, trying to distract himself from a growing sense of queasiness. Alan Lee did not look good.

The inspector grinned at him, not un-kindly. 'First body, eh? I remember my first — it must be thirty-five years ago now. A woman killed by her jealous boyfriend. Blue, puffy face. The butterfly-shaped strangulation marks. You never forget the first.'

Attention back to the body, he continued, 'I would say that the person who killed him knew him. The killer must have stood in front of him, spoken to him and then shot him. They were face to face when it hap-pened. Alan Lee was not expecting violence. Otherwise, he would have been on his guard and unlikely to have been shot so cleanly.'

Sergeant Shukor nodded his agreement, getting caught up in the analysis.

'Also, I think it was an amateur . . . rather than a professional hit.'

This surprised Shukor.

'Only an amateur would have chosen to

shoot him in the chest. He might have survived. The bullet might have missed the heart outright or been deflected by the sternum. A punctured lung is a lot less likely to be fatal if there is quick medical intervention. No, a professional always goes for the headshot. Unless, of course, it was a professional pretending to be an amateur.' His belly laugh reverberated through the cold room. 'That's what makes this job so challenging.'

Shukor grinned and said, 'Where to now, sir?'

'Back to the beautiful widow.'

'There is a possibility that the Syariah court will place the boys in a home,' the inspector said brutally.

For a moment it seemed that he had not penetrated the thick haze of her isolation. Then Chelsea Liew looked up, sunken eyes staring at him unblinkingly.

'What are you saying?'

'The Syariah court might take them into care.'

'But my mother has them.'

'She is not Moslem.'

'Neither are they.'

The inspector shrugged. 'They are the under-age offspring of a Moslem man who

71

declared them Moslem before he died.'

Through dry lips, the accused spat. The saliva trickled down her chin. Her mouth was too dry for this expression of anger.

She snapped, 'I won't let them have my children!'

It was the first real emotion she had shown the inspector. He was delighted but he hid his pleasure. He said brutally, 'You won't be able to stop them if you're dead.'

She was silent so he continued. 'And you will be dead if you are not prepared to defend yourself. You know they will hang you. The judge has no choice if you are found guilty of murder.'

She nodded, more to herself than in acknowledgement of his remarks.

The inspector felt confident enough to persevere. He seemed to be getting through to her, chipping away at the protective wall to provoke an emotional response. It was a cruel thing to do — to use her children as a tool to break through her defences. Inspector Singh acknowledged the fact to himself as he looked into her wide, frightened eyes. He did not hesitate, however, to press home his advantage.

He said, 'Don't imagine there will be any mitigation. He might have beaten you but the killing was a cold-blooded execution.'

Chelsea was silent but her eyes flickered like those of a trapped beast.

Inspector Singh continued, this time sympathetic — a one-man 'good cop, bad cop' routine, 'You need to be there for your children — and I can help you.'

Chelsea whispered, 'I'm so tired. I didn't want to fight any more. After all, who would believe that it wasn't me who killed him? After what he did to me, after he tried to take my children away . . .' She paused for a moment and added bitterly, 'Besides, I thought if I kept quiet, they would leave the children alone. Forget about this whole Moslem thing . . . I can't believe they're still trying to take the kids. He's dead for God's sake!'

Singh seized the moment. He asked, 'Did you kill him?'

She looked at him as if seeing him with new eyes. She said firmly, 'I didn't kill him.'

The inspector looked sceptical.

'I did not kill him — although he deserved to die a thousand times.'

'Why didn't you kill him, if that's how you feel?'

Sergeant Shukor, standing quietly to one side, looked startled. Was the inspector advocating murder as a solution to marital difficulties?

Chelsea Liew appeared to take the question quite seriously. 'I considered it,' she said.

'Why didn't you?'

She smiled wryly. The first emotion other than anger she had shown to him.

'Someone else got there first? No, I did not kill him because I did not want to end up here, like this — separated from my children.'

Singh nodded. 'Well, whoever did kill your husband hasn't done you any favours. You need to help me find out who did it if you want to get out of here.'

It was her turn to nod.

Inspector Singh could see the glimmerings of the woman who had fought her powerful husband tooth and nail for custody of her children. He could see the woman who had the courage to take on the whole Malaysian establishment and challenge her husband's conversion to Islam. But had this strength also led her, when other avenues were proving to be dead ends, to kill her husband?

He asked now, 'Why did you stay with him?'

Again her bleak sense of humour showed. 'You see me sitting here and you ask me that?'

His lips curved a little — a small, unintended, answering smile.

She sighed and continued, 'At first I loved him, believe it or not. I was very young when we married. Twenty-one. He swept me off my feet. The newspapers and magazines at the time, I used to read them and think that for once, they did not have to exaggerate — it *was* a fairy tale. Rich man meets poor girl, showers her with gifts and flowers, takes her on exotic holidays, treats her like a queen. I was so naïve.'

'And then?' the inspector asked quietly as she fell silent, lost in her memories.

'He started to hit me — even when I was pregnant.'

The awareness of what her husband had been capable of still had the capacity to shock her.

'Why didn't you walk out then?'

'I'm not sure. Why don't women walk out? I used to read all the women's magazines — full of good advice to women trapped in abusive relationships. I didn't even *really* believe I was one of them. I remember thinking to myself, he might hit me once in a while but at least I'm not one of those battered wives. Of course, in reality, I was a textbook case. In denial, for my own sake, for my self-respect. For the sake of the

children. I don't really know. Alan' — it was
the first time since meeting the inspector
that she had used her husband's name and
he duly noted it — 'would always have some
excuse — he was stressed with work and
just snapped, I had spent too much time
talking to some man at a party . . . He was
always apologetic afterwards. He would
bring me gifts, take me out, he would even
cry with remorse. I doubted myself. Perhaps
it *was* somehow my fault. He had seemed a
good man when I married him. Perhaps I
was a really lousy wife, a lousy person to
have changed him into something so awful.
Maybe I was a slut — talking to men at
parties.'

She tossed her head, a glint of pride. 'It's
hard to believe now, but there was a time
when men would seek my company.'

He looked at her. Hair drawn back. Pale.
Hollow cheeked. Defiant. Meeting his eyes
— challenging him to disbelieve that the
wreck she was had been a new model once.

'I imagine men would seek your company
if you walked out of this prison today,' he
remarked.

She was embarrassed. A hint of pink, the
first colour he had seen, flushed through
the translucent skin.

She said, 'Oh! Those would just be the

reporters.'

He felt the first stirrings of genuine engagement with the welfare of this woman.

A loud knock on the door put an end to the conversation. It was time for her to go back to her cell.

They both stood outside the prison, young policeman and old. The inspector squinted against the sun. Sergeant Shukor pulled a pair of sunglasses out of his pocket and slipped them on. His wrap-around, ski-style, black shades added to his air of danger and competence. The inspector tried to recall if he had ever looked the part of a professional policeman in the way that the younger man did. He doubted it. He looked down at his sneakers, having to crane to see past his ample stomach. They were extremely grubby after a few days in the dust and grime of Kuala Lumpur. He looked around. The entire city had the feel of a place where contracts for upkeep and beautification were handed out to companies with connections rather than competence. The pavement on which he stood had been relaid with shaped tiles intended to create floral patterns. Most were cracked, some were missing — tiles were unevenly laid or had popped up under the intense sun. It was impossible to walk along and think — every moment had to be spent avoiding twisting an ankle. Instead of leafy trees to provide some shade, palms were planted at regular intervals. These were a recent addition, propped up with lengths of wood. Fairy lights were decoratively coiled around each trunk. The wires made the tree look like it was set up for death by electrocution.

The inspector sighed and kicked at a protruding piece of pavement. 'Whose bright idea was this anyway?'

Sergeant Shukor shrugged, a gesture of resignation made powerful by the breadth of his shoulders. He was not going to defend the uneven pavements from criticism. No sense of misplaced national pride was called for — especially as he himself had just stubbed his toe.

And yet, the inspector thought, Kuala Lumpur had a certain something. It was difficult to put his finger on what it was exactly. There was a sense of freedom perhaps, of anarchy even, that Singapore so sorely lacked. Perhaps it was the lack of deference to authority, the physical space, the ability to take a step back and enjoy a moment of quiet that lent Kuala Lumpur its atmosphere. Singaporeans were always adding to the list of reasons each one kept to hand, in case they met a Malaysian, of why it was so much better on the island than the peninsula. They ranged from law and order to cleanliness, from clean government to good schools, and always ended on the strength of the Singaporean economy. But in the end, the Malaysian would nod, as if to agree to the points made — and then shrug to indicate that they probably wouldn't trade passports, not really. And if pressed for a reason they would fall back on that old chestnut which somehow seemed to capture everything that was wrong about Singapore — but your government bans chewing gum. The nanny state and the police state all rolled into one.

Singh dragged himself back to the issue at hand and said, 'OK, let's start at the top. If Chelsea did not murder her husband, who did?'

'You believe her, sir?'

'Yes, I do,' said Inspector Singh firmly.

Shukor sighed. He could smell trouble. One blundering Singaporean policeman stampeding all over a cut and dried case was not what Inspector Mohammad had wanted when he assigned Shukor to babysit. He liked the policeman from Singapore — he was honest, direct and seemed to care about the people involved in the case. They were not just ciphers to him. But this bee in his bonnet about Chelsea's innocence was unhelpful. They only had her denial to go on. How was it that was enough to convince the senior policeman? He came with a big reputation for success and a bad one for being his own man. He hadn't got either by being gullible.

Singh interrupted his train of thought. 'Well? Who else do we have?'

Shukor said, 'I have no idea, sir.'

'All right. There's work to be done then. Let's go find out who killed Alan Lee.'

Six

The lunchtime meal of the Lee family had evolved substantially over time. The staple of the early days, when the Lee patriarch used to preside over the table, was the mega-meal of the food-loving Chinese. In his day, the senior Lee would arrive home for lunch in a chauffeured limousine, the Mercedes Benz so beloved for the status it conferred as well as its robust build. One of his two wives would have cooked. Numerous dishes would be served — all designed for general health and well-being. Judicious use of longevity herbs and a sprinkling of powders purchased from the apothecary — selected after careful consultation from the rows of jars behind the counter — would, when combined correctly, give the body the perfect balance of elements.

Chelsea Liew, product of a different generation, would usually have a sandwich, carefully crafted by the maid — tuna mixed with onions and garlic diced fine, a hint of lime squeezed in — or perhaps a baked vegetable sandwich — aubergine and pumpkin taken out of the oven when softened to perfection, crispy round the edges, sprinkled with sesame seeds and served between two slices of brown bread, a far cry from her childhood meals of *congee* with fried anchovies.

Alan Lee would usually eat at one of the high-end Kuala Lumpur restaurants — fine *dim sum* at the Mandarin Oriental Chinese restaurant with a view of the Twin Towers — tallest buildings in the world in the recent past, now superseded by the national equivalent of penis-envy in some other country with big ambitions. Or Alan would eat Western food, a sign of personal success, indicating to the world that he did not merely have wealth, but class as well, as manifested by his cosmopolitan tastes. Even French *nouvelle cuisine* was available to the new élite of Kuala Lumpur. Gone were the days when the only 'Western' dish available was the chicken chop and chips at the Coliseum café on Jalan Tuanku Abdul Rahman. Despite this, quite a few members of this select, wealthy club would stop at a stall on the way back to the office to purchase a top-up meal of *laksa* or *roti chanai*. Alan Lee himself had not been averse to substantiating a meal with a packet of noodles bought on the way back to his gleaming office.

Kian Min, the workaholic, ate little and usually at his desk. His secretary would buy a packed lunch before she left for her own break. She had long since given up trying to work out what it was he wanted or liked. Now, keen that purchasing lunch for the boss should not encroach on her own free time, she usually bought him something from a nearby food court, her choice as to his meal based entirely on the length of the queues at the different outlets. Kian Min was indifferent and did not seem to notice if he was fed a leathery lamb steak, an oily biryani rice or fried noodles.

Much had changed recently in the dining habits of the Lee family. Chelsea was in prison, picking over a mess of white rice and unidentifiable gravy. The two younger children of Alan and Chelsea were being served bowls of *congee* with finely sliced ginger and fish cakes. The eldest, Marcus Lee, had refused lunch because he had a hangover.

Jasper Lee, back from his fleeting visit to Borneo, was at a Chinese coffee shop. Since leaving the family business, he had managed on a shoestring budget, eschewing by choice his prior lifestyle. He sat on a stool at a brown, Formica-topped table. The four-legged stools were from Ikea. Their aluminium stools with plastic coloured seats were cheaper than the rattan or wooden ones that used to adorn cheap restaurants. Jasper paused to regret yet another casualty of globalisation, unnoticed and hardly regretted, but affecting some of the charm that had once been prevalent at food outlets, even those as grubby as this one.

The smell of *koay teow* frying, the flames leaping around the wok, perched on a portable stove and attached by a rubber tube to a nearby gas tank, triggered an explosion of gastric juices in his stomach and sent a sharp stab of acidic pain towards his chest. The meal, with a glass of fresh icy soya bean juice, would cost less than five ringgit. Despite this, Jasper knew he would enjoy it far more than the expensive dishes of exotic, endangered species with self-consciously lyrical names that an expensive Chinese restaurant would offer him.

The cook wiped the sweat from his brow and a few drops fell into the wok, sizzling against the hot sides. He said to Jasper, 'Want extra chilli?' and when Jasper nodded, scooped up a gob with a spatula from a large plastic container and flicked it in.

Jasper tucked in heartily. In the old days, he would have been unable to eat under pressure as great as he was suffering now. But years on his own had taught him that a failure to eat regularly only exacerbated the nature of the problem he faced. He picked the mussels out of his food carefully. One slipped through his guard, filling his mouth with its stale metallic taste — like the warm iron taste of blood. He almost gagged but managed to spit it out, half chewed.

A cat slipped out from a drain where it had been waiting for just such a moment. Heavily pregnant with large teats almost brushing the ground and a mangy coat through which ribs were visible, the cat was no different from the hundreds of other strays that lived in the vicinity of hawker centres and fought over scraps while avoiding the odd kick from a disgusted patron. Jasper felt sorry for the beast. Leaving money wedged under his empty glass, he quickly tipped his plate onto the floor. The cat barely waited for him to step away before attacking the food with the ferocity of a mother driven by a biological imperative to look after her unborn young.

Crudely, it put him in mind of his brother's wife, Chelsea. It was no hardship for anyone to believe that she had gunned down his brother to protect her children. He did not feel any anger towards this woman accused of killing Alan. Instead, he wondered what she had eaten for lunch. He had no idea what prison food in Malaysia involved. He shuddered and then steeled himself. He had made up his mind what to do. There was no turning back now.

His father had accused him of being feckless and disloyal when he had walked out of the family home. He had always felt that it was the ounce of truth in those accusations which had made them so hard to bear. Perhaps his principled stand about the family business, his desire to wash his hands of what he saw as tainted money, tainted wealth, boiled down to his inability to live up to his father's expectations. It was easier to walk away than admit failure.

He would run away now if he could.

'Let's start at the beginning and do things the old-fashioned way,' said Inspector Singh.

Shukor hazarded a guess. He had begun to understand the other policeman's elliptical references. 'Who gains from the death of Alan Lee?'

'Yes.'

'No will has turned up.'

'So the kids get everything? How old are they?'

'The oldest boy is seventeen, the others are twelve and seven.'

'Three boys, huh? I suppose that the oldest might have fancied some spare cash if his father kept him short?' The inspector did not sound convinced by his own accusation.

Shukor said, 'It's more complicated than that, sir.'

'What do you mean?'

'If it is finally agreed that he died a Moslem, the Islamic laws on intestacy are not the same as for non-Moslems.'

Singh rolled his eyes. 'Give it to me straight. Who gets the incredible wealth of Alan Lee under Islamic law?'

'To be frank, sir, I don't know. But I think there will be shares for all the family — the brothers as well as the sons, maybe even Chelsea.'

'Let's not bring Chelsea back into it. She has motives to spare. But the brothers might get something?'

'I'll check with a lawyer, sir — but probably, yes.'

The inspector looked thoughtful.

Shukor said diffidently, 'There's one more thing, sir.'

'One more thing? What is it this time?'

The younger man smiled. 'The family holding in Lee Timber . . . It was placed in a trust by the father. Kian Min inherits after Alan.'

'What?'

'Kian Min gets Lee Timber, sir. It is only the rest of the wealth, cash, property and so on, that is divided up amongst the rest of the family.'

'You know something, Shukor? It sounds to me like Lee Kian Min had a damn good motive to do away with his brother.'

Jasper Lee walked to his appointment concentrating on the here and now. He walked along the kerb in dusty shoes looking at his feet as he put one ahead of the other. He noticed that he walked with quick, small strides and consciously slowed down. There was no particular hurry. He noted the plastic bags and cans collected around the base of every tree. He listened to the horns blaring on the road beside him. He looked at the passengers interestedly, absorbing their uniform expressions of frustration and anger at the traffic jam they found themselves in. The fumes from revving cars with nowhere to go made him feel lightheaded. He breathed deeply. Not even the perfect dawn air, deep in the jungles of Borneo, had filled him with such a lust for life as the whiff of carbon monoxide that afternoon. The evening sun's rays, peeping through the forest leaves and turning everything to gold, did not have the same power to enchant him as the blazing afternoon sun on his bare head.

Jasper understood now why people talked about their lives flashing before their eyes. In his case, it was not so much his whole life but a highlights reel. Peculiarly, he was neither seeing his past nor reliving it. It was the sensations associated with significant moments that flowed over him. He heard the door slam behind him as he left home for the last time, smelt the scent of the woman he loved the first time he met her, felt the wind rush through his hair as he piloted his little plane high above the rain-forests. It was a mosaic of emotion and experience, a reward for doing the right thing.

Jasper Lee walked into the Bukit Aman police station and cleared his throat to catch the attention of the duty sergeant, who was immersed in the sports pages of the afternoon tabloid, his half-eaten packet of rice and curry, wrapped in banana leaf and newspaper and tied up with a rubber band, on the desk in front of him. The policeman dragged himself away from his newspaper long enough to look up and ask grumpily, 'Ya?'

Jasper Lee said firmly, without hesitation, 'I have come to confess to the murder of my brother, Alan Lee.'

SEVEN

The young man of mixed parentage looked at himself in the mirror. It was a full-length, teak-bordered mirror set in the lightest part of the room. Ravi liked what he saw. His stone-washed jeans were moulded across his thighs and artistically frayed at the knees. He had bought them like that, of course. He'd never worn a piece of clothing long enough to wear it out. He wore a black T-shirt firmly tucked into low-cut, hip-hugging denim jeans and a broad belt with a square, masculine buckle. His hair was cut close to a well-shaped head. He looked good, he thought. He took care of himself. He exercised daily at a big, glass-enclosed gym. He looked after his skin and his hair. But he made sure to keep his look natural. Only he knew the effort that went into his careless good looks.

Looking at his reflection with admiration, he could not understand why Chelsea had refused to see him. After all, he had taken a big risk asking for her. Nobody knew about him. About them. He had been willing to take a chance on being found out but she had rebuffed his attempt without even the courtesy of seeing him first. A policeman had broken the news to him, the smirk on his face suggesting he was being laughed at because a woman in jail, whose options for company were limited, did not want to see him.

Mind you, she had rebuffed his early efforts to get to know her as well. But he had played his cards well. He, Ravi, was experienced in the ways of rich, lonely women. He had maintained a physical distance. He had treated Chelsea with studious, old-fashioned courtesy, listening to her stories with a sympathetic ear. He had never once put himself first in his dealings with her. Finally, she had started to open up, unburden herself. Really talk to him. As he had guessed from the start — it was the same with the other abused women he had targeted — she was only too willing to sleep with him the moment she started talking to him. For women like Chelsea Liew, the commitment was communication. Sex was a reward to men who had earned her trust.

They had managed their relationship very

well. The husband had never suspected. Alan Lee had been a little bit too confident that he had beaten his wife into submission. It was easy to arrange assignations. Interludes between shopping trips while the kids were in school. He had Chelsea precisely where he wanted her — dependent on him for emotional solace and physical pleasure. The small gifts she gave him had turned into cash handouts.

But to his intense annoyance, she had broken off all contact the minute the custody battle for the children had begun. He had protested that they were discreet, nobody need find out about their liaison, but she was firm. She was not going to give her husband any ammunition in the battle for the children. She, who was alleging adultery as grounds for divorce and custody, did not intend to be caught, literally, with her pants around her ankles. Ravi had hoped to go back to the well a few more times. But if it was not possible, he could live with that. He knew when to cut his losses and walk away. There were plenty of other rich, lonely women in Kuala Lumpur.

But then Alan Lee had been killed. What a euphoric moment. He smiled at the recollection of his own short-lived delight. He had sent her a letter immediately, professing undying love, predicting a future together, talking about his willingness to be a father to her children. She did not respond but he had not been worried. He knew she had been too busy and careful during the divorce and custody hearings to have replaced him. With the husband out of the way, he would soon insinuate himself back into her good graces, her bed and hopefully marriage — his ticket to the good life.

He could not believe it when Chelsea was arrested for murder. His golden goose was about to be hanged from the neck. And to add insult to injury, she would not even see him. He kicked the bed in frustration and scuffed one of his ankle boots. Taking a piece of cloth, he sat on the bed and started polishing the spot with neat circular movements.

Sergeant Shukor's mobile phone rang. He extricated the phone with his left hand. His right hand was still soiled from tucking into his lunch of *roti telur* and dhal curry. He was sitting across from Inspector Singh, the table so small that they were generating static between their trousered knees. The inspector ignored the contortions of his Malaysian colleague as he tried to answer the phone with one hand. He wiped his

plate clean with his last piece of *thosai* —
an Indian bread made with rice and lentil
flour. He had eaten three without pausing
for conversation. The sergeant was nodding
his head, listening to the man at the other
end of the phone. He waved his hand in the
air, signalling for the bill. Inspector Singh
glared at him, indicating with a curt shake
of the head that the sergeant was being
premature, the older policeman fancied
some dessert.

But his subordinate tapped the phone suggestively. Whatever the message was, it could
not wait. As the bill arrived, Inspector Singh
took a handful of grubby ringgit from his
pocket and tossed them on the table. With a
nod to the old Punjabi man with a snowy
white beard to the middle of his chest,
Inspector Singh followed Shukor out into
the blazing sunshine and blinked as his eyes
watered in the unexpected light. They were
standing close to Masjid Jamek or Jamek
mosque, built at the confluence of two rivers. The rivers themselves, small and muddy
brown with concrete embankments, looked
like large drains. Any romance attached to
their presence in the heart of Kuala Lumpur had been ruined by the need to shore
them up to prevent landslips. But the
mosque itself was an exquisite building,

Moorish in design and perfectly proportioned.

Sergeant Shukor stood with pursed lips and hands on hips.

'What's the matter? What's happened?' asked the inspector.

'There's been a confession.'

'A confession? Chelsea has confessed?' Singh's heart sank. He had been quite wrong about her.

'No. Not her. The brother! Jasper Lee has just confessed.'

'Confessed to what?'

'His brother's murder!'

'But why? Why did he kill Alan Lee?'

'No idea, lah!' exclaimed the young policeman. 'Let's go and find out.'

The Malaysian police now had two people in jail for the murder of Alan Lee and Inspector Singh was incensed.

'Why can't you just release her?' he asked angrily.

'You should understand, Inspector. We cannot release her until the prosecutor drops the charges or the judge dismisses the case. The prosecutor won't dismiss the case yet because he doesn't know the details of this new confession — maybe Jasper Lee and the widow were working together?'

'Don't be ridiculous!' snapped the inspector.

Inspector Mohammad shrugged.

'OK, why doesn't the judge order her release?'

'Holiday, I'm afraid,' he said laconically.

'What?'

'The judge is on holiday.'

Inspector Singh kicked the table. It was the height of rudeness to his Malaysian counterpart but he could not bottle up his frustration. Chelsea Liew was innocent but they would not let her go.

'What about another bail application?'

'Her lawyer is working on it, I believe. I wouldn't worry, Singh. She'll be out soon enough.'

The fight went out of him. Singh, of all people, knew the bureaucracy of a police force. He, who always found himself swamped by paperwork. The Malaysian police were not going to come out of this smelling of roses having incarcerated the beautiful mother of three children while a murderer roamed free. They were not going to compound any errors by acting hastily at this late stage. He would have to bide his time. More importantly, Chelsea Liew would have to bide her time until her release.

Inspector Mohammad was looking at his Singaporean colleague with interest. 'You were convinced she was innocent, weren't you? I mean, even before this confession from the brother.'

Inspector Singh nodded.

'Why? On what grounds?'

Singh thought hard, understanding that the policeman was asking him a serious question, genuinely wondering why the Singaporean had been so sure that Chelsea was innocent, when all the facts pointed the other way. Finally, he said, 'I'm not sure I was convinced, to be honest. But she had so much strength and what looked like . . . integrity, I thought I'd take her word for it and look around for another possibility. And there seemed to be a few about — although I never suspected Jasper.'

Mohammad nodded ruefully. 'Well, I owe you an apology, I suppose. I was sure she'd done it. Didn't look under many rocks after that . . .'

It was handsomely said and Singh's respect for the man increased. He shook the Malaysian's hand and realised there was nothing to prevent him catching a taxi to the airport and hopping on a shuttle back to Singapore. His work was done albeit without any actual input from himself. He had been sent to see that Chelsea got a fair deal. The outcome was even better than that. She would walk free. His superiors in Singapore would have to find some other way of forcing him into early retirement. He debated asking Shukor to take him to the airport and then thought better of it. He had a curiosity to see how things turned out. He would hang around for a few days.

Inspector Mohammad, with that perspicuity that Singh was beginning to recognise, must have guessed his reluctance to leave just yet.

He said, 'Would you like to sit in on the interview with Jasper Lee?'

It was an olive branch to the Singapore police officer. Inspector Singh seized it at once. The men set off for the labyrinth of detention cells. It was not hard to believe that anyone incarcerated here would be prepared to confess to just about any crime. It was harder to see why Jasper Lee, a free man, had decided to subject himself to this place.

It was an interview with Jasper Lee but he was not saying much. The Malaysian policemen were persistent, repeating themselves, demanding answers — pointing out that he was putting his head in a noose. The self-confessed murderer was indifferent. If anything, he seemed slightly amused by their efforts.

He said again, 'I've told you I killed him, shot him in the chest. What more do you want?'

'What weapon did you use?'

'What do you think?' asked Jasper cuttingly. 'A gun, of course.'

'What sort of gun?'

'How do I know? The kind you point and shoot.'

'Where did you get it?'

Jasper shrugged. 'You can always buy these things if you really want to.'

His insouciance was starting to visibly irritate the policeman asking the questions. Inspector Singh suspected that if he had not been there, they might have considered roughing him up by now. And he could see why they might be tempted. This man, voluntarily confessing to murder and somehow finding it amusing, *was* extremely tiresome. Or perhaps he was doing the Malaysian police a disservice. He could not picture the placid Sergeant Shukor beating up a prisoner. As for Inspector Mohammad, he was the most correct gentleman Singh had ever come across. The idea of him laying a finger on anyone was ludicrous. On the other hand, Singh reminded himself, this was the country where a top policeman had given the deputy prime minister a black eye. It would not do to be sanguine.

Inspector Singh looked at Jasper curiously. He had, in all his experience, never met a self-confessed murderer who took such pleasure in his role. Jasper Lee was still in civilian clothing. Despite his confession he had not been charged yet. The police preferred to ask him questions first — so unexpected was his arrival on the scene. He was a small, plump man. Conservatively, but casually, dressed. Not handsome like his brother Alan had been. In fact, fate had rather cruelly made him a caricature of his good-looking younger brother. He was shorter and rounder, with receding hair and protruding ears — like the drawings done on the spot at tourist venues for easily amused visitors. Jasper had a mole on one cheek from which grew a couple of 'lucky' hairs. Traditional Chinese believed that a mole with hair brought luck. It was not uncommon to see older men twirling those strands of hair in the same way that men of other cultures twirled their moustaches.

Despite his bravado, there were bags under Jasper Lee's dark eyes and, behind his black, plastic frames, he looked tired.

He was cheerful now but he had been losing sleep in the recent past, perhaps weighing up his decision to come in and confess. It took courage to face a mandatory death penalty.

Inspector Singh asked, 'Why did you kill him?'

Inspector Mohammad's lips thinned with displeasure that the inspector from Singapore was taking advantage of the situation to insert himself into the interview process. He did not, however, interrupt. He was curious to hear the answer to the question. None was forthcoming. Singh asked again, 'Why did you do it? There must be some explanation! He was your brother.'

Jasper Lee shrugged. 'Any number of reasons actually. Alan Lee was cruel and corrupt. I despised him for what he was doing to the environment. He deserved to die for that alone.'

'What?' ejaculated Inspector Singh. 'You killed your brother to stop him cutting down a few trees?'

'Yes. It's not just a few trees, is it? He and his cronies are cutting swathes through the jungles of Borneo. Bribing, or if that fails, intimidating everyone who gets in their way. Men like him are destroying the rainforests. Sometimes, if you want to protect something you care about, you have to take extreme steps.'

Sergeant Shukor had the last surprised word in the face of the unexpected motive. He said, *'You dah gila, ke?'* Have you gone quite mad?

EIGHT

'He's lying,' said Chelsea flatly.

The inspector stared at her in surprise. He asked, 'What do you mean?'

She said again, 'Jasper's lying. He did not kill Alan.'

'He confessed!'

She shook her head angrily. 'I don't care. Jasper is not capable of killing anyone. He's far too gentle. He wouldn't know where to begin!'

'Why would he confess then?'

'How do I know? Maybe one of your chums beat him up.'

Inspector Singh took a deep breath, trying to keep a lid on his temper. This woman was being incredibly obtuse. And he didn't understand why. She might be a former model. But she did not fit the stereotype. She was far too smart not to see the implications of what she was asserting so forcefully.

He said patiently, 'For your information, I've just been with Jasper Lee while the Malaysian police interviewed him. No one laid a finger on him. They didn't have to. I've never seen anyone confess to premeditated murder with such enthusiasm.'

Chelsea Liew snorted. A derisive, disbelieving sound.

The inspector continued, 'You do realise what you are saying, don't you? His confession gets you off the hook. Your lawyers are applying for bail again. The prosecutor is bound to drop the charges. Or the judge will dismiss them. You will soon be a free woman!'

Chelsea Liew looked at the inspector in disgust. 'You think I'm better off because some *other* innocent goes to the gallows?'

The fat man said indignantly, 'Actually, yes — I do think it's better that they hang the man who confesses to a murder rather than a battered wife and mother of three who has protested her innocence all along!'

Singh was alone in the cell with Chelsea. The Malaysian police had left it to him to break the news of Jasper's confession to her — quietly washing their hands of the Singaporean whom they had wrongly held in custody for one long month. He was more than willing to be the bearer of such good news to a woman who had given up hope. He had pictured her surprise as colour flooded back into her pale face. Instead, he had this unexpected, persistent denial. The worry lines between her eyes had deepened. He did not understand it. He tried again.

'Nobody who's innocent confesses to a murder where the penalty is certain death.'

'In your experience?' she asked, her voice tinged with sarcasm.

He was stung by this and snapped angrily, 'In my many, many years of experience, yes!'

She was sitting on her chair, sunk slightly into it, knees higher than her lap with two arms around them. Now she uncoiled and stood, looking down at him from her greater height.

She said, enunciating each word carefully, as if talking to a child or an idiot, 'Jasper Lee did not kill anyone.'

He grabbed her arm. 'There is only one way you could know that for sure!'

She wrenched free angrily. 'Now you are accusing me of murder again? No! I am not confessing . . . unlike the combined talent of the Singapore and Malaysian police force, I just know an innocent person when I see one.'

He changed tactics. 'Fine! What does it matter to you whether he did it or not? You get out and go home to your kids!'

She sat down heavily on the seat again, adopting her previous upright, semi-foetal position. Defensive, tired but not quite defeated.

She said, 'I will. I will do that. I owe it to my children not to walk away from an open door. But then I will work to clear Jasper's name!'

Singh said tiredly, 'That could land you right back in here.'

'So be it.'

'Jasper has confessed!'

The man at the other end of the phone could hear the excitement in Kian Min's voice. He asked, 'That means we can go ahead?'

There was a silence punctuated by static crackling on the line.

Again the question was asked. 'Mr Lee, are you there? Can we go ahead?'

After a few more long moments of hesitation, 'Yes, OK. You can go ahead!'

Wai Ming, who preferred to be known as Bruce — after his boyhood idol, Bruce Lee — punched the air once. Then he walked out of his trailer and shouted in dialect, 'The time for waiting is over!'

For those among the band of ruffians

lounging around outside who did not understand him the first time, he repeated himself in Malay. A muted cheer could be heard from the men. One or two stubbed out cigarettes, a couple of others went back to the job of oiling and cleaning their guns with extra care. Someone switched off the TV, powered by an outdoor generator that drowned out the sound of the Malay-dubbed Brazilian soap opera which was playing grainily. A native Iban sharpened his *parang,* a powerful blade ten inches long, against a stone. The metallic sounds and flying sparks scared away a pair of hornbills sitting on a branch overhead.

The dew hung like individual teardrops at the tip of each leaf. A fine mist reduced visibility slightly. It was still cool. It would take a while for the sun to penetrate the canopy and warm the jungle at ground level. A nightjar brushed the cheek of one of the men as it rushed home to bed. He flinched slightly. It was an unlucky bird, an ill omen to see on an expedition. They were walking single file along the riverbank. On their left, the muddy brown Rajang moved sluggishly through Borneo towards the South China Sea. A sudden excited chattering broke the stillness of the jungle. The men, acting of one mind, stopped in their tracks. Overhead, a group of macaque monkeys, disturbed by the appearance of their simian cousins, gesticulated excitedly. They soon got tired of this sport and made off as a unit deeper into the jungle. The men started again, keeping their eyes peeled, scanning the horizon for telltale signs of human activity. They kept a close eye on the river, wary of crocodiles masquerading as logs, on the lookout for an easy breakfast.

Chelsea Liew's eyes flashed. There were spots of high colour on her cheeks. She was wearing a head-scarf, worn by pious Moslem women to indicate modesty and religiosity. It was a common enough sight in Malaysia where growing numbers of Moslem women had adopted the headdress worn around the head, all hair tucked away and invisible, with a full cloak reaching almost to waist level, draping the upper body. Pressure from menfolk, peer pressure, genuine choice — it was difficult to know why so many women had adopted the stricter Islamic code of dress, although the full burqa was still fairly uncommon. Those dressed in the black, shapeless gowns, with black socks, shoes, gloves and an opaque veil, tended to be part of the huge contingent of oil-rich, Arab tourists who came to

Malaysia to shop for designer clothes to wear under their black coveralls.

Chelsea Liew wore a transparent gossamer head-scarf lined with beads. Her hair peeped out enticingly. It could hardly have been the intention of the Syariah court, in insisting on a mandatory head covering for women appearing before the court, whether Moslem or not, to enhance the appeal of the wearer. But that was what they had achieved in the case of Chelsea Liew. The difference between observing the letter and the spirit of the law was crystal clear when viewed in the context of Chelsea's headgear.

Chelsea's relief at her release from prison had immediately turned sour. She had gone home to her children. They had asked her no questions, too thankful to have their mother back to question the manner of her return. It was as if the boys had decided that to know too much would tempt fate — they sealed themselves from the past by remaining ignorant of it. Chelsea knew that at least Marcus, the eldest boy, knew that she was out of jail because their uncle had confessed — it was in all the newspapers. But she acquiesced in his withdrawn silence, thankful for the respite from the immediate past.

And then she had received an official

document from the Syariah court requiring her presence at a custody hearing regarding her children. Apparently, the Islamic Council felt it necessary to seek custody of her children, the offspring of a Moslem man, rather than have them brought up by a non-Moslem mother. It was their view that the children would be better off fostered in a Moslem home and they had applied to the Syariah court that the children be placed with Moslem caregivers.

Chelsea had frantically consulted her lawyers only to discover that they did not have *locus standi,* the right to appear, before the Syariah court. Their practice was wholly before the parallel civil jurisdiction that held sway in Malaysia over most matters except that of Moslem family law. Her lawyers could advise but they could not appear. Finally, she had found a Moslem lawyer to represent her and they had arrived for the hearing only to be barred at the door. Her clothing, knee-length skirt and jacket over long-sleeved blouse, was not modest enough for the presiding judge. Her lawyer had hastily arranged a twenty-four-hour adjournment. Chelsea was now dressed in the customary Malay dress, the *baju kurung,* a shapeless long-sleeved knee-length blouse with a closed neck, a long maxi-skirt and the required scarf.

In the end, in the manner of all courts, religious or secular, the hearing was postponed. The judge, dressed in long black robes and sporting the fist-length beard believed by some Moslems to be required of their religion, was anxious to usher them all out of his courtroom. The law and his personal sympathies were pulling in opposite directions. He would give everyone a few weeks to mull things over.

Outside, the rain beat down. The sky was an impenetrable dark grey. Crashes of thunder followed hard on the heels of bolts of lightning that lit up the heavens and caused the air around them to tingle with electricity. The weather required a grander denouement than a postponement of a hearing. This was a storm more appropriate to families pulled asunder by the majesty of the law. At least the rain had thinned the ranks of waiting reporters. A few stood huddled together, under voluminous raincoats, next to the main entrance of the beautiful courthouse building. Chelsea deliberately unwound her head covering, shook out her hair and stuffed the scarf into her handbag.

The inspector had found out about the hearing from the newspapers and decided to attend. He had a curiosity about this woman as well as a concern. Looking at the teeming downpour, Singh did not have much hope of summoning one of the beat-up red and white taxis that plied the streets. There was hardly any traffic on the roads, an unusual occurrence in Kuala Lumpur. Everyone was driven to look for cover — trying to avoid one of the flash floods that regularly beset the city, a foreseeable, but ignored, consequence of the continuous frenzied building without adequate drainage for the monsoons. The inspector glanced at Chelsea and caught her eye. She shouted to be heard above the rain and beckoned imperiously, her summons emphasised by a clap of thunder. 'Come with me. I want to talk to you!'

Docilely, he walked over and her chauffeur held a large golf umbrella over his head and ushered him into the Mercedes Benz. This was a different woman from the creature whom he had first met behind bars. That Chelsea had been tired, defeated and regretful at having tilted against her husband's wealth and influence. But now, free, rested and in a battle to maintain custody of her children, the indomitable woman he had sensed even in her darkest hours was back. And, free from prison and no longer a suspect in her ex-husband's murder, she had been allowed to resume the trappings of his wealth — the car, the clothes, the chauffeur. He did not begrudge her a cent of it. She had paid for the accoutrements of the rich in blood and tears. Of all the things that Alan Lee had done to thwart her, Shukor had told him, he had not made a will, and her children were now entitled to much of his money, except for the ownership of Lee Timber, which went to Kian Min. She, Chelsea, had her divorce settlement. If it was determined that Alan had died a Moslem, his money would devolve in accordance with Syariah rules and include chunks for his parents and siblings. However, most of it would be reserved for his children. Even if he had left a will, as a Moslem he would not have been permitted to give away all of his property as he wished. No doubt an unforeseen consequence of his conversion, thought Chelsea cynically. Even if a will did turn up and he had left all his money to whichever woman he was sleeping with at the time of making it, his becoming Moslem would protect the children. Not that having access to his money would be of any use to her if her ex-husband managed to extend an arm from beyond the grave and snatch her kids away. Her lips thinned into a straight line. She was not going to lose her children.

Inspector Singh sat next to her on the cream leather seats in the back of the car but did not say a word. He was happy to let her break the silence when she was ready. There was a reason she had asked him along. She would come to it eventually.

The inspector's superiors in Singapore had got wind that Chelsea was a free woman and were insisting that he get back to Singapore. He was booked on an evening flight that day. He was glad that he would have a chance to speak to Chelsea Liew before he left. He needed to get a sense, for his own peace of mind, that she had the tools and courage to fight.

The electric gates of the Lee residence drew open and the Mercedes purred into the driveway. The gates immediately closed behind them. He could see the closed-circuit television cameras on every promontory, covering every angle. In the distance he could hear the deep sound of big dogs barking. There was a guard dog contingent on the premises.

Chelsea must have guessed the direction his thoughts were taking because she said, 'Didn't do him much good, did it?'

She nodded her head in the general direction of the barking dogs to indicate what she meant.

'Where exactly was he killed?' asked the inspector. 'I know it was in the vicinity of the house.'

She nodded coolly. 'Yes, he was shot about two hundred yards down the road. If the car was needed to go and pick up one of the children from school, the driver sometimes dropped him off at the bottom of the hill. Whoever killed him knew that.'

They were out of the car now and walking in the main door. Two children ran down the stairs and then pulled up short when they saw their mother had a guest. The inspector tried to smile at them in a friendly manner, but it was more of a nervous grimace. It was a long time since he had interacted with children. They glared at him, indifferent to his overtures.

Chelsea said, 'Boys, I have a guest I need to talk with. Will you both go upstairs and play for a while?'

The younger boy asked, 'Is he going to take you away?'

She said calmly, 'Of course not.'

Beside her, the inspector shook his head to emphasise her denial.

The boys turned and went back up the stairs, dragging their heels to indicate a general reluctance. Chelsea watched them go, an indecipherable expression on her face.

Then she turned to the inspector and said in a sprightly tone, 'Tea?'

She was interrupted by the appearance of a surly youth.

Chelsea said, 'Inspector Singh, this is my eldest son, Marcus.'

Singh stood up and held out his hand. Marcus looked at him in disdain and walked out of the room.

Singh watched him go. He turned to the widow. 'Kids, eh?'

Jasper still had the courage of his convictions but his physical courage was flagging. He was photographed, thumb-printed, had his rights read to him and was charged with the murder of his brother. Now he was in a holding pen with various members of the Kuala Lumpur criminal fraternity and they scared him. He sat on the floor in the corner of the cell trying not to catch the eye of any of his cellmates. They ranged from a Chinese gang member, whose dragon tattoo foraged up his arm and curled around his neck, to a large, Indian man with a jet-black moustache and pockmarked face, brooding in a corner. The majority of his cellmates appeared from their accents to be Indonesians, part of the large contingent of illegal immigrants in Malaysia. Some turned to crime to supplement their income from the menial jobs that Malaysians, after fifty years of economic growth, felt were beneath them. Others were merely convenient scapegoats. These wiry, brown men with lined faces worked on construction sites, manned the rubber and oil palm plantations and operated the pumps at petrol kiosks the length and breadth of the country. They were both relied upon and abused at the same time. Those who turned to crime gave the rest a bad name. Jasper was reminded of the line from the movie *Casablanca* where the police 'rounded up the usual suspects'. It seemed the practice was still rife. At least, he thought, the government should be proud that their efforts to integrate the various races in Malaysia into a cohesive society were bearing such fruit. It was a very multi-racial group that was penned in together.

NINE

Inspector Singh sipped his tea from a delicate bone-china teacup. The fragile thing looked out of place in his large, grubby hand and his forefinger barely fitted through the handle. However, he was a guest and the Indonesian maid who ran the kitchen knew better than to exercise discretion in the choice of crockery.

Across from him, Chelsea also sipped her tea. He could smell it — it was a fragrant green tea. He hated the stuff, give him a strong black tea any day, but the smell was like a slice of heaven. Singh noticed that Chelsea's fingernails were trimmed and glossy, but colourless. She had found time for a manicure. Her hair too was trimmed and shining although still coiled in a bun on her head. As he stared at her she pulled off the jewelled clips and her hair cascaded down her shoulders. He was sure that he had seen a TV shampoo advertisement once where she had done the same thing. The hairclips looked like rabbit traps with their long teeth and spring-loaded action.

Chelsea shook out her hair and said, 'You have no idea how wonderful it is to be clean! I've been scrubbing for days to get prison off my skin.'

He did not respond. Inspector Singh was not the sort to indulge in small talk. Not when murder was the subtext of the conversation.

Chelsea changed tactics smoothly. She said, 'You must be wondering why I asked you back here. Now that you've done your job and I'm free.'

He shrugged to indicate a willingness to hear her out but also to deny anything as crude as curiosity.

'I need your help.'

'What can I do?' he asked, puzzled.

'I want you to clear Jasper. You know, find out who actually killed Alan.'

'I am a policeman from Singapore, not a private investigator for hire,' he said crossly. 'My flight back is booked for tonight.'

'You have to stay.'

'I can't! And anyway, even if I did, I would be of no use to you. I was sent here to look after your interests. You're out of jail. My job is done.' He added as an honest after-

120

thought, 'Not that your getting out had anything to do with me in the end.'

She did not say anything. The rigidity of her shoulders was the only sign of her tension.

The inspector asked, 'Why me?'

She looked at him, eyes pleading. 'I don't know anyone else with the skills to find a criminal, a murderer. And I trust you to look out for my interests.'

'What makes you think you can trust me?'

She did not answer. He knew she was right though. She could trust him. Somehow or other she had gotten under his skin.

He said heavily, 'I could lose my job!'

A twig snapped underfoot and the leader turned to glare at his companions. He was distracted from censuring the culprit by the sight that he was looking for — a thin, curling wisp of smoke in the distance. He pointed at it with his thumb, an affectation belonging to a past where he had been punished for pointing because his parents thought it rude. The men made their way until they could smell the cooking fire. With a wave of one hand, the leader indicated that the men were to spread out. They did, splitting into two columns and surrounding the small native encampment. The Penan, a nomadic tribe who wander about the Borneo rainforest in small communal groups, were gathered around a small river turtle being turned on a spit. Except for one or two young men who were wearing T-shirts, the men wore loincloths and the women were bare breasted. All were barefoot. It was a cheerful breakfast get-together. Old women cackled with toothless laughter. A wizened old man was telling a story in a high, quavering voice to a group of young men who were largely ignoring him. A young woman deftly lifted the spit and sliced the turtle onto a large banana leaf.

The men surrounding them waited for the signal. It came in the form of a sudden yell from their leader. They rushed into the encampment, scattering the gathered crowd. Women fled into the jungle clutching their children. A few men tried to protest. They were thrown to the ground and clubbed with thick wooden staffs. The old Penan man sat cowering, never moving from his spot. One of the men unstrapped the jerry can on his back and began to pour petrol over the area. He set the whole place on fire, stopping for a moment to admire his handiwork.

The leader grabbed the old man by the arm and yanked him to his feet. He shouted at him in Malay, 'You understand me?'

The old man nodded, his terror showing through cataract-filled eyes.

A young, pregnant woman, with long black hair and a gentle face, rushed over to his aid. She stood in front of the old man and glared at the intruders.

The leader grabbed her by the arm and yanked her towards him. He said, 'Go! Take your filthy kind and leave this place. If we see a Penan in this jungle, we will kill him. And we will hunt down his tribe and kill them too! Do you understand?'

The woman managed a nod.

She was flung back to the ground. She landed awkwardly and yelped with pain. The old man bent over her. The leader kicked him once in the knee for good measure. He fell. The man aimed another kick at him. He rolled over to escape. The pregnant woman took the whole weight of the boot. She curled up silently, trying to protect her stomach and the unborn child within.

The leader gave a whistle and his men fell in behind him. He led them back into the jungle, well satisfied. That had been quick and easy. But there were other communities to track down.

The Penan do not have many possessions.

They have lived for generations in the Borneo forests in harmony with their environment, taking what they need from the jungle, leaving no footprint but that of bare feet on muddy earth washed away with each rain. It was not difficult for them to regroup and move deeper into the forest. They would not be missed and traces of their ephemeral presence would soon be erased.

Inspector Singh took a leave of absence. He had accumulated a lot of leave — hardly ever having taken time off in the course of his career. His superiors did not ask him what he intended to do. If they had and if he was honest, they would have ordered him back to Singapore at once. Instead he implied that there was some sort of family crisis involving his sister. And since he was on the spot, he felt he should take a few days off and try and fix the problem.

Having been sent to try and avert a scandal, Inspector Singh was now well placed to become one himself. For, against his better judgement, he had agreed to Chelsea's request to stay on and try and help Jasper Lee. It was an absurd assignment. Even more ridiculous than his original remit to keep an eye on Chelsea and make sure she got a modicum of due process. At least she had always protested her innocence. Second time around, he was being asked to look out for a man who had blithely confessed to being a murderer. Singh had heard Jasper with his own ears — unforced, willing even — admit to shooting a man. Not just any man but his brother. Surely a man deserved to hang for holding his own blood so cheap?

But Chelsea Liew pleaded with him, urged him to believe that he was the only one who could help, that if he turned his back on her she would have nowhere else to go. She appealed to his dormant masculinity. It was a long time, the inspector thought, since any woman had made him feel needed. Chelsea explained her concerns in hushed, heartfelt tones. The Malaysian police were not going to look any further for a killer. They were embarrassed at having charged the wrong person once. She could not turn to any private investigator. She could not be certain that they were on her side. They would be in it for her money and the kudos of such a high-profile job. Probably they would sell any dirt they dug up to the tabloids.

She needed a professional. And he was it. After all, she pointed out, he had been sent to help her in the first place. She did not realise perhaps the large element that politics had played in the decision of the Singapore government to send him — corpulent knight to the rescue. Singh had no doubt that she sensed that he was emotionally embroiled in her affairs. Finally, he agreed. He could not quite remember the point that the conversation ceased to be about whether he would help but about how he would help.

She put a slender hand on his arm and said, 'Thank you. You have no idea how much this means to me.'

And he could see both that she meant it and that he was trapped.

Singh had no idea how he was going to proceed. He had no *locus* to ask questions. He had Chelsea's support which might open a few doors but not many. And he would certainly need the cooperation of the Malaysian police if he was going to try snooping around. He did not even know if Jasper would be willing to see him.

'Mum, is Uncle Jasper in jail?'

Chelsea looked at her eldest son. Marcus was a thin and wiry seventeen-year-old with a teenager's quick passions. But of late the feisty, combative youth had become quiet — his eyes always on the ground in front of him. She told herself that it was inevitable that recent events had taken their toll. Marcus had been very unhappy with his father

— coming to her defence when he had started to hit her. He would pit his strength against the grown man and be brushed aside. But when Alan had died it had still hit Marcus hard. She had not understood his reaction, fluctuating between despair and anger. But she had tried to give him the confidence that they could carry on, that time would make them whole again — until she was arrested for murder and dragged away from her children. She had no idea how the boys had coped. The wounds were so raw that she had refrained from discussing her ordeal or theirs but just tried to compensate them with love.

She had not answered his question and Marcus asked again, 'Is Uncle Jasper in prison?'

She nodded and tried to put her arms around him but he resisted and pulled away.

'For killing Daddy?'

'Yes,' she said.

'Do you believe he did it?'

She shook her head emphatically.

Marcus punched a door, hard.

Chelsea looked at him, her face creased with intense concern. It was a fleeting snapshot of what she would look like as an old woman.

Of her three sons, it was Marcus she was

most worried about. The other two, with the resilience of children, were recovering from their ordeal. They were insecure, clinging and demanding — punishing her for having left them. But she did not doubt that time would restore their equilibrium. Marcus was another matter. He was the one who had understood a little of what she had gone through being married to Alan Lee.

It had started to affect his behaviour well before the divorce. Seventeen years old, with a driving licence and the Mercedes sports car his father had bought him as a birthday present over Chelsea's angry protests, he was always out or locked in his room. She knew he went clubbing. She could smell the stale cigarettes and old beer on his clothes and his breath in the morning. She knew he had girlfriends, impressing them with his fast car, moneyed background and devil-may-care attitude. She could see the hatred he felt for his father, as well as a burning anger at her, Chelsea, because she was his mother and she had let herself be hurt and there was nothing that he could do.

As the divorce had approached, Marcus calmed down — relieved perhaps that his mother was finally taking steps to leave his father. He was still out of the house at all hours but seemed calmer and happier.

Chelsea had wondered if he had found a serious girlfriend. Marcus needed all the affection he could get. Chelsea knew that a mother's love was not proving enough to stop her firstborn from losing his way.

But during the custody hearings, Marcus had reverted to his old ways. She had found bottles of alcohol in his room. He never washed or changed his clothes. She had asked him whether he was worried that his father might get custody, assured him that she was going to win.

He had laughed bitterly and said, 'I'm seventeen, Mum. Neither of you has any control over me — it doesn't matter a damn which of you has "custody".'

She had not been able to work out what was upsetting him. She could not find a way through the wall her son had erected around himself — to keep her out.

She tried again. 'Marcus, what's the matter?'

He shook his head.

'Don't shut me out. Let me help you.'

'You? You can't even help yourself!'

Inspector Singh still had the file on the murder. It was time to look at it again — this time with a view to exonerating Jasper. He sat down at the desk in his hotel room.

129

Three hours later he stood up, felt his knees creak with the effort, and left the hotel in one of the red and white taxis that spread like a rash across Kuala Lumpur. Any plans to think about the contents of the file he had just read were soon lost in the important business of hanging on to his seat as the driver weaved his way through traffic, missing each motorbike by inches and every car by less.

He stopped some way from the scene of the murder. Singh told himself this was in order to understand the general environment of the crime better but it was actually because he was starting to feel carsick. He got out, gave the driver a few ringgit and looked around him.

In every direction, rows of terraced houses stretched. Each one had started identical but the owners had used the many years since their homes were built to express their individuality. In Singapore, house renovation had only one goal — to convey wealth. He had seen houses that appeared huge, with a vast amount of road frontage, only to pass by another day using another route and discover that the same house was narrower than a long boat.

In Kuala Lumpur, thought the inspector, the personalities expressing themselves in architecture were unique.

In many of the homes, charming well-tended gardens were the owners' innocuous way of stamping personality on their abodes. Rows of heliconia, pots of hibiscus and hedges of bougainvillea adorned many houses. Large mango or guava trees, sometimes outgrowing their small gardens, loomed large and dark over the road. Other householders had decided bricks and mortar were the best way to assert themselves and had built a puzzling array of additions to their tiny houses. Roof tiles had been swapped from the traditional rust to blue or green. Balconies with balustrades protruded. Ponds with carp and complex water features took up all the available garden space. Gates were wrought iron and picked out in gold. One house had stone elephants on the roof. Another had ceramic peacocks. An otherwise normal home had chickens pecking about in the garden. Bird flu was apparently less of a concern in Kuala Lumpur than back in Singapore.

Despite the poor architectural judgement, the streets had a certain charm. Singh supposed it was because, however peculiar, each addition was designed to reflect the owner's taste, rather than his wealth. Besides, many of the houses were rundown and needed a coat of paint. The brightest colours on the street were still the flowers, not paint jobs that looked like cake icing, as would have been the case in Singapore.

Inspector Singh got his bearings in consultation with a road map and set off towards the murder scene. It was a quiet part of the morning. There was not much traffic on the road. The school and work rush was over and the lunch rush had not started. He would have to come back in the evening and gauge the traffic. Was it likely that nobody had seen anything or were witnesses reluctant to come forward and be associated with this notorious case?

It took him five minutes to reach the spot where Alan had been shot. Here it was easier to imagine that the murderer had gone unnoticed. It was a quiet cul de sac. The crowded terraced houses had given way to individual bungalows hidden behind high walls and security cameras. The blue from swimming pools could be seen through front gates. Balinese-style villas complete with stone gargoyles and frangipani trees stood next door to mansions that had evidently used the White House as their design inspiration.

Inspector Singh dragged himself away from an awed perusal of the houses to contemplate the crime that had taken the life of one of its residents. According to his chauffeur's testimony, Alan Lee had alighted from his car, waved his driver away and turned to walk up the hill along the broad, quiet road leading to his unhappy home. He had not gone further than fifty yards when he met the person who had shot him. The murder weapon had not been recovered although the police had scoured the drains and the rubbish tips over a five-hundred-yard radius. Alan Lee's valuables, from his watch to his gold cufflinks, were left untouched. The murderer had wanted the only thing that a man of his wealth could not replace — his life.

The inspector stood silently, looking around him. Trying to understand, trying to visualise the murder. He was convinced, based on the forensics, that Alan Lee had known his killer. It was possible that the perpetrator had been frightened off before he had completed the robbery. But it struck the inspector as improbable. It was such a risky murder. It seemed farfetched that robbery was a motive or, if it was, that the killer would have abandoned his crime before completing it.

Singh walked all the way up to the gates of Alan Lee's residence. He did not know if

Chelsea was home and he did not seek to find out. He had nothing to report. There would be time enough to visit the widow when he had made some progress in the investigation into the murder of her ex-husband. She wanted him to exonerate her brother-in-law, Jasper Lee. The inspector did not conduct murder investigations based on who he most wanted to exculpate. He conducted investigations to find a murderer.

In his heart he knew he would be pleased if he could find proof, contrary to the widow's wishes, that implicated Jasper Lee. If he could prove to Chelsea that Jasper had done it, his confession was in earnest, she would abandon this effort to prove him innocent and get on with her life. Inspector Singh was not of a mind to contemplate the alternatives. If Jasper had not done it, the prime suspect would once again be the ex-wife of the victim.

Singh decided he needed access to Jasper Lee. He dug out his mobile phone and called Sergeant Shukor.

He said without preamble, 'Singh here. I need to see Jasper Lee!'

'Why?'

'Chelsea has asked me to look into the murder. Find some mitigating circumstances if I can.'

He decided the complete truth — that he was seeking to absolve the eldest brother — would be too much for the young sergeant to stomach.

There was hesitation at the other end. At last the policeman said, 'I can get you in. But if Inspector Mohammad finds out, I'll be in big trouble.'

'I won't tell him if you don't.'

The men sitting around the polished wood table, made from the cross-section of a single massive tree, were pleased. Things were going well. China's need for wood products was inexhaustible. Ever since the severe flooding around the Yangtze River a few years back, the Chinese government had cracked down hard on excessive or illegal logging on the mainland. But this had not in any way dampened the demand for wood for the massive ongoing construction site that was modern China. And the authorities, so belatedly mindful of the degradation to their own environment, turned a blind eye to wood sourced from overseas. As a result, primary forests across Asia, from Papua New Guinea to Borneo, were being denuded at a rate that would soon see the end of the great jungles of Asia.

None of these things were a concern to the men in the room. They were at the profitable end of the destruction. The four of them were fellow directors of Alan Lee's timber company. The boss was dead but the men were still doing their best to make money for the company under the guidance of their new boss, Lee Kian Min. Besides, Kian Min had been running the show for years. It would have been much harder to carry on if he had been the one killed.

Kian Min walked into the room, took the seat at the head of the table, received their respectful greetings and said, 'We are increasing our production out of Borneo.'

There were nods of approval all around.

'How come? I thought we had logged all the non-reserve land?' asked one of the men with nonchalant curiosity.

'Don't worry about it,' said Kian Min. 'We have found new areas.'

The others understood the implications of this. They had been in the timber trade their whole lives and their fathers before that. New areas after generations of intense logging could only mean wildlife reserves and protected forests.

'You need to be careful — there is a lot of concern. Those Penan are in the news every day,' said one of the men worriedly.

'I said no need to worry about it. I have everything under control.'

'What about the bio-fuels project?'

'That is also under control.'

Inspector Singh's sister was hanging clothes out to dry on the washing line attached to two iron T-shaped poles at the back of her house. She had a clothes dryer indoors. Her son had bought it for her as a present. She loved showing it off to people. 'That clothes dryer, my son bought for me as a present. He is doing very well, you know, and doesn't want his old mother to work too hard.'

But she never actually used it. Baljit was not convinced that clothes squashed into a dryer would get a proper airing. She was sure that the dark recesses of the machine's gaping maw contained mould and germs. The sun and wind had dried her family's clothes for generations and she was not going to change that. But she was very proud of the modern equipment taking up space in the laundry room and the son who had bought it for her.

Across the fence, her neighbour was also hanging clothes so it was natural to gravitate to the boundary to exchange words as they had done for the past twenty years.

Baljit opened the conversation with her

usual directness. She had something to boast about. 'My brother got that Chelsea Liew out of jail, you know.'

'What brother?'

'Singapore brother, lah. He's a very senior policeman!'

'That fat one is your brother, ah?'

'Yes. He got that girl, the one who killed her husband, out of jail.'

'I thought someone else confessed what?'

'Yes, yes. But why so suddenly — after my brother came from Singapore?'

'You think he made him confess? But in Singapore, police are not allowed to beat people.'

Baljit nodded her head. 'I still think the wife did it. Maybe she bribed the police to let her out?' She added as an afterthought in case this should reflect badly on her brother, 'Malaysian police, I mean. Singapore police cannot bribe, also.'

They both stopped to ponder this incorruptibility.

The Chinese woman across the fence said, 'My son says very easy one to bribe when you are caught in a speed trap.'

This sentiment drew no censure from the policeman's sister. 'Ya, you are right, but speeding . . . murder, different, lah!'

TEN

'Chelsea does not accept that you killed your brother.'

'And you believe her rather than me?' Jasper's question to the inspector seemed reasonable.

'Actually, no,' said the inspector.

'Then why are you here?'

'I'm not sure,' the inspector confessed with a sigh, rubbing his eyes with stubby fingers. 'I am going to lose my job when my bosses get wind of this . . . I guess I could never resist the request of a pretty woman!'

'Tell me about it,' said Jasper. 'Chelsea can be very persuasive.'

The inspector was quick to latch on to this. 'Are you saying that she persuaded you to confess?'

Jasper looked pained. 'Don't be ridiculous! She would never do that. She didn't try. And anyway, why would I agree?'

The inspector changed tactics. 'Look, I

accept you murdered your brother. At least tell me why. Then I can convince Chelsea you did it and go home. She does not seem to be prepared to accept your word for it.' He added a sweetener. 'Maybe I can find some mitigation — save you from hanging at least!'

'Like what?'

'I don't know. I came here from Singapore last week, for God's sake! Anything — self-defence, provocation, accident. Anything!'

Jasper looked at the inspector long and hard.

The policeman could see that prison was taking its toll on the man. He was pale. He had lost much of the colour of the outdoors-man in a few short days. His skin sagged, the weight loss too sudden for the elasticity of his skin. In prison clothes, his tragicomic face emphasised the tragic.

At last, he seemed to come to a decision. He took a deep breath, squared his shoulders and said, 'There is something.'

'Well, that's nice,' said the inspector dryly.

The prisoner ignored the sarcasm. He sat in the plastic chair, elbows on the table, deep in thought.

The inspector thought that Jasper's receding hairline had more grey in it than the first time they had met. He wondered again what led men to commit crimes when the physical and mental consequences were too much for the frailty of the human body and spirit. With Chelsea, at least he had been able to understand why she might have turned to murder as a solution. She must have felt there was no other option to keep her kids away from Alan Lee. But the inspector could not see what might have driven Jasper to such an act.

The inspector waited for Jasper to speak. He was used to these moments. The quiet had a pregnant quality, like a city just before dawn, teetering on the edge of a noisy awakening. Singh had been in innumerable interviews with prisoners as they sat silently pondering what truths to tell and what lies to invent. Eventually, they would make up their minds and start to speak, uttering carefully honed exculpatory sentences that they had played in their minds over and over again in the long days and nights in their cells, clinging to the hope that one of the words would be the 'Open Sesame' that got them out of jail.

The act of speaking, the release from silence, invariably meant that the prisoner would say too much, give something away, let slip an honest truth in the midst of the self-justification. Inspector Singh, like a fine piano-tuner, could listen to these verbal outpourings and pick up those hints of expression or emotion that were off-key and those that rang true. And so he waited for Jasper Lee to open his mouth, and a door to the truth, at the same time.

'There is someone to see you, ma'am. He says it's urgent.' The maid managed, in the great tradition of household workers, to convey far more than she said in words. Looking up at her, Chelsea could tell, from the slight emphasis on the word 'someone', that she did not know and did not approve of the guest who was waiting to see her employer. From the hint of a raised eyebrow she knew that her helper did not believe for a second that the matter on which he wanted to see her was urgent. Nevertheless, the maid knew better than to substitute her own judgement for that of Chelsea's, especially in these difficult times. She stood waiting for instructions.

Chelsea got out of the easy chair she had been lying in to read court papers. She went to the window and parted the curtains slightly. A short, overweight Chinese man stood at the entrance holding a file.

She said, 'Let him in.'

The man was sweaty. The few strands of

hair he had left were arranged carefully across his scalp. His eyes had disappeared so far into the rolls of fat on his face that only two small, black pinpricks remained. Despite all this, he managed to convey, through a puffed chest and a big smile, that he was pleased with himself.

Chelsea said, 'Good morning, Mr Chan. What can I do for you?'

'Nothing, nothing! But I can do something for you, yes, yes.'

Chelsea waited politely.

'You remember you ask me to investigate your husband Alan Lee? Find out what he was up to . . . about other women and things?'

The maid, having made a tactical decision to dust the next room, heard this and nodded her head wisely. A private investigator — that made sense.

Chelsea said, 'Yes, of course I remember — but you might not have heard that my husband is dead. So, if this is about your fees, please send me your bill for the hours you worked.'

Mr Chan had one very long nail on his left hand. It curled. He used it carefully to pick his nose. He said, 'I know Mr Alan is dead. I found out some things — I was going to pass them to you — but you also went to jail.'

Meeting with silence, the private investigator became garrulous. He realised that the tactics he used to provoke reminiscences from cheating husbands were now being used on him. It did not stop him talking. He said, 'When you come out of jail, I thought better to pass you the file. You can read it. Always good for the wife to know everything. I know Mr Alan dead . . .' The man wiped his brow with a short shirt sleeve and got to the point. 'My bill is on top.'

Chelsea nodded, keen to get rid of this gross little man. She said, 'All right, I will look at the file. If the information is useful, I will send you a cheque.'

'Cash, please.'

She raised an eyebrow.

'Otherwise, my wife will take the money.'

Chelsea nodded abruptly. Mr Chan understood that he was being dismissed and walked out of the door, smiling broadly. He did not doubt he would get his money.

The widow watched him go. She felt another blast of anger at her dead husband for putting her in a position where she had been forced to consort with lowlifes in an effort to dig up some dirt that she could use in the custody hearings.

144

Mr Chan had not been the only one she had hired — and a few of them had come back with enough information for her to prove adultery. She remembered how she was so absolutely sure that she was going to win custody of the children and put the whole unhappy history of her marriage to Alan Lee behind her. And then he had dropped his bombshell. He was Moslem, so were the kids — he should have custody. Chelsea Liew, surrounded by uncertainty, fear and doubt, was convinced of just one thing at that moment in time — Alan Lee had deserved to die.

It was not apparent that the man was Caucasian. He was burnt nut brown by the sun. This was not a superficial tan but deeply embedded into his skin which was leathery and lined like cured animal skin. His hair was unkempt, streaked with grey, greasy and tied back with a length of twine. His clothes were worn through with make-shift patches over the knees. It was only when he looked up — as he did now at the policeman behind the desk — that his piercing blue eyes gave his race away.

The accent was pure Queen's as well — England not Brooklyn. 'These people are being terrorised and I want to know what you are going to do about it.'

The policeman said, 'I will report to the senior officer when he comes in — for now you fill in the incident report. That is our procedure.'

'I tell you that the weakest members of your society are being hounded off their land and this is your response?'

'You are foreigner — why you come here and shout at me? You do not understand the Malaysian way. These Penan are trouble-makers. You should not believe everything they tell you.'

'Tell me? I've seen the destruction with my own eyes. A pregnant woman died!'

'I will report it, sir.'

'You do that.'

The policeman watched the Englishman walk out the door, slamming it behind him. As if the exit was his cue, the senior officer, wearing a tan bush jacket with the gold frame of his reading glasses poking out of a pocket, appeared at the door to his office. He had been listening to proceedings quietly in his room. The two men looked at each other.

'What should we do?' asked the junior man. 'If he calls the newspapers . . .' He trailed off into silence.

They both knew the consequences. There

146

was no need to spell it out and leave the words hanging like prophecies in the air.

'He must not go to the newspapers. You know what to do.'

The senior policeman went back into his office and closed the door with exaggerated care.

The younger man sat quietly at his desk for a moment. He looked at the screen saver picture of his wife. She was smiling shyly at the camera — pretty, demure, deeply honest. She was pregnant with their first child now. He wondered if it was true that a Penan woman had lost her life. He wished that there was something he could do to rewind the clock. To crawl back up the slippery slope that had led him to this point. Be the husband and father his family deserved. It was too late. All he could do now was try and keep from being found out. Keep the family safe and happy in their ignorance. He unbuttoned his holster and slipped his revolver out. He had never used it except on the firing range. He checked that it was loaded, slipped it back into its case and walked out of the door onto the dusty street.

Rupert Winfield was staying at a Chinese lodging house in Kuching. It was a favourite haunt of backpackers. It was cheap and had in residence a loudmouthed Chinese woman. She collected the rent, kept the place spotless, wore nylon floral dresses and fake pearls all day and in all weathers and cooked up cheap but tasty meals of fried rice in the café she ran on the ground floor for any of her guests who needed an inexpensive meal to go with their cheap room. She was known as Mrs Wong although in the many years that she had run her establishment, there had never been any sign of Mr Wong. She had a large notice board on one wall of her café and it was covered with photos and notes from the young men and women who had passed through her doors on their way to or from the Borneo interior. All were messages of thanks for a motherly outpost in a threatening world.

She was always proud to receive a new memento for her wall and the little ceremony with which she greeted an addition never varied. She would slit open the envelope, remove the picture or card, put it carefully on the table, cut out any return address, placing it in a box on her desk already filled with yellowing paper, walk down to her wall, examine it carefully, smile as one or two faces brought back an amusing memory, pin her new addition carefully in a vacant spot, take a step back to admire her handiwork and then sit down to a cup of coffee in a clear glass mug — stirring the thick layer of condensed milk at the bottom until it was thoroughly mixed with the jet black, bitter coffee on top.

A policeman walked into the café. He looked around carefully, searching for someone, and then walked out again. Mrs Wong, watching the street with the contented pleasure of a hardworking woman who knew this was a deserved interlude before she went back to iron-fresh sheets, could see him on the road, a dark silhouette against the bright sun. He tapped his foot impatiently, as if his body was annoyed at the indecisiveness of his mind. At last he came back in and walked over to the small desk that served as a reception for the hotel. It was unmanned and he looked around — seeking someone to attend to him. Mrs Wong waddled over. He looked at her and asked brusquely, 'Mr Winfield — he stay here?'

She nodded.

'Which room?'

'Why you ask me that?'

'None of your business!' The young man's hand caressed the butt of his gun for a second and she could see the beads of sweat on his hairline and upper lip.

He asked again, 'Which room? I know he stay here.'

She said, 'One, one, five.'

He made for the stairs.

'Where are you going?'

'Stay out of police business, old woman!'

She said mildly, 'He is not in his room.'

This stopped him in his tracks. Mrs Wong nodded to the little pigeonholes behind her. His strained eyes found the slot marked '115'. A key was bundled into it.

'Do you know when he will come back?'

'Not sure.' She shrugged, indicating that her rules were easy and her guests independent.

The policeman said firmly, 'Don't tell him that the police are looking for him. I will come back later.'

He did not go far. She could see him standing under the limited shade of a casuarina tree across the road, watching the entrance to the hotel. Occasionally, he would glance up and down the street. Mostly, he kept his eyes trained on her front door. She went back to her cup of coffee, grown cold in the interim, and made a face of disgust when she had a sip. She put it down, went to a cupboard, took out a mop and bucket, shouted in Cantonese to the staff that she would see to the bathrooms upstairs and started up the stairs. She could feel the eyes of the policeman on her back. As she reached the semi-cool darkness at the top of the stairs, out of sight of the road, she hastily put down the bucket and hurried to Room 117, tapping gently on the door. Rupert Winfield opened it, looking haggard and dishevelled. She looked past him into the room lit with a single, bright fluorescent tube. His clothes were scattered on the bed. An empty suitcase on the floor suggested that he was starting to pack.

She said, 'You better hurry, lah. The police are looking for you.'

Chelsea opened the file the private investigator had given her. There was a note on the top with the name and address of a woman, 'Sharifah Abdul Rahman, #04-04, Rose Condominium, Ampang'. It was stapled to the investigator's bill for two thousand ringgit. Her eyebrows went up. Mr Chan must be convinced of the value of the information he had provided and expected her to be willing to pay handsomely for it.

The only other thing in the file was a CD. Chelsea held it in her hand, watching as the light caught the gleaming surface. Did she really want to see what was on this recording? Presumably, it was yet more evidence of Alan's adultery. She had always known and never needed proof. The courts had required evidence, so she had found it for them. None of it mattered any more now that Alan was dead. Reluctantly, Chelsea decided that she could not ignore it. It might contain something as simple as Alan tucking into a plate of *char siew* — roast pork — after his so-called conversion to Islam. It might eventually be good evidence, assuming one of the courts would actually look into the matter, that religion was purely a matter of convenience for Alan Lee.

She ran up the carpeted stairs lightly and soundlessly. She went into the spare bedroom and locked the door. There was a television and DVD player, rarely used, in there. The state of her marriage had not allowed for many guests. Steeling herself, she slipped the CD in, grabbed the remote controls and perched on the edge of the bed.

The images had been shot on a recording device with fairly low resolution — a mobile phone, Chelsea decided. She had no difficulty recognising her husband as he sat on a bar stool watching the dancers at a club. Chelsea could not tell if it was because of the quality of the recording but the air seemed smoky. Flashing lights in many colours punctuated the scene and she could almost smell the perspiring dancers. The sound was largely muffled but Chelsea could make out the persistent beat of loud music. She wrinkled her nose in disgust. Alan had been so pathetic, going clubbing to places where the average age was twenty years younger than him. She continued to watch, wondering if all there was on the tape was Alan sipping a cocktail.

A young woman walked up to Alan. She was exquisite. Tall and thin, with beautifully made-up features, she strode into the shot like a model. With a start, Chelsea realised that the woman bore a strong resemblance, in height and style, to herself. Alan had not seen her as she walked up to him. He was concentrating on the dancers. She slipped a long, thin arm around his neck and he swivelled on his stool. Standing over him, she leaned down and kissed him full on the mouth. It was a smooth, sensuous action — even on a phone recording. Alan responded by standing up and folding the woman in his arms. Chelsea felt her stomach muscles clench. Knowing your husband was adulterous and watching him were two different things. Public displays of affection — or lust, thought Chelsea dismissively — were not common in Malaysia. A few people had turned to look at the couple kissing so uninhibitedly. This was Sharifah, whose address was in the file, she supposed. The screen went blank. She wondered why Mr Chan thought she would be willing to pay two thousand ringgit for what he had provided.

The camera came back on. Perhaps he had been trying to conserve the battery. A young man had marched up to the couple. He was slim, dressed in black with short, dark hair. He grabbed the woman by the arm and yanked her away from Alan. She turned in surprise, and then seeing who it was, took a step backwards and said something — it was impossible to hear over the music. It was obvious that she knew the young man. He grabbed her by the shoulders and shook her — not roughly, almost pleadingly. It was clear to Chelsea what had happened. Alan had stolen this girl from the young man and he was desperate to win her back. Seeing the woman's face for the first time, Chelsea realised that despite her dress and make-up she was very young. She was not in Alan's usual style at all. He liked his women to be practised. No doubt she had been swept off her feet by an older man with money who knew how to be charming. Chelsea could almost feel sorry for the girl.

Alan had grown tired of the young man's

impassioned pleading because he grabbed him by the arm and pulled him away from the girl. The girl put out a hand, a gesture of sympathy, an apology — it might even have been a sign that she knew deep down that her affections lay with him. Alan must have recognised the possibility because he put both hands on the stranger and shoved. The boy stumbled backwards, found his balance and would have charged forward to attack Alan if the girl had not stepped between them. She shook her head at the young man. He said something and she shook her head again, more firmly this time. The boy raised an angry finger — pointing at Alan over the girl's shoulder. Chelsea could just make out the words, 'I won't let you get away with this!'

And then he turned and almost ran away from the couple. But not before he had looked directly into Mr Chan's camera.

Chelsea collapsed backwards onto the bed. She buried her face in a pillow.

ELEVEN

'I killed him.'

The inspector said testily, 'Yes, yes! I've heard this part before. I am asking you why!'

'His job . . . his business.'

'You wanted his business?' There was no disguising the puzzlement in the inspector's voice. 'But I thought you walked away from all that. Chelsea told me that you had no interest in money matters.'

Jasper said impatiently, 'Not to get his business, to stop Alan running it!'

'Why?'

'Everything he has ever done is illegal and destructive.'

'I'm not sure what you mean.'

'The family business is logging — my father was the original timber magnate. He built an empire cutting down trees from coast to coast.'

The inspector nodded to indicate that he knew the potted history of the Lee family.

'Alan was expanding operations to Borneo. That is where the best logging is — most of the old-growth hard wood on the peninsula is long gone. What is left is on nature reserves and fairly well-policed.'

'I still don't know what you're driving at.'

'He was logging illegally. Destroying the rainforest ecosystems. Driving species to extinction. Hounding the indigenous tribes and chasing them off the land they have used for thousands of years.'

Jasper Lee's voice was rising with anger — his genuine disgust at his brother's actions apparent in the reddening face.

The inspector's voice dripped with sarcasm. 'Are you trying to tell me that you're some sort of ecoterrorist?'

Jasper was stung into a reaction. 'I don't care what you believe! You asked me for an explanation and I've given you one.'

The inspector snorted.

'What do you want from me?' asked Jasper tiredly.

'The truth would be a good place to start.'

The self-confessed murderer stared past the policeman at the grimy walls of his cell.

He said, 'You ask me for the truth but you don't believe me when I tell you. I know it sounds farfetched, when you live your life in air-conditioned cities — shopping and going to the movies — that I could have killed my brother to save the rainforests.'

The inspector was silent. This did not seem the time to point out that he hadn't been shopping or to a movie in years.

Jasper continued, 'But if you're out there, in Borneo, you would understand.'

Inspector Singh raised one of his expressive eyebrows.

Jasper hung his head, refusing to meet the policeman's eyes.

Finally, the inspector said, 'All right — let's say I take your word for it — you killed your brother because of these . . . jungle people. Why now?'

Jasper looked at him, brow wrinkled with perplexity.

'Presumably Alan has been up to no good for years. Why did you kill him now? Besides, I understood it was your other brother, Lee Kian Min, who was the brains behind Lee Timber anyway. Haven't you just made things worse? You killed the wrong brother.'

Kian Min was frankly mystified. He had no idea why his brother Jasper had confessed to the murder of Alan. Even if he had committed the murder, which Kian Min thought highly unlikely, Jasper wouldn't have had the balls, surely there was no reason to implicate himself by confessing so dramatically.

Kian Min had taken Alan's messy divorce and lengthy custody battle in his stride. When Alan had asked him to testify as to his good character, to nullify the damage Jasper had done by appearing for Chelsea, he had laughed out loud and then agreed to help — for a price. He remembered the occasion well. Alan had summoned him on the office intercom. Even when he wanted a favour, he still demanded that his brother come up to the big office to see him. Kian Min would have wagered money that Alan did not even know where, in the huge Lee Building on Jalan Raja Chulan, he had his modest office. But he had trotted up dutifully and agreed to help — if his brother would cease objecting to his big idea to expand the business.

He had never understood Alan's reluctance to adopt his most recent business development plan. Alan rarely got involved in planning and never had a view on prudent policy. Every now and then though, to Kian Min's intense irritation, he would step in and veto some plan. Or more rarely, as it required work, propose some seat of his pants idea to turn water into wine. Kian

Min was certain that Alan did it just to yank his chain, stop him getting ideas above himself about where he belonged in the company's hierarchy, remind him who, by an accident of birth, was the boss of Lee Timber.

Alan's most recent effort had been to veto Kian Min's plans to turn the land they logged in East Malaysia into oil palm plantations. Kian Min firmly believed that the future of the business was in bio-fuels. And the company had a huge advantage muscling into the market because of the land concessions they had and could easily buy from corrupt government officials. But Alan had refused. He had asserted that Lee Timber was a timber company and he was not going to compromise on the legacy his father had left him. He had implied that he, Alan, had inherited the trade because his father had trusted him with the family business. In vain had Kian Min pointed out the advantages of diversifying and the dangers of staying hooked on a logging industry that was fast running out of trees. Alan was obdurate. Until, that is, he had needed his brother to testify at the custody hearings. Kian Min had spelt out the cost of his co-operation — setting up of the bio-fuels unit. Alan had agreed immediately.

'What happened to all your big talk about protecting Father's legacy?' Kian Min had asked snidely.

'I couldn't care less. I just love that look on your face when I screw up one of your pretty little business plans.'

Kian Min, standing before his brother's desk like a schoolboy summoned to see the headmaster, had grown pale with anger, but had not said anything.

Alan had waved his hand to indicate that his brother could leave the room.

His parting words were, 'Get out! That sour face of yours is going to put me off my lunch.'

Inspector Singh looked mournfully at his shoes. His snowy white sneakers were streaked with mud and covered in a fine film of grey dirt. In Singapore, where one could eat lunch off the pavements, he never had any difficulty keeping his footwear pristine. But Kuala Lumpur was a more challenging proposition. The density of cars on the complex network of roads, its location in an airless, windless valley and the largely sporadic tree cover meant that there was always a layer of grime on his clothes and footwear. He wondered whether the time had come to abandon this affectation and buy a pair of black, leather shoes. He scratched his chest through the white vest he always wore under his shirt. A bead of sweat rolled down from his turban and left a moist trail all the way to his collar.

He watched a young Malay woman with a baby under one arm try and heave a pram onto the high pavement. He got to his feet and went over, helping her lift the pram up. She gave him a grateful look and then scurried into the nearest air-conditioned shop, desperate to get out of the sweltering heat. The infant in the pram wore a full body suit, mittens and a cap over his head. His small face was red and dazed. Her toddler was dressed in jeans and a long-sleeved shirt. A mini-man with damp hair plastered to his forehead.

Inspector Singh shook his big head to himself. He knew what these observations were about. He was taking in detail, scrutinising his surroundings, immersing himself in his environment. All his detective skills and instincts were in overdrive. But he was impeded by his lack of status and his peculiar remit. He picked up a newspaper and settled back into his chair, waiting for his coffee and his guest.

Moving quietly as he always did, Singh did not notice the young sergeant until he was right in front of him. The older man gestured at a chair, inviting Shukor to sit down. He did not. He stood looking down at the inspector, a troubled expression on his face.

'What is it?' asked Singh.

'There's another man.'

'What do you mean?'

'Chelsea had . . . has maybe, a boyfriend.'

'How do you know?'

Sergeant Shukor slipped a letter across the table. It was handwritten with looping juvenile strokes and much underlining for emphasis. The inspector picked it up gingerly and read the enthusiastic plans of a young man composed on the demise of his lover's husband.

'Where did you get this?'

'We were putting together the stuff we took from searches of the Lee residence after Chelsea was arrested. I came across this while I was tidying.'

'Alan Lee didn't know about this enthusiastic young man!'

'Why do you say that?'

'Well, I suspect it would have come up in the custody battle. It might even have stopped him from converting to Islam. Adultery is never viewed with enthusiasm by the courts. She might have lost custody without any of these religious episodes.' Singh continued thoughtfully, 'In fact, if she was still in the dock for murder, this letter would have been the final nail in the coffin.'

'Are you going to ask her about it?'

Singh grimaced and gestured at the letter. 'I would very much prefer to know as little as possible about the repulsive creature who wrote this piece of epistolary art.' He picked it up again and looked at the signature. 'One Ravi, apparently. But you're right. We do have to make sure this has no bearing on the case. Chelsea may not be a suspect any more. But she seems very sure that Jasper did not do it. Maybe she knows something we don't about this boyfriend of hers! If his literary effusions are to be taken seriously, he is a creature of strong emotions.'

Chelsea got up off the bed, walked to the bathroom and splashed cold water over her face. She took the soft bath towel and scrubbed herself dry. She looked at herself in the mirror. Her eyes were those of a cornered wild beast. She sucked in a few deep breaths. Everything she had ever done, she had done for the children. They needed her more than ever now. She did not know where she was to find the strength. She felt physically sick, cowed by what she had just discovered on the disc from the private investigator.

A pounding on the door distracted her.

Her youngest son was yelling for her to come out. He wanted to show her something. It was important. She unlocked the door and he came tumbling in, all excited about the grasshopper he had caught in the garden.

She said distractedly, 'That's very nice. Remember to be gentle with it. Mummy can't come to look at it now. She has to go out for a while.'

The boy looked rebellious and Chelsea put her arms around him and hugged him tight.

She said, a little catch in her throat, 'I'll be back soon, honey.'

The chauffeur was outside but she waved him away and grabbed the car keys. She did not want anyone to know where she was going. She nosed the car out of the garage and into the street. She drove past the spot where Alan had been killed. The notepaper with the address jotted down on it lay on the passenger seat. She knew where she was going. She was not sure what she was going to do when she got there.

Rose Condominiums turned out to be an

elegant, low-rise development some distance away from any main road. Chelsea took the elevator up to the fourth floor and hurried down a wide, well-lit corridor until she was outside apartment #04-04. She hesitated. She noticed the number four, considered unlucky by the Chinese as signifying death, and made up her mind. She put a finger on the doorbell and pressed firmly. She could hear the faintest of rings through the heavy door.

A few moments later the door was opened a crack and a young face peeped out. Her mouth rounded into a literal 'o' of surprise when she realised who it was. The older woman's recent notoriety meant she was instantly recognisable wherever she went. She stood there uncertainly. Chelsea took a step forward, signalling her intention to enter. The woman shrugged and stepped aside. Chelsea walked into the apartment. It was a pleasant, airy place with watercolours on the walls and Persian carpets on the floor. A very large, smoky cat twined itself around her legs, mewing softly.

Chelsea remarked calmly, 'Nice place. Did my husband pay for it?'

The girl, she was no more than a girl really, did not say anything but her guilty face spoke volumes.

Sharifah picked up the cat and hugged it to her cheek. She asked quietly, 'What do you want?'

Chelsea wandered over to the dining table. It was piled high with books and papers. The girl was studying — they were mostly science texts.

She asked, genuinely curious, 'Why in the world did you get involved with him?'

'I don't know really. He was so kind. He bought me so many things. He seemed so worldly.'

Chelsea could have screamed at the other woman for being so naïve. The only thing that held her back was the knowledge that she had fallen into the same trap herself so many years ago.

Sharifah said defiantly, 'He said he would marry me. I believed him. He said he was divorcing you. It was all in the newspapers so I knew it was true.'

Chelsea shrugged. 'He might have done, I suppose.'

'He even agreed to convert to Islam because I'm a Moslem!' insisted Sharifah, stung by the disbelief in Chelsea's voice.

Chelsea looked up sharply at this. 'He did convert,' she said abruptly. Could it be that he had done it to marry this woman? If he had really intended to marry her, he would have had no choice. It was the law. Marriage to a Moslem in Malaysia required the non-Moslem to convert to Islam. That would destroy her case that the conversion was a cynical ploy to get the children, that Alan had not been a genuine Moslem and therefore the kids weren't either. The Syariah court would almost certainly take the kids away from her. She looked at Sharifah, trying to decide if Alan had really fallen in love with her. It was not impossible. There was no fool like an old fool. And she really was beautiful — young, fresh, with that gentle voice.

Sharifah said, 'I really believed he wanted to marry me. But then someone killed him. I heard at first it was you . . . but then they arrested the brother.'

'Jasper confessed.'

'I see,' but it was clear that she didn't.

'Were you upset when he died?' asked Chelsea.

'Of course,' asserted the young woman, but she looked down, sleek hair falling over her face like a veil.

Chelsea looked at her pityingly. Her regret did not ring true. Perhaps she had begun to suspect that a relationship with an older man, however rich, was not all it was cracked up to be. Probably Alan had started to hit her. Possibly she had woken up in his arms one morning and realised that things were not going to be so rosy when she was still a young woman but her husband had become an old man. Or perhaps she really cared about that young man who had begged her so passionately to come away with him.

Sharifah screwed up the courage to ask again, 'What do you want? Why are you here?'

'It's not about my husband, actually. It's about my son.'

TWELVE

Sharifah looked frightened. 'What do you mean?'

'I am not interested in your sordid affair with my ex-husband. I want to know about your . . . relationship with my son.'

'How do *you* know about it?' Sharifah's hair was tinted with a hint of auburn and she pulled at strands of it nervously.

Chelsea waved the question aside with a well-manicured hand. 'Tell me the truth.'

Sharifah's voice, when she spoke, was the merest whisper. She said, 'Marcus and I were at school together. We started going out. He didn't want to tell anyone because I'm a Moslem and he was afraid we would get into trouble. For a while, we were very happy.' She looked up defensively. 'I don't mean that we were making long-term plans or anything — just that we hung out and had a good time, that's all.'

'Then what happened?'

'Once, when the driver came to pick him up from school, I got in too. We were planning to go to the movies. Marcus never wanted to go home so he was always making plans.'

Her words hurt but Chelsea gave no outward sign of it. She listened impassively.

Sharifah continued, 'His dad was in the car. It was just a coincidence. He had a meeting nearby or something. He chatted to me a little bit. Not much. Marcus was always telling me how much he hated his dad but he seemed all right to me.'

Chelsea knew just how good Alan Lee had been at dissembling. Few people would suspect him capable of the cruelty he had shown her on meeting him for the first time.

'I guess he must have found out who I was . . . he pursued me.'

'And you swapped the son for the father?'

'Marcus was just a boy. Alan seemed so grown up. I didn't know what to do.'

Chelsea was silent.

Sharifah said, 'When Alan was killed, I was so worried that Marcus had done it. But then they arrested you . . . and now you say his brother has confessed?'

It was a prosaic escape. Mrs Wong led him downstairs — he stayed behind her, hidden from view by her wide girth and floral skirts. On the ground floor he fell to his knees, scurrying after her on all fours like a dog on heat. She did not say a word but marched down the corridor to the kitchen. There they both ignored the bemused stare of the toothless old man who washed the dishes. She opened the shutters. Rupert Winfield climbed out of the window, only standing up when he was outside and on the opposite side of the building to the watchful policeman.

He said through the open window, 'Thank you!'

She was more practical. 'Money, passport?'

He patted his breast pocket to reassure her and himself. 'Yes, I'm OK. I have everything.'

'Don't go to airport, lah!'

It was good advice. He nodded. She put up her hand in a tentative gesture of goodbye. He clasped the raised hand in both of his, bringing them close to his chest. She understood that his thanks were heartfelt.

The airport was out of bounds but he had to get back to Kuala Lumpur. In Kuala Lumpur, he knew people who knew people. He would get in touch with that wildlife activist, Jasper Lee. He was a good guy and he was related to the Lee family. He was pretty sure it was them who were behind the shocking events he had witnessed. Jasper might have some idea who was ultimately responsible for the attack on the Penan. But first he had to get there. And it was not going to be easy with a crooked policeman on his tail. He had no illusions. He was a threat to a multimillion dollar industry. They feared he would approach the newspapers with his story or seek out policemen and government servants who had not been bought. He could spread the story of the treatment of the Penan at the hands of the logging industry and allege indifference and corruption on the part of the police in Borneo.

The policeman who had tried to ambush him at the bed and breakfast was not pursuing him for a chat. If he disappeared here in Borneo, it would just be one more tale of a white man who had mistakenly believed he could tame the jungles. The Englishman slipped on a pair of shades. With his blue eyes obscured, his race was indistinguishable to the casual observer. It was his best chance of escape.

Rupert flagged down a taxi and headed to a fishing village a few miles outside Kuching. The men were out to sea. In the distance he could see boats bobbing up and down on a fractious ocean. There was only one boat tethered close to the river mouth. The fisherman on board was cleaning his nets and whistling through the gap in his teeth. It was a cheerful vessel, gleaming with a coat of fresh paint. It looked reasonably seaworthy as well. A Malaysian flag fluttered merrily at the helm. Rupert asked the man in broken Malay, 'Why you not go out today?'

The fisherman shrugged. 'Engine no start!'

'Is it working now?' The fisherman looked confused. 'Engine OK now?' he asked again.

The man grinned. 'Yes, OK now!'

'You want some money?' asked Rupert, taking off his glasses so that the man could see that he was foreign. In the eyes of the locals, most foreigners were wealthy tourists.

The fisherman gazed out to sea, looking at his compatriots making their way slowly back to shore with the day's catch on board, a shiny, silvery mass of fish wriggling against each other in tanks on board each boat.

'Every day I go to sea. There is so little fish left. I got five children. Of course I want money!'

'Good.'

■ ■ ■ ■

He was back again, the young policeman.
Mrs Wong was not surprised.

He asked, 'Where is he?'

She feigned ignorance. 'What do you
mean?'

'Rupert Winfield — in Room one, one,
five?'

'He not in one, one, five, he in one, one,
seven. He check out already!'

The policeman hit her. The blow was so
unexpected that she staggered backwards
and sat heavily in her chair, holding her jaw.
Leaning forward towards her shrinking
form, he said, 'If I cannot find this man, I
will come back for you.'

It was not difficult to work out what had
happened. He guessed that his prey had
slipped out the back — with the help of the
fat woman. His lip curled. If he failed to
track down his quarry, he would go back
and make her understand that it had not
been prudent to get in his way. The policeman thought hard. He knew because he had
warned the airport that Rupert Winfield had
not escaped that way. The only other possibility was a boat. The policeman climbed
on his motorbike and headed out of town

on the coast road. He stopped at the first fishing village. The men were just coming in to shore and denied seeing any *Mat Salleh,* a local term for white man, around their village, let alone taking him out to sea. Their wives, tying up their sarongs and getting ready to help with the fish, backed up this story. They had no reason to lie to him. It seemed likely that Rupert had either gone further up the coast looking for a ride out of Sarawak or he had headed out of town in the opposite direction, east rather than west. There was no way to know for sure. The sergeant shook his head. He was not getting the breaks. At this rate, he might be too late. Forewarned, Rupert Winfield undoubtedly recognised the need for urgency. It seemed doubtful that he had bothered to go further up the coast without at least stopping at this village first to seek a way out. The policeman decided. He would go back the way he had come.

He struck gold immediately. A small boy skipping stones into the water at the pier agreed at once that a white man had passed that way. '*Mata biru macam* David Beckham!' Blue eyes like David Beckham, he said in awe. The sergeant handed him a coin.

'Where did he go?'

The boy nodded nonchalantly in the

direction of the sea. *'Pergi sampan Pakcik!'* He left on the old man's boat.

'Ke mana?' Where to?

The boy shrugged. He did not know and did not care.

The policeman headed back to town. He would have to report failure.

Sergeant Shukor knew that it would be best for his career to maintain a distance from the maverick Sikh. Instead, he was getting involved in the details of the case against Jasper Lee. His official remit was to shadow the troublesome policeman from across the border. His unofficial mandate was to encourage him to leave as soon as possible by any means, including being obstructive. But he found himself actively helping out. He had already got the inspector in to see Jasper Lee on a number of occasions.

He had listened in on the interviews — admiring the way the inspector had mastered the use of silence as a weapon. He just sat there quietly in the cell, patiently waiting for Jasper Lee to start filling the empty spaces with words. There were no threats, no brutality expressed or implied. Just a gradual getting under the skin of an imprisoned man until he talked to pass the time or distract himself from the loneliness of certain death. And from this idle conversation had come nuggets of information. The most peculiar of which was this assertion that Jasper had killed his brother to stop his destruction of the environment. It was a lesson in interview technique that Shukor looked forward to testing the next time he was asked to interrogate a suspect or a witness. And the more the young man learned, the more he felt compelled to return the favour by arranging access for the Singaporean policeman. He knew that, when his superiors got wind of it, as they inevitably would, he would be in a difficult position, but he hoped by then something concrete would have resulted from their efforts.

He and the inspector sat in what was now their favourite restaurant, sipping hot sweet tea and watching the street vendors flog their wares that ranged from prayer mats to holy beads. All the products were geared towards the Friday prayer crowd who would soon be overflowing from the mosque, forming lines on the pavement facing Mecca and chanting praise of God.

Shukor was deep in thought.

At last he said, 'It is possible.'

'What?'

'It is possible that he killed his brother

because of what he was doing in East Malaysia, especially Sarawak.'

'What makes you say that?'

'I've been looking at his history,' replied Shukor.

He seemed to hesitate for a moment but then slipped a folder across the table to the inspector. Another breach of protocol, handing over confidential police files. It was the haul from Jasper's second-floor shophouse office in Chinatown. The police were thorough. They did not want the prosecution of Jasper for his brother's murder to end in failure. They had a confession. They wanted background information as well. After all, he would not be the first accused to retract a confession at the eleventh hour and insist it was provided under duress — whether true or not.

The inspector looked through the file with interest. The majority of papers were innocuous enough. They indicated an interest in conservation issues in Malaysia. There were World Wide Fund for Nature reports printed off the Internet, various flyers pleading for logging to be stopped in Sarawak, newspaper cuttings on the plight of every animal, from the orang utan to the pygmy elephant, as a result of deforestation. A draft research paper on a nomadic tribe in Borneo

— the Penan — was written by one Rupert Winfield. There was also correspondence between Jasper and Rupert Winfield on the problems faced by the indigenous peoples as their symbiotic relationship with nature was thrown out of kilter by the logging industry.

'I guess it shows he genuinely cared about these issues, but that is a long way from murder,' remarked the inspector.

'That's because I haven't shown you the best part,' was Shukor's response.

'What do you mean?'

Another folder was slipped across the table.

The inspector picked it up and flipped it open inquisitively. He started leafing through the pages, his bending posture indicating his progressive interest in the contents.

At last he looked up at the young man across the table. Shukor was looking a trifle smug. It was not often in their relationship that he was one up on the fat policeman.

'Where did you get this?'

'At his office as well.'

'Well, it is not quite a smoking gun but it does lend some credibility to his claims about his brother.'

Sergeant Shukor nodded.

They both looked down at the papers in front of them. It was a miscellaneous collection of company annual reports, government survey maps, handwritten notes, printouts of commodity prices and columns of numbers. It was difficult to see at first what Jasper had been driving at with his careful highlighting of maps and scribbled margin notes. But a careful look made it clear that by putting together the company returns and estimating the volume of wood that had been sold over the various years, more wood was sold by Lee Timber than appeared in their books. They had systematically inflated the prices they received for the timber and processed wood they exported to justify the large income flowing in. This combined with survey maps showing logging areas, conservation areas and marked with the results of Jasper's own aerial reconnaissance showed that logging had encroached deep into protected areas.

There were also letters written by Jasper to various authorities in Sarawak pointing out these findings, but the appended responses were always polite denials that there was a pattern of illegal logging going on under their noses. Their officers had checked out the allegations and found no truth in them.

In the margin of one of these replies, Jasper had scribbled angrily, 'How much did you get for this?'

'It was certainly a subject he cared about,' remarked Inspector Singh.

Shukor nodded. 'I can almost believe that he killed his brother for this.'

'A man on a mission?'

'Yes, if he had proof that his own family company was involved in the activities. You know what these Chinese are like — it's all family honour and saving face.'

'Surely he would have confronted his brother, not killed him!'

'Maybe he did.'

It was a pertinent point and well made, thought the inspector. It was quite possible that Jasper had confronted his brother and been given short shrift. What was the next step? Murder? Surely, trial by publicity first.

'Wouldn't he have gone to the newspapers?'

'He might not have had much luck.'

'What do you mean?'

'Plenty of cronies around. The newspapers might have refused to publish.'

The inspector pulled at his beard, now flecked with grey. It was possible that Jasper had tried all these options first, failed and then decided to kill Alan. But something did not ring true. He was still not confident that Jasper Lee had killed his brother over such an abstract issue. He thought of the murderers he had caught over the years. Crimes of passion and crimes of greed. He had never come across an altruistic murderer before. He still thought the boyfriend a more likely suspect. But Ravi had not confessed. And Jasper had.

'I do not believe that he was a genuine convert so what is the use of trying to take the children from the mother? It is cruel.' The thin, ascetic man in white robes and thick glasses spoke in a measured tone.

'We cannot question the conversion. It will open the floodgates for friends and relatives to argue the real intention of a convert after he is dead. People will doubt every new Moslem.' A young firebrand with flashing eyes and a black beard thumped the table to emphasise his conviction.

'We have to pursue the matter. We cannot set a precedent where we choose if and when to uphold Syariah law. That is not Islamic justice,' he continued.

'If it was not a genuine conversion, Alan Lee will have to explain his actions to God. We are not the judges of what is in a man's heart. He went through the necessary steps.

He professed to convert to Islam. He declared his children to be Moslem. We have a responsibility to see that his children are brought up in a Moslem household.'

This assertion was by the president of the Council. He was a venerable scholar and well respected by his colleagues even when they disagreed with him.

There was a small sigh from the ascetic as he saw which way the Council was leaning. He said, 'May Allah forgive us.'

Could she risk losing? The first hearing had been postponed. They were due back in court the following week. Chelsea sat in the waiting room of her Syariah lawyer's office — impatiently waiting to hear his advice. The waiting room was small and cramped. There were a couple of worn sofas — Chelsea could feel the springs through the floral fabric, yearning to break free. The carpet was stained with coffee or tea, perhaps tears too. There were a couple of Arabic phrases, she assumed from the Quran, framed and hung on the walls. A plastic ashtray with cigarette burn marks all round the rim sat in the middle of the glass-topped, cane coffee table. Next to it was a vase of cheap plastic flowers in those luminescent shades of pink and green which

Chelsea, rightly or wrongly, always associated with poor manufacturing standards in China. She knew the lawyer was both senior and successful. Why couldn't he clean up the filthy waiting room?

Finally, she was shown in. It was another small, cramped room. This one came with a desk piled high with books. Gold-trimmed black court robes, fraying around the edges from years of use, hung from a coat stand in the corner. The lawyer himself was small, almost gnomic, largely hidden by the piles of paper on his huge desk. He had large, pointy ears poking out on either side of the white cloth cap worn by Moslems who had performed the Hajj in Mecca. He stood up as she came in and she held out her hand, expecting the usual handshake.

He shook his head slightly. 'As you know, Mrs Lee, my religion forbids me from having contact with a woman who is not my wife.'

Chelsea's hand fell to her side. She was embarrassed, immediately on the defensive.

As if to accentuate the cultural gap between them, her lawyer walked around the desk, avoiding brushing against her as he did so, and opened the door that she had closed behind her. He pushed a doorstop into place with a slippered foot. He was not allowed to be alone with a woman who was not his wife either, not behind closed doors anyway. The preliminaries dealt with to his satisfaction he smiled, baring large coffee-stained teeth, and said, 'May I offer you a cup of tea?'

She shook her head mutely. She needed to get down to business. This man was the most senior practising member of the Sya-riah bar. He came highly recommended and, despite the slippers and fraying gown, he was expensive. She was not interested in tea-breaks.

He understood because he said, 'I know the background to your case, of course.' Left unsaid was that he would have had to be a hermit to avoid the details of Chelsea's recent exploits.

Chelsea nodded. 'What are my chances? Can they take my children from me?'

She was not in a mood to beat around the bush and her lawyer looked a little pained at being put on the spot so quickly.

He said, looking thoughtful, 'This is a very unusual confluence of circumstances.'

Chelsea glared at him. Apparently it did not matter whether it was within the Sya-riah or civil jurisdiction, all lawyers charged by the hour and would not answer a direct question.

She asked, 'So what does "unusual con-fluence of circumstances" mean for me and my children?'

Her lawyer sighed and looked up. She saw a sincerity in him that reassured her for a moment. His answer however did not. 'I don't know. I don't know what the outcome will be.'

There was a tense silence between them as they both digested his admission of ignorance as if it was an unripe fruit, sour and unpalatable.

The lawyer spoke first. 'It is always unfor-tunate to be precedent-setting in a case that is in the public eye. All the parties involved feel that they have to adopt the harshest line because they don't want to be seen to be weak.'

She nodded. She had always lived her life on the front pages of the tabloid press. But now she had gravitated to the broadsheets and the reputations of powerful men were at stake.

He continued, 'My contacts at the Islamic Council inform me that they are split on whether to pursue this custody matter in the first place. Not everyone is convinced that your husband's conversion was genuine.'

'Of course it wasn't!' snapped Chelsea.

'Unfortunately, the Council does not want to set a precedent of doubting the authenticity of a religious conversion. You can see why that would be. Whenever any non-Moslem converts, objecting family members will turn to the courts. A matter of faith will become a matter of evidence.'

Chelsea slumped back into her chair. 'What are you getting at?'

'The court might not let us introduce evidence that Alan was not really a Moslem. He followed the legal procedures to become a Moslem. They might take it at face value. If they do that — well, then strictly as a matter of Islamic family law, the children should be brought up as Moslems . . . and by Moslems. The court could take the children away from you.'

'What can we do?'

'There is one sure way to avoid losing your children,' the lawyer replied gently.

She looked up hopefully. 'What is it?'

'You could convert to Islam too.'

Chelsea said quietly, 'I've thought about that, of course.'

'Then why don't you do it?'

'Do you think that two conversions of convenience are really the solution?'

The lawyer steepled his fingers and looked at her ruefully. 'It's best if you don't reveal to me that any conversion to Islam by you would not be genuine. It is important that your adoption of the religion appears credible.'

Chelsea snorted. 'Like Alan's?'

The lawyer could not meet her eyes. He looked down, shuffled the papers on his table and sighed.

Chelsea spoke in a quiet voice. 'If I convert, it means Alan has won. He has reached out from beyond the grave to control what I do and how I live my life with my kids. I don't want to give him that victory . . .'

'It might be the only way of keeping your children.'

She nodded. 'I realise that. But for now I am still hoping for some justice from the courts.'

THIRTEEN

Singh was not looking forward to his appointment with Chelsea. To ask this woman about her Achilles' heel would not be pleasant. He was forced to concede that he was shocked to discover that she had a boyfriend on the side. He would not have thought it would be in her character. He supposed he was just not in a position to understand a vulnerable woman. He had no doubt in his mind about Ravi. He was a slippery character on the lookout for women he could exploit. It was his job — the way he made a living. Singh had come across many of his ilk over the years. He would have assumed they were too cowardly to commit murder for gain. But Chelsea's potential wealth and anticipated gratitude, if her husband was removed from the picture, might have tempted Ravi to overreach.

There was another possibility. Perhaps Chelsea Liew had provided the backbone

Ravi lacked to kill her husband. Singh wiped his face with a big, white handkerchief. He really did not want to contemplate Chelsea's involvement in the killing, whether she pulled the trigger or not.

Singh sat, wedged into a spindly, cushioned chair, waiting for Chelsea. He had turned down offers of refreshments, tea, freshly squeezed watermelon juice or coffee, from the demure, uniformed Indonesian maid. The best place to get honest impressions of people, as long as you could persuade them to talk, decided the inspector, was from the domestic help. Quarrels took place in front of them. Secrets were revealed as if they were not there. They were the most likely members of the household to pick up the phone when a boyfriend called, the most likely to discover the lipstick marks on a straying husband's shirt.

Singh decided to test his theory. 'Tell me about your boss, Alan Lee,' he said.

The Indonesian housemaid in her frilly apron was cagey, reluctant to speak.

She said at last, 'Nothing to tell, sir.'

'Nothing?' The policeman's tone was disbelieving.

She spoke more firmly this time. 'Nothing!'

In the inspector's experience, sometimes

those who tried to help did the most damage. Their attempts to mislead often flagged new avenues of investigation.

He persevered. 'The whole family must be very sad that the boss was killed,' he remarked.

He could see her struggle between the desire to agree with everything he said and the temptation to say what she really felt about her dead employer.

Finally, she said, 'Sometimes he had a very bad temper.'

'I know, I know! I heard that he hit his wife, Mrs Lee. But maybe she asked for it?'

The domestic help was not about to lambast him for being politically incorrect. Instead, she assured the policeman in hushed tones that Chelsea was a wonderful wife and mother who had never done anything inappropriate that could have provoked her husband to anger.

The inspector knew this was not true because he knew about Ravi. The sheer emphasis in the Indonesian's voice as she painted a picture of a paragon who could do no wrong made him suspect that the maid knew about the boyfriend too. Her loyalty to Chelsea impressed him. She was prepared to lie to a policeman to protect her, a courageous decision for a foreign

worker in Malaysia dependent on the goodwill of the authorities for her livelihood.

The door opened and Chelsea came in.
Dressed in a pair of white linen trousers,
with an equally cool sky-blue shirt worn
open over a white camisole, she looked fresh
and well — a far cry from the traumatised
woman of a couple of weeks ago.

She said now, as if theirs was a relationship of casual, gossipy friendship rather than
a bond forged in the most unusual of
circumstances, 'How are things going?'

He shrugged, bearded chin sinking against
his chest as if he was trying to avoid speech.

She looked at him quizzically. 'Go on, you
can tell me! I've had my fair share of difficult news in the past few months. Have
you found some evidence against Jasper? I
won't believe you if you tell me you have.'
She smiled to rob her words of offence.

The inspector said heavily, 'Not as such,
no. He says he killed his brother because he
was cutting down the rainforests.'

'Really?' She shook her head, disbelief
tinged with affection. 'I know Jasper takes
these things seriously but surely that's a bit
farfetched?'

Singh nodded. 'It strikes me as a bit odd
too.'

There was an awkward pause between

them. Singh tried to look competent and menacing at the same time, sitting up straight and stroking his beard.

She said, holding his glance, 'That's not really what you came to discuss, is it?'

He was the first to look away. He stared past her, looked at the ceiling briefly, tied a shoe-lace and then sat back up in his chair.

Chelsea said, half amused and half worried, 'For God's sake, how bad can it be?'

Singh said brusquely, 'We know about your boyfriend.'

It was her turn to sit back in her chair and avoid meeting his eye.

She said quietly, looking down at her hands, 'Ravi was the mistake of a woman with nowhere to turn . . . and no one to turn to. He is not relevant.'

'On the contrary, aside from Jasper, he's the best suspect we have.'

Chelsea looked at him directly. 'I've told you — Ravi meant nothing then and means nothing now.'

'Have it your way. But that leaves Jasper in the frame — by himself.'

'You've forgotten someone,' Chelsea said.

'Who?'

'Kian Min, Alan's younger brother. He's taken over the company. It's been his life's ambition to do that. Who is to say that he didn't kill Alan to inherit Lee Timber?'

'It's interesting,' remarked the inspector, 'that you are so anxious to help one brother, Jasper, but have no qualms about pointing a finger at the other brother, Kian Min.'

'It's not interesting at all,' snapped Chelsea. 'Jasper is a kind, decent man. Lee Kian Min would make Alan look like the good guy.'

Singh put up a hand. 'Fine, I'll look into it.'

They hauled Ravi in for questioning. Sergeant Shukor was only too pleased to lend a hand. He did not even mention the possible reaction of his superiors or indulge in his usual angst about getting into trouble if he continued to help the Singapore policeman. Like the inspector, he was curious to see the man who had cuckolded Alan Lee.

Ravi was extremely good looking, the fat policeman acknowledged to himself a little ruefully. He was in perfect physical condition — strong without being excessively muscular. With his mixed Indian-Chinese parentage, he had even features, warm eyes and flawless skin.

Nevertheless, it did not take them long, either of them, to get the measure of the man.

Ravi started out blustering. 'How can you arrest me? For what? I haven't done anything!'

'You were having an affair with a wealthy woman whose husband has turned up dead,' pointed out Singh.

Ravi turned pale. His eyes shifted from one policeman to the other. He stammered, 'I . . . I didn't do it. You can't go around accusing people of murder just like that. I want a lawyer. I won't say anything more until I have a lawyer! You're violating my rights.'

Singh suspected that Ravi's knowledge of police methods was derived entirely from American television drama.

Shukor said patiently, 'You've not been arrested. This is just a chat. You can walk out if you like.'

Ravi considered his options. The policemen watched him silently. Ravi decided belatedly on cooperation, no doubt afraid, thought Singh cynically, of the police proceeding to use the evidence of others without giving him a chance to put his side of the story forward.

'She pursued me, of course,' he offered as his opening remark in the cooperative phase.

Inspector Singh took a deep breath. He said, 'In what way?'

'We met at a party. I could see she was attracted to me.'

'How could you tell?' asked Shukor.

The inspector wondered whether the policeman was wasting valuable interview time trying to pick up tips about women from someone who fancied himself an expert.

Even in the company of two men, Ravi could not help running his fingers through his hair. A practised, flirtatious gesture.

He said, 'Well, she couldn't take her eyes off me. I noticed that right away. And when we were introduced and shook hands, she held my hand for just that bit longer than necessary.' He continued smugly, 'You can always tell, can't you?'

'Moving on,' said Singh brusquely, 'what happened next?'

'I gave her my phone number.'

'And she called you?'

'Not exactly, no. But we . . . er . . . bumped into each other a couple of days later at the Marriott and had coffee together.'

Singh had seen it so many times before. A man, little better than a gigolo, setting his sights on a rich, lonely, unhappy woman and engineering coincidences until he had wormed his way into her affections and her bed. He was just surprised that Chelsea had fallen prey to such a predator. He supposed that he had no idea what she had been through. And she was evidently an appalling judge of the male character. She had married Alan Lee, after all.

'Go on,' said Shukor brusquely to the boyfriend.

When discussing his successes with women, Ravi was not reluctant to talk.

'It was the usual story,' he continued, smirking slightly. 'She pursued me. We ended up having a relationship. I was reluctant because she was married, but in the end I could not say no.' Ravi stopped to admire the picture he painted of a moral man tempted too far by a determined woman.

'How much did you take her for?' asked the inspector abruptly.

Ravi looked pained. 'I have no idea what you are talking about.'

'How did you feel when she called off the relationship?'

'Who said she called it off?'

'She did!'

Ravi looked unsure whether to contradict this version of events, but decided against it.

'She was worried about the custody battle.'

'So how did you feel when your meal ticket was threatened?'

'She was not a meal ticket. She was the woman I loved!'

Sergeant Shukor snorted derisively. Ravi looked at him angrily and then, taking in the policeman's physique, decided that discretion was the better part of valour.

He said again in a quiet tone, 'I loved her. I would have married her and been a father to her children.'

Singh could not resist sarcasm. 'You mean you would have been willing to marry an extremely wealthy and beautiful woman? You amaze me!'

Ravi started to say something and then thought better of it. He slumped in the chair, looking sullen. This was not going the way he planned.

Singh asked, 'So did you kill him?'

'What?'

'Did you kill Alan Lee?'

'Of course not!'

'You had every reason.'

'I did not kill him. Anyway, I thought the brother confessed.'

The policeman did not answer him and he said again more plaintively, 'But I

199

thought the brother confessed!'

Later, when the policemen were alone, Shukor asked, 'Could Ravi have done it?'

Inspector Singh shrugged. 'He strikes me as a coward, but people have surprised me before with the lengths to which they will go for a few bucks. He had an excellent motive. Without Alan in the picture he must have felt secure enough of Chelsea to think that he had found the pot of gold at the end of the rainbow.'

Shukor said tentatively, 'But we've still got Jasper's confession, lah.'

Singh sighed. 'You're quite right. There is still that damned confession.'

The office was closed. Rupert leaned his forehead on the grimy wall and closed his eyes. He was too tired, too dirty and too worried to face another hurdle. Jasper Lee was his best hope. He needed someone with access and information. A conduit who knew the issues would have been perfect. Someone who he had worked with and trusted was an additional plus. But the door was locked and the place musty and damp. No one had been in for a while. He tried to peer through the tinted glass. It was dark inside the room. He could not even make out the silhouette of furniture. It was impossible to know when the office had been abandoned. There was certainly no way of knowing where Jasper Lee had gone.

Rupert suddenly wanted to be somewhere else. This narrow corridor at the top of a stairwell felt too much like a dead end. He ran lightly down the stairs. It was dangerous in the half-light cast by a single bare light bulb but he was determined to get back to the bustle of the street. Once down again, and feeling the safety of anonymity in a crowd, he walked into the coffee shop at the base of the building and asked an old crone chopping vegetables where Jasper had gone. She cackled at him, showing gold teeth sporadically protruding from red gums but did not answer. A harassed woman, sautéing vegetables in a big pot of boiling water and then deftly flicking them onto a row of plates while another worker squirted soy sauce and a spoonful of fried garlic on each, said, 'She no speak Engris one!'

He turned to her gratefully. 'Maybe you can help me? I am looking for Jasper Lee — the man with the office upstairs? He might have come here to eat.'

She looked at him curiously, pushing a strand of hair, damp with sweat, behind her ear.

'Why you want him?'

'He's an old friend of mine.'

'He not here any more.'

Rupert nodded encouragingly, willing her to continue. He could tell that Jasper wasn't around any more. He needed to know where he had gone.

Answering the silent question, she said, 'He go to jail!'

'Jail?'

Rupert's first thought was that somehow the police had guessed where he would be going and had deprived him of his one ally in the battle against the logging companies. Then he realised that was farfetched.

He asked, 'Why is he in jail? What did he do?'

'He kill his brother. He go to jail. They sure hang him!'

She seemed to relish this unseemly end to her neighbour's career. The pleasure in being the bearer of such unique news overcame any sympathy she felt for a man facing such an unpleasant fate — even one she had served in her coffee shop on numerous occasions over the last few years.

She continued, pointing to a small table, 'He always like to sit there and eat noodles.' For a moment she must have felt some pity for Jasper because she said in a soft voice, 'He always like my food.' But then she shrugged and went back to her task of scooping vegetables out of the boiling water, scowling when she saw that her thirty seconds of conversation had resulted in limp, overcooked greens.

Rupert walked down the street. He did not notice the noise or the crowds. He did not flinch from the buses thundering down the roads and brushing the pavements. He was too shocked at what he had just heard. He could not believe for a second that the gentle man he had known, with his overwhelming compassion for every living thing, could have taken a life. He of all people knew the time and effort that Jasper had put in to protect those who were weaker than him in society. What could have led him to kill his brother? Possibly it was some sort of trumped-up charge by the police to get Jasper Lee out of the way. That would not have surprised the Englishman, who had spent the last twenty-four hours escaping from corrupt policemen. He knew that Jasper's research was getting closer and closer to proving the extent of the illegal logging going on in Borneo. Someone might have seen fit to frame him for a murder he had not committed.

How was he to find out more? Rupert Winfield set out for the library newspaper archives. Sitting there half an hour later, scrolling down the history of Jasper's internment, he was not a happy man. It seemed that the person he had hoped to turn to in his predicament was in a lot of trouble. So much for his theory, formulated on his walk through town, that Jasper had been framed because he was causing trouble for the logging industry. The man had confessed to killing his brother. Alan Lee, the man he held responsible for the events in Borneo, was dead. He, Rupert, would never have the opportunity now to confront him with the consequences of his actions. But he still found it hard to believe that Jasper had killed him.

He stretched and sneezed. Even when the old newspapers were on screen they seemed to exude mustiness. It reminded him of his time researching dusty books when he was studying the indigenous tribes of Borneo. He had never anticipated that his academic interest would be so bound up in his own fate. But his life among the simplest of folk, first as a researcher, then as a defender, had completely changed his career path. Not for him, he had decided, the ivory towers of academe. He had traded it for a cause. And it had left him with a strong sense of fulfilment over the years.

He looked around him. An empty, soulless room with a bank of computer screens and a network of wires running across the floor, along the walls, taped down to the carpet with strips of brown packing tape. It reminded him of the squirming mass of black baby cobras he had once found under a rock. He sat lost in the past, forgetting his immediate troubles in memories of the jungle.

It would not have been Inspector Singh's choice to move in to his sister's house. But now that he was no longer in Kuala Lumpur in his official capacity as a Singaporean policeman seconded to a Malaysian case, his budget did not stretch to a hotel. He had called his sister and told her he would be coming to stay for a few days. She seemed indifferent rather than enthusiastic. But there had never been any danger of refusal. The right of family to come and stay indefinitely, whatever the inconvenience and expense, was hardwired into her brain. It was the Asian way. Hospitality was paramount — especially to relatives. They might bitch about each other, nag, complain and occasionally quarrel. But the door was still open if you wanted to stay.

He was at her door now with his small

suitcase. She let him in and he sat silently in the gloomy living room waiting for her to make him a drink. It did not take her long to return with the cup of tea, tepid from the addition of cold milk.

She asked, 'How come you are not staying at the hotel?'

He debated telling her that he was freelancing and decided against it. It would give her too much ammunition with which to nag at him for the duration of his stay. She would go on and on about the importance of staying on the good side of one's employers — with her usual sprinkling of judicious anecdotes about her late husband's talent in this field. Singh, who remembered her husband as a gruff, choleric man whose temper had led to an early heart attack, wondered what his sister would have done if he had still been alive to give the lie to all the numerous stories she made up about him to make a conversational point.

He said instead, 'If I stay here they will still pay me the hotel allowance.'

She nodded approvingly, sipping her tea from a mug with Avis emblazoned on both sides. 'That is good!'

Singh did not know if she was referring to his cunning in getting some spare cash or the generosity of the government of Singapore in letting him get away with such an old-fashioned expense fiddle — but it was apparent from the mug that she did not disdain a freebie.

'What would you like for dinner?' she asked.

He shrugged indifferently. He was a fat man with a fat man's lack of fussiness over his diet.

She continued, 'I am making *chapattis*.'

'Why did you ask me what I wanted then?'

She did not answer but wandered back into the kitchen and he could hear the preparatory clanging of pots and pans. He dragged himself with some difficulty out of the too-soft sofa seat and wandered in after her. She was placing a heavy flat iron skillet on the stove. She lit the fire under it and wiped the surface with a brush of coconut fibre which she had first dipped into a bright green tin of ghee. She picked up a *chapatti*, prepared earlier in the day, with a thumb and forefinger and flipped it onto the flat pan. Immediately, it started to heat up, bubbles of air forming beneath the surface and then sinking back down. She flipped it over like a pancake and the surface was browned with scattered darker spots. She spread some ghee. The rich smell of toasting ghee and baked bread filled the air and Inspector Singh realised that he really fancied *chapattis* for dinner after all.

'Smells good!' he remarked.

She did not acknowledge his comment but flicked the *chapatti* onto a plate and set another one on the skillet. The rolls of fat hanging off her arms wobbled with effort and the kitchen was growing hot. Beads of sweat gathered on her forehead and his. Singh was cast back fifty years. He remembered his own mother, doing much the same thing with a similar skillet and identical rolls of fat. He had wondered at the time how his mother could perspire so much and still be so overweight. Now he knew. A rich diet, little exercise and a genetic disposition to fat. No doubt his sister's weight was the product of similar flaws in habit and design. He remembered the last time the family had got together for the wedding of a niece. The whole clan was overweight, with the exception of his own stringy wife. There was much amusement when the women confessed that they had all taken to waving goodbye like royalty, with minimum movement. Otherwise, the swaying of fat under the raised arm was just too pronounced. Singh watched his sister flipping *chapattis* and felt a rush of fondness for her. She had done so much more than him to preserve family traditions and pass them on to the next generation. But he would not have expressed those thoughts in words for anything in the world.

Instead he said again, 'Smells good!'

She nodded to the plate where the *chapattis* were piling up.

'You can eat.'

'Did you do it?' asked Rupert without preamble.

Jasper looked amused. 'I confessed,' he pointed out.

Rupert nodded. 'I know that. I read the newspapers. I just can't believe you would kill anyone.'

'Not even Alan?'

Rupert smiled suddenly at his friend. It was true that they had shared many a cup of *arak,* fermented coconut wine, over a campfire while Jasper had complained bitterly about his brother.

Jasper said now, 'What are you doing here anyway? Last I heard you had vanished into the jungle with a beautiful Penan girl!'

Rupert shook his head. 'It's called research into a disappearing people.' His face became serious. 'I barely got out. Thugs attacked the camp. Just after daybreak.'

'Thugs?'

'A group of armed men. I was away having a piss. I heard the commotion. I dashed back. Armed men were attacking the Penan. They were just leaving as I got there.'

'Did they kill anyone?'

Rupert's voice cracked. 'A young woman. She went into early labour and mother and baby died.'

'What did you do?'

'I hid. There was no point letting them see me. I was afraid they would kill everyone if there was a non-Penan witness. You know they don't really fear that the authorities will take the Penan seriously if they complain. But they might not be so sanguine about a foreigner. I didn't know what had happened to the girl at that point — or I would have confronted them whatever the consequences.'

Jasper nodded thoughtfully. 'What was it about?' he asked but he knew the answer. He wanted to see if Rupert had come to the same conclusion separately.

'I would guess — in fact, I know — it's the timber companies. They want to log the area. It's off limits, in a nature reserve. Difficult to log illegally with a nomadic tribe in your midst.'

Jasper was struck by something that Ru-

pert had said earlier. 'I agree with you —
that must be the reason for the attack —
but why do you say you know, rather than
guess?'

'You're not going to like this, but I recognised one of the toughs.'

'Who was it?'

'That big chap with the tattoos — the one
who used to work as foreman of the Borneo
operations of Lee Timber.'

Jasper nodded slowly. 'You're sure it was
him?'

'Positive! I remember him from that time
we went to the site to protest something or
other — do you remember? — and he had
us thrown out.'

'Well,' said Jasper, 'it looks like my brother's ghost still walks!'

'Is he employed by Lee Timber still?'

'I think so,' replied Jasper.

Rupert sighed. 'I cannot be upset that
Alan Lee is dead — but I would have liked
to have forced him to acknowledge what he
did.'

'I know what you mean,' said Jasper. 'The
fact is, though, Kian Min — my other
brother — has been running the show at
Lee Timber for a long time.'

'Really?' asked Rupert, staring at Jasper
fixedly.

'Oh, yes. So if you want to confront someone, the right person is still alive and well.'

Chelsea could not pray. The gods were fighting over her children but she could not seek the help of any of them. And she had so much choice. She had grown up a Buddhist, her ex-husband was allegedly a Moslem when he died, her own sister was a Christian — so many options for salvation. Her sister, Ruth, had said that prayer was a weapon and a shield. Chelsea would have settled for solace through prayer. But she did not believe that there was an invisible hand behind the farce that was her life's play. At the very least she did not believe in a benevolent God. She could be convinced, she thought, of divine caprice. She shook her head. Surely it was better to lay the blame for the machinations of fate at the door of chance? She did not think she would have the strength to fight back if she thought that there were all-powerful, omniscient beings ranged against her. To those to whom much is given, more is taken away, she thought grimly. Alan was reaping what he sowed — writhing in the literal flames of hell if her sister was to be believed or soon to be devoured by worms. Either was a fitting end.

FOURTEEN

Each episode began with a certain rhythm. A quiet, repetitive grunting that she would have got used to and then, no doubt, slept through. But that was not the end. The noise grew louder and louder and, as it did, the rhythm started to break down. Snorts and snuffles added variety to the theme. Eventually, the snoring would reach a crescendo of coughs and grunts, followed by a sudden abrupt cessation of sound. She would slowly relax into her pillow, her neck muscles would ease and then it would begin again. Baljit did not know what to do. She could wake him but, from the persistence of the sound, she suspected that he would begin again the minute she was back in bed. Presumably he was waking up intermittently as well. No one could sleep through the ghastly noise. She had never liked her brother's wife — a feeling, she suspected, that she shared with her brother — but she felt a pang of sympathy for her now. No wonder she was so bitter and twisted if she had to listen to this cacophony every night.

Baljit thought of her dead husband for the first time in months. She invoked him regularly in conversation — whether with her neighbours or her children. Many sentences began with 'If your father were here . . .' But that was habit. It did not require an independent memory of the dead man. Now she remembered vaguely but fondly that he had never snored. She got to her feet, rolled up a towel and placed it along the bottom of her door. That would muffle the sound slightly. She crawled back into bed and covered her head with a pillow. She really, really hoped that he would catch his murderer soon.

Subhas Chandra placed another pencil in the sharpener on his desk and turned the little handle furiously. He tested the nib, honed to a fine point, on his finger. The slight sting convinced him it was sharp enough. He picked another one out of its case. Sharpening pencils was what he did repetitively when things were not going well. And things were not going well. He, who was not in the habit of losing, was being defeated at every turn.

He remembered that he had been pleased to be asked to represent Chelsea Liew during her divorce and custody battle. He would have preferred Alan Lee as a client — it was always better to represent the half of the couple that had the majority of assets. Still, he had been confident of winning, which meant that Chelsea would have got a substantial part of the family wealth in a settlement. Either way, his name and picture were in every newspaper in the country for weeks. His was one of the inevitable photos accompanying each salacious detail of the Lee marriage and subsequent breakdown. Allegations and counterallegations were revealed first in court and then through the press to a wider audience. Publicity like that was hard to come by. He could have waived his fee for the amount of indirect value he was getting from the case, but of course he hadn't. That was not the sort of precedent that any self-respecting lawyer would set. He had played his cards well — allowing Alan Lee to wash all his dirty linen in public. He had kept Chelsea above the fray, a mother fighting for her children — not a wife looking for revenge. Public opinion was on Chelsea's side — battered, long-suffering wife against violent timber tycoon. And then the rug was pulled from under his feet.

Alan Lee's conversion to Islam was a master tactical stroke and he, Subhas Chandra, the foremost divorce lawyer in the country, had been taken completely by surprise. It rankled. He sharpened another pencil and then rifled through his papers until he found the cutting from a newspaper that he had kept. It was a picture of him on the steps of the courthouse. He remembered the moment well. He was rushing to avoid reporters, something he had never had to do before. He did not want to be asked any questions about Alan Lee's conversion to Islam. This was quite contrary to his usual practice of holding an ad hoc press conference outside the court to make sure he, and of course his client, got the best press. His billowing gown had snagged the stair rail and he had turned in surprise. That was the moment he had been photographed: mouth slightly open, eyebrows raised, eyes wide. The caption had read, 'Lawyer struck by bolt from blue!' Clever, really.

And now there was more bad news. He reached for the phone and then sat back in his chair again. It was the most expensive orthopaedic chair that money could buy — but he shifted uncomfortably. He would have loved to resign from the case but headlines about the lawyer who abandoned his client just when the going got tough would not endear him to any future clients. He would have to stick it out.

He reached for the phone again and rang Chelsea Liew's mobile. She picked up immediately. Her 'Hello' sounded strained.

He said, 'What is it?'

She did not answer his question directly. 'Nothing in particular. What do you want?'

He paused and could sense her growing impatience on the phone. He screwed up his courage, put on his most lawyerly voice — deep, slow tones usually reserved for when he was in court — and said, 'I have some bad news. I'm afraid the court has released the body of your husband for burial in accordance with Moslem funeral rites.'

'So?'

'They've released the body to the Council to bury.'

She said, 'I could not possibly care less.'

The lawyer wiped a moist hand on his trouser leg and reached for another pencil. This was not easy. 'I realise that you are not particularly concerned about what happens to the body and I understand that. But the court's decision does have legal consequences.'

'What do you mean?' Her voice was hard

and suspicious.

'The civil courts did not choose to hear us on the matter. They decided, based on the affidavits, that the matter was out of their hands.'

Chelsea said firmly, 'I have no idea what you are talking about!'

Her lawyer swallowed a sigh and started again, reminding himself that, despite the amount of time she had recently spent within the judicial system, she was a layperson. 'If you will recall, we asked the judge in the civil custody hearing to examine the conversion to Islam of your ex-husband. The idea was that if his new religion was not genuine, then his children were not Moslem — and therefore you should keep them.'

'Yes, I understand that.'

'Well, the judge, when releasing the body, ruled that he had no authority under the Constitution to look behind a conversion to Islam to determine whether it was genuine.'

'So?'

'It will affect the decision about the children.'

'What do you mean?' Chelsea was getting angry. It was all so damn complicated and appeared to be designed only to separate her from her children.

'The civil courts have set a precedent saying they will not question the genuineness of a conversion to decide whether Alan Lee should be buried with Moslem rites. In other words, if he claims to be Moslem, that's enough for them. They could use the same logic about your custody claim. And the Syariah courts will be predisposed to accepting any conversion to Islam as genuine.'

'I see,' said Chelsea, slowly. 'What do you suggest I do?'

'Appeal!'

'Can I win?'

'It is difficult to say. These are uncharted constitutional waters . . .'

Chelsea rolled her eyes. She would dearly love a lawyer who gave her a straight answer but suspected that this restraint was endemic in the profession. She said, 'What's your best bet?'

'There is a certain safety in numbers. The Court of Appeal might be more willing to make a controversial decision than a judge sitting alone. It is not impossible that we will get a favourable result.'

Chelsea said, 'All right, go ahead and appeal,' and terminated the call.

Her lawyer carefully filed the newspaper clipping away and put another pencil into the desktop sharpener. He turned the little handle mechanically, watching the fine shavings fall into the clear plastic receptacle.

Sergeant Shukor was the point man. He had to be. These tycoons were far too well-funded and well-advised to subject themselves to questioning by a Singapore policeman freelancing in Malaysia. They had agreed between them that Singh would come along and remain in the background — unintroduced unless it became necessary. His Singapore origins were not to be revealed under any circumstances.

They had made an appointment and were shown in to see Lee Kian Min. Kian Min was running Lee Timber, just as he had done for his father willingly, and his brother unwillingly. His appointment as managing director of Lee Timber had not been formalised. The company thought it would be better to wait until Alan Lee had at least been buried before the official handover. There was no difficulty with the present arrangement anyway. Kian Min did not require official titles — power and wealth were sufficient.

Kian Min did not know why the police wanted to see him but he had nevertheless choreographed the encounter to ensure that his questioners were made to feel at a disadvantage. He sat behind the huge desk. On the other side there were two much smaller chairs.

Kian Min stood up as they came in and ushered them into the two chairs facing the desk. His slightly nasal voice suggested roots that were not quite as polished as his dress and surroundings implied. Unlike Alan, who had ironed the Chinese *towkay* out of his voice during the course of an expensive education, Kian Min had stayed close to home and sounded it. He said, 'So why the police want to see me?'

'We just have a few questions,' said Sergeant Shukor reassuringly. Singh sensed he was intimidated by the tone of wealth and felt like an intruder rather than a policeman on righteous business. He wished he could take part in the interview. He would soon have the little bastard by the balls. He ground his teeth in frustration and the two other men turned to look at him in surprise. In the quiet room, it was audible. Singh patted his stomach apologetically and succeeded in their pre-arranged plan that he act the buffoon.

Kian Min, his confidence increased by the embarrassment of the two policemen, said, 'What questions you want to ask me? Is it about my brother? If so, I can tell you straight that I have no idea why Jasper killed Alan.'

Shukor said quietly, 'We have received reports that Lee Timber is logging illegally in East Malaysia.'

'There are always reports. People don't like our business. But they like what we provide.' He ran a hand lovingly over the polished surface of his desk. A man whose uncultured background rang in every cadence of speech took a spontaneous pleasure in beautiful things.

'We have evidence that Lee Timber is logging illegally.'

He looked up at this. 'What evidence? Cannot be!'

'We have maps and aerial photos showing that you have been logging on areas gazetted as national park land in Borneo.'

'Let me see it then if you say you got evidence.'

Shukor shook his head firmly. 'We will look into it further first.'

'You cannot simply come here and make accusations. The Sarawak police have investigated and found nothing.'

'So you deny that Lee Timber is involved in anything illegal?'

'Of course I deny it.'

'Well, this is the thing,' said Inspector Singh, unable to obey his own rules about keeping out of trouble, 'Jasper claims he killed your brother to stop his illegal activity in Borneo. If what you say is true — there is no illegal activity — Jasper Lee has no motive . . . unlike another brother of Alan who did rather well out of his untimely demise.' As he said this Singh looked around at Kian Min's office trappings contemptuously and then turned back to look at the man he had just implicitly accused of murder.

To his surprise, Kian Min looked unperturbed, amused even. He ignored the allegation and concentrated on Jasper's story.

'So Jasper say he kill Alan to stop him cutting down trees?' He laughed, a derisory sound. 'You know, he's so screwed up he maybe believes it. But that's not the real reason.'

Shukor jumped in. The inspector would have preferred to let Kian Min keep talking off his own bat. 'Why then? Why did he kill Alan?'

Kian Min eyed them. The interruption had given him pause for thought. At last, he said, 'Well, it's obvious, right?'

This time both policemen kept silent.

'He did it for Chelsea.'

■ ■ ■ ■

It was the first time she had gone to see him. She had stayed away for as long as possible but then guilt had driven her to prison. She could not abandon her brother-in-law without at least a visit. He was the reason she was free. Remembering her own experience she was pleasantly surprised when she saw him. He looked thinner and tired but there was a bounce in his step when he came into the room. Jasper had an inner resilience which she had not suspected. They sat in silence for a while. He looked at her with a mildly amused expression on his face, guessing her conflicting emotions — relief not to be incarcerated herself, guilt that he was there. Chelsea looked around, not saying a word, struggling to believe that a few short weeks ago she had been sitting in this room as the accused, not a visitor.

She screwed up the courage to ask, 'How are you managing?'

He shrugged. 'Well, it's not the Mandarin Oriental — but I'm fine!'

She said, 'Why did you confess?'

He looked at her, meeting her eyes fearlessly. 'Because I killed Alan.'

'I don't believe you.'

'I know. You even have that fat policeman trying to persuade me that I'm not guilty. But really, I killed Alan and I don't regret it.'

This last was said with a stubborn look, defying her to contradict him.

She shook her head gently. 'I won't pretend that I have any sorrow at Alan's death. The man I thought I married died for me a long time ago.'

In the silence, they were both remembering a wedding day from many years ago — where the radiance of a young bride had transcended the kitschy white wedding and turned it into something truly beautiful. Jasper had not been asked by his brother to be the best man. The relationship between them had soured by then. Jasper would have refused anyway. Instead, he had sat in the front pew of the big church and watched his brother marry the most beautiful woman he had ever seen.

He looked at the woman across from him, seeking in her features something of that young woman, girl almost, he had watched that day. She had grown older, of course, and developed an air of sophistication as the wife of one of Malaysia's leading businessmen. There were a few faint lines on her face, erased to some extent by make-up.

He thought to himself that Chelsea had aged in the manner of expensive wine — her face had developed in character what it had lost in beauty. The fine bones were still there and the iridescent, almond eyes. He thought her more attractive now than he had done on that wedding day when his envy of his brother had formed a physical constriction in his throat.

He was lost in the past and did not hear Chelsea speak.

She said again, 'Jasper!'

He looked up at her, taken aback by her changed appearance, so immersed had he been in his memories.

She looked worried and he smiled re-assuringly. 'I'm fine.'

This made her angry. 'How can you say that?' she snapped. 'I was sitting in that chair not long ago — looking forward to a dawn walk to a hangman's noose. There is nothing fine about this situation!'

He did not know what to say. Her anger was palpable. He understood that it was concern for him. But he did not know how to deal with this fiery-eyed, assertive woman. All the years he had known her she had been retreating further into a shell until he had become accustomed to the quiet, polite but basically secretive woman. Her release from prison into a world where there was no dominating husband had removed emotional shackles too.

He changed the subject. 'What's happening with the custody thing?'

She said, 'It doesn't look good. The civil courts released Alan's body to the Council for burial in accordance with Moslem rites.'

Jasper was no fool. He said thoughtfully, 'I see — and that might be a precedent they use for the custody issues?'

Chelsea nodded. 'Which leaves me entirely at the mercy of the Syariah court. They must surely be even less inclined to examine whether Alan was actually a Moslem or just faking it.'

Jasper said, 'It's possible, I suppose, that they will be more willing to preserve the sanctity of the religion — by not allowing a conversion of convenience to carry any weight.'

'That's my last hope!' said Chelsea, an edge of desperation in her voice. 'The worst part is that, if Alan was alive, I might have stood a better chance. The judges would have seen with their own eyes that he could not possibly be a genuine convert. We both know Alan. It's not an act he could have sustained for very long. Can you imagine it — going to the mosque every Friday, fast-ing during Ramadan? But now, with Alan dead, it has become a matter of principle — not of people . . .'

Jasper asked, 'Are you sorry he's dead then?'

Chelsea did not answer for an interminable moment. Then she said quietly, 'No, I'm not.'

Jasper reached out and took one of her hands in his. She noticed abstractedly that his nails were not clean — residue from his first week in prison.

He said, 'You need not worry about me. Really, I'm OK. If they hang me, so be it. I did what I did knowing the consequences.'

When she did not respond, he continued, 'I just wish there was something more I could do to help you.'

'You need to concentrate on helping yourself!' said Chelsea, squeezing his hand to rob her words of the harshness. She rose to her feet, picked up her small clutch purse, put out a hand and touched his cheek fleetingly — a small, sad farewell gesture — and knocked on the door to be let out.

He did not protest her departure. This was no place for her. It was imagining her in a cell like this one that had given him the strength to come in and confess to the murder in the first place. He did not want to see her here, even as a visitor.

Singh held a handkerchief to his nose and stared in disbelief at the misty outlines of the Twin Towers. The sun, struggling to penetrate the gloom, was a pale moonlike orb.

The streets were almost empty — a few dispatch boys on motorbikes scurried along, hankies tied firmly around their noses and mouths. The smell of burning was pervasive and Singh could almost feel the soot clogging his nostrils.

'They will have to close the schools again,' said Shukor.

'Airports too, I suspect,' was Singh's response. 'The haze is bad this year, isn't it?'

'Forest fires in Indonesia. When the wind changes, it blows here directly from Sumatra, Borneo, Java and gets trapped in the Klang Valley,' said Shukor by way of explanation.

The Malaysian suddenly turned on his heel and headed back into the building they had just exited. Singh hurried after him.

'Where are we going?' he asked, surprised.

The young policeman, face grim, did not answer. He headed straight for the elevator, impatiently jabbing the buttons with a blunt, angry finger. The lift 'pinged' and Shukor hurried towards it.

The doors slid open and Kian Min walked out. He was surprised to see the policemen still in the building — but his expression of discomfiture was quickly smoothed into the inquiring mask he had presented to them upstairs. It did not last.

Shukor grabbed him by the arm and dragged him towards the exit.

'What are you doing? Let me go!' shouted Kian Min angrily.

People in the lobby stopped and stared at the sight of a leading business figure being frog-marched out of their building. Singh, breathless at the pace, was trying to catch Shukor's eye. He had no idea what had got into the sergeant.

They stopped just outside the main entrance. Shukor let go of the slight Chinese man's arm.

He said, 'Look around you!'

Kian Min complied, rubbing his sore arm.

'What do you see?'

It was clear that Kian Min did not know what the right answer was.

'What do you see?'

He shook his head. 'I don't know. I cannot see much. Very hazy!'

Shukor grabbed him by the lapels and

held him on tiptoes, Kian Min's face inches away from his own.

'Yes, you can't see anything — because of this haze. Because you and your cronies are clearing land all over — burning the rain-forests . . . And here in Kuala Lumpur we cannot see to the end of the street!'

Kian Min shook his head feebly. 'It's not me. I am not the one who does it.'

Shukor said, 'Yes it is. It is you and men like you. You wear your expensive suits and you hide in your expensive offices while your gangsters chase people off their own land so that you can log it and burn it to plant oil palm.'

Kian Min was over his initial shock. He realised the policeman could not do any-thing to him. They were in a crowded place with plenty of witnesses. He hissed, 'I will have you kicked out of the police force.'

Shukor said, 'Well, you'd better be quick — because I am going to prove that it is you and your company that has caused this.' One arm took in a wide arc that indicated their surroundings and its thick veil of haze. The other let go of Kian Min's lapels so suddenly that the smaller man stumbled backwards and almost fell before righting himself.

Shukor gave him a last meaningful glare

and then walked off at a great pace with the inspector struggling in his wake.

'What was that about?' he asked when Shukor slowed down enough for him to catch up.

'I just got angry, lah.'

Kian Min recovered his equilibrium slowly. His back straightened. He dusted off his jacket and straightened his tie, wincing at the soreness in his arm. He smoothed his hair carefully and then reached into his pocket and slipped out his ultra-slim mobile. He rang a number and listened calmly, timing his breathing with each ring to regain mastery over his emotions.

A man picked up the phone and said 'Hello' in an impatient voice.

'We have a problem,' said Kian Min.

Chelsea wandered around the living room, straightening ornaments that were perfectly aligned and reorganising photographs on the mantelpiece. All the pictures of Alan had been removed. But still she looked around the room in disgust. If she had a chance, she decided, after this whole thing was over and there was no longer a threat to her children, she would have this room gutted, erasing every trace of the past. In fact, she would have the house gutted and start again from a clean slate. She considered moving instead. That would surely be the easier, more sensible option. She thought about it for a moment and then shook her head and said loudly and firmly, 'No!'

Moving would be like running away, letting Alan have the last word. His presence was everywhere in the building, festering as if his corpse was rotting under the floor. Alan had chosen the interior designer and agreed the plans and slapped her when she had suggested that the opulent furnishings were not appropriate for the climate or young children. Chelsea made up her mind. She would erase every trace of him. Nothing should remain of Alan — his tastes, his past, his preferences. She would have every piece of furniture he had ever touched destroyed. She would repaint every wall. She would even strip out the marble flooring and carpet over every footstep. This house would not just have every memory of Alan destroyed but every thumb-print as well. And when she had finished, he would be well and truly gone. There would be nothing of him left to haunt her.

The flaw in her plan said tentatively, 'Mummy?' And then as she did not answer, again and louder this time, 'Mummy!'

She looked down at the youngest of her three sons. Her son, but also Alan's — a flesh-and-blood creature who carried the imprimatur of his father's genes. She realised that she could wipe away the physical traces of her husband in the house, but these living symbols would remain. Perhaps she would leave the house as it was. Alan was gone. The memory of him would fade. She did not need an exorcism by interior design.

She smiled at her son, who said, 'I want to play with my Lego. Will you help me?'

She nodded and walked out of the room with him.

Both policemen were standing, both of them looked sheepish. Inspector Mohammad was livid. His face was contorted with rage and it was only with the greatest difficulty that he was able to squeeze words out from behind his clenched teeth.

He said, 'Let me get this straight: although we have a man in custody who has confessed — confessed! — to killing Alan Lee, you two, a rookie and a foreigner, decided to keep investigating?'

Sergeant Shukor said smartly, 'Yessir!'

'And then you went to see Lee Kian Min, one of the most powerful men in the country, and accused him of murder?'

'Yessir!'

'And finally, you attacked him in a public street.'

Shukor did not feel able to speak, he simply nodded.

Mohammad steepled his fingers and looked at them in disbelief — genuinely at a loss for words at the magnitude of their insubordination.

Finally, he said, pointing a finger at Shukor, 'You're suspended for two weeks. You'd better hope Lee doesn't take it further. As for you' — he turned his attention to the fat man — 'I want you on a plane to Singapore this evening.'

The steady whirring of the stand fan was the only sound to be heard in the room. Singh looked Inspector Mohammad in the eye and said, 'No.'

FIFTEEN

'What do you mean, "no"?' yelled Inspector Mohammad.

'I mean no — I'm not leaving. If you want to get me off the case, you'll have to arrest me.'

'Fine — have it your way. Shukor, arrest him.'

Shukor took an uncertain step forward, stopped, looked at the inspector from Singapore — a short, fat man with a determined expression and dirty white shoes — turned to his boss and said firmly, 'I can't, sir. I've been suspended.'

Singh understood what the word 'apoplectic' meant for the first time. Mohammad's face was mottled red right up to the roots of his peppery hair. In contrast, his lips were pale and bloodless, he had them pursed so tight.

Singh stepped in. He could not let the younger policeman ruin his career over his,

Singh's, stubbornness. He said, 'Look, Mohammad. You're quite right. We were completely out of line. I was just sniffing around and things snowballed.'

Mohammad's jaw muscles unclenched slightly. Shukor heaved a tiny, inaudible sigh of relief.

Singh continued persuasively, 'Listen, if you'll just hear us out, I'll get on a plane if you insist. But I don't think Jasper Lee killed his brother. And I know you don't want to hang an innocent man.'

Inspector Mohammad exclaimed, 'What's the matter with you chaps? Chelsea Liew didn't do it. Jasper Lee didn't do it. Alan Lee has a bullet in his chest. Someone did it!'

Singh relaxed. Inspector Mohammad was listening now.

He said, 'Look, I think I can get Jasper Lee to retract his confession. Will you let me try?'

Mohammad laughed. 'Well, that's an unusual approach. Here we usually work to *extract* confessions from suspects — by fair or foul means — not persuade them to retract. We leave that to the damned lawyers.'

Singh laughed too. Shukor didn't dare. He was quiet, hoping to keep his job.

Mohammad said suddenly, slapping the table with both hands and standing up, 'All right, it's a deal. If Jasper Lee recants, I'll reopen the investigation *and* let you stay.'

The private investigator was angry. The disc he had given Chelsea Liew was worth its weight in gold. He had expected her to pay up and pay up quickly. But days had passed and no messenger had arrived bearing a sealed envelope stuffed full of cash. Mr Chan had a long fingernail and a comb-over — but he also had pride. When he performed the task to which he was assigned he expected more than a pat on the head or a quiet dismissal. He thought back to his interview with Chelsea. She was repulsed by him and his dirty job. He had sensed that immediately. These rich people and their marital problems. They wanted to know the truth. They asked people like him to do the digging so that *they* did not get dirt under their manicured fingernails. But when the information was brought to them, they were disgusted. They treated him as if he had tramped mud across their expensive carpets. Perhaps he had, but it was their mud, not his.

He could not let this pass. If word got out that he, Mr Chan, could be cheated of his rightful fee, others would not be slow to follow suit. He thought hard, the long fingernail gently scratching a patch of eczema on the side of his bulbous nose. The idea came to him — the perfect punishment for rich bitches who didn't understand hard work. And the best part was that he could pretend that he had done it for all the right reasons. It would be a useful card to have up his sleeve if ever he needed a favour. Mr Chan picked up his mobile phone and rang one of his contacts.

Jasper Lee was in the interview cell. He looked even thinner — but still cheerful. He looked at the trio, Inspectors Singh and Mohammad and Sergeant Shukor.

'And what can I do for you, gentlemen?' he asked. 'Crime must be a bit slow at the moment if the police can waste three of their top cops on a confessed murderer.'

None of the men said anything and Jasper's face grew worried. 'Has anything happened?' he asked. 'Is Chelsea all right?'

It was Singh who responded. 'Oh yes! She's fine. Relieved to be out of here. The kids are OK too.'

Jasper visibly relaxed. He said, 'That's great, I'm glad she's recovering.'

Singh said, as one musing aloud, 'I would

go as far as to say she's happy.'

'Oh? Why do you say that?'

'It's a great relief for her to be able to shack up with the boyfriend, I think. You know her better than I do — but she does not seem to be the sort who would want to hide a relationship.'

'What are you talking about?'

Inspector Mohammad shifted in his seat slightly, his eyes fixed on the accused. Jasper did not notice. All his concentration was on the fat policeman from Singapore.

'Ravi, of course,' said the inspector, feigning surprise at Jasper's ignorance.

Shukor, watching the performance, felt almost sorry for Jasper Lee. He was no match for the Sikh policeman's low cunning enhanced by his dramatic abilities.

Jasper looked annoyed, like someone who suspected that the joke might be on him but could not quite put his finger on the punch line. He said, as coolly as he could, 'Who is Ravi?'

'Don't you know? I thought you were bound to be in on the secret — seeing how close you and Chelsea are.'

Jasper was not so lost to his agenda that he was ready to forget his lines. He said automatically, 'We were not that close.'

Shukor thought that they were both actors, the policeman and the accused, but they were playing parts from different scenes.

Jasper asked with a valiant effort at a nonchalant tone, 'She's met someone, has she?'

'More than that!' exclaimed Singh. 'She's had a bit on the side all this while.' His tone was deliciously gossipy. 'What's sauce for the gander is sauce for the goose, eh?' And to Shukor's amazement, he winked at Jasper Lee.

Jasper's shock was palpable. Shukor could have reached out and touched it, kneaded it into shape — a permanent monument to a man surprised. 'What are you saying?'

'You need me to spell it out? All this while she's been playing little Miss Innocent, she's had a tasty bit on the side.' Singh stopped and appeared to think about his statement for a moment. Then he said, 'Well, I may be being just a bit unfair. It does seem she really loves this guy. They've been inseparable since she got out.'

Jasper had turned gallows pale. Shukor doubted he could look more deathly if he was swinging at the end of a rope.

Jasper said, more to himself than anyone, 'I don't believe it.'

'Well, look at this then . . .' And Inspector

Singh slid Ravi's love letter across the table to Jasper.

It had turned the inspector's stomach to read the lies that the boyfriend was willing to tell to get his hands on some of Chelsea's money. It had a different effect on Jasper.

He let the letter slide through numb fingers and said in a voice that was so thick and choked, it sounded like his tongue had inflated suddenly, 'So what are you doing here anyway?'

'We just wanted to ask you again why you killed Alan Lee.'

Jasper didn't answer. He stood up and said, 'Can we do this another time please?'

They left Jasper to his thoughts and walked out.

'Why didn't you ask him if he was sticking to his story?' asked Shukor.

'Too soon,' said Singh, and Mohammad nodded his agreement. 'In my experience, a mistake like he's made — it will take a while for him to move from disbelief to denial and then, of course, to anger. I give it about twenty-four hours — and then he'll be asking to see us.'

A young uniformed policeman came up to them and muttered something to Inspector Mohammad. A vertical line appeared between the inspector's eyebrows. The policeman handed a package over to him and, saluting smartly, retreated into the depths of officialdom from which he had come.

Singh asked, 'What is it?'

'A tape from an informer. It might have a bearing on the Lee investigation apparently.'

'Convenient!' remarked Inspector Singh. 'Any idea what it's about?'

'Not a clue. But we can find out.'

The men walked purposefully towards a room with audio-visual equipment. Mohammad led the way, walking with long-limbed elegance. Shukor padded silently in his wake. Singh lumbered after them. A study in physical contrasts, they looked like a procession that was not just walking along a corridor but up the evolutionary chain as well. But, despite appearances, it would have been a brave man who bet against Inspector Singh if it came down to the survival of the fittest.

Mohammad opened the package and handed the disc to Shukor, who organised the equipment efficiently. The three men sat down and the whole episode at the night club unfolded before them. The wealthy Alan Lee, just a few weeks before his death, his plaything and the irate young man shunted aside.

Shukor felt it was like an MTV rock video with the repetitive bass, the strobe lights and the excessively beautiful woman.

Singh, from an older generation, was reminded more of silent movies with their painted dolls and exaggerated acting.

It was left to Mohammad to say something and he did. 'Jasper hasn't even changed his mind yet and new suspects are crawling out of the woodwork.'

'Maybe that woman had some reason to be jealous?' suggested Shukor.

'Yes, although more likely that young man had a surge of testosterone,' was the Malaysian inspector's response. 'We need to find out who he is.'

Singh said unexpectedly, 'Oh no we don't!'

'What do you mean?' asked Inspector Mohammad testily. 'You're convinced he's innocent? Leave me some suspects, for God's sake.'

Singh grinned, baring his small, even teeth, stained with nicotine and coffee. 'No, I don't know that he didn't do it. But I do know who that young man is. I met him only last week.'

The other two turned to him, the inspector in surprise, the sergeant, who was beginning to see the Singapore policeman as omniscient, in expectation.

'That there,' said Inspector Singh laconically, 'is Marcus Lee — the murdered man's son.'

Twenty-four hours later, Jasper Lee asked to see Inspector Mohammad. Mohammad summoned Singh and they set off for the cells. There was no talk now about Singh returning to Singapore. Although there was no official reason for him to stay, not unless Chelsea was rearrested, he was too involved. Mohammad had changed his tune. He treated the inspector from Singapore as an ally in a hunt for the truth, not an adversary in a battle for kudos. Singh admired him for it but did not expect it to last past their next dispute over culpability. Still, it was much more pleasant doing investigative work with the authority of a police department behind him. Singh, the maverick, had suddenly been made aware that the bureaucracy he despised served a very useful purpose. It gave him power and access, without which no amount of investigative acumen was of any use.

Jasper Lee was a pale imitation of the man he had been a mere twenty-four hours earlier. His thinness was cadaverous. His eyes were bloodshot and his hair lank. Singh thought he looked like someone he had seen recently and was debating whether it was a resemblance to his nephew, Marcus, that he perceived or the other brother, Kian Min. It came to him with some shock. Jasper Lee looked like Alan Lee — as he had seen him in the morgue, three weeks dead and waiting to be buried. Up until he had heard about Ravi, Jasper had been waiting for certain death with dignity — now he looked like it had caught up with him.

Singh flicked on the tape recorder and said with cruel humour, 'You asked to see us? Decided why you killed Alan yet?'

Jasper sat sullenly. He had called them in, but his heart still shrank from what he intended to do. The policemen saw the doubt and anxiety flit across his face. And also the disappointment. Jasper Lee had screwed up the courage to be a hero — and had only managed to land the part of the fool.

Singh sensed it was partly a reluctance to admit that his great sacrifice was a mistake. This was a man who had been branded a failure by his father, his brothers and his peers. He was vilified as being weak, unable to carry things through, lacking the hard head needed to make intelligent business judgements. Jasper Lee had chosen his moment to confront his secret fear — that these accusations had more than a grain of truth in them. He must have felt secretly proud — proud of his capacity for self-sacrifice, proud of his courage in the face of death, proud of his ability to take a decision of principle and stick to it. And it had all been for nothing — merely vindicating the family view that he was a gullible idiot.

Singh said almost gently to the tortured man, 'It's not too late, you know.'

Jasper looked up at him and there were tears in his eyes. Mohammad shifted uncomfortably. He was of the old school — grown men didn't cry and boys shouldn't. Singh was from the same generation. But to him, tears were an honest reflection of emotion. And honesty led a policeman like him to the truth.

'Not too late?' asked Jasper. 'I'm afraid you're quite, quite wrong. It was too late twenty years ago.'

'Too late to have her — not too late to save your life,' urged Mohammad.

'Save it for what?'

'For the things you care about,' said Singh.

'I was going to sacrifice it for the thing I care about.'

'We know,' said Mohammad gently.

Jasper looked at them and saw from their

sympathetic expressions that they did know. It made it that much easier for him to put his errors into words.

He said carefully, looking down at the floor, noticing that it was bare cement and hard and cold and grey like the world as it appeared to him, 'I did not kill my brother, Alan Lee.'

'Why did you confess?'

'I wanted to protect Chelsea. I was afraid she would be convicted of the murder.'

'Can you tell us why you wanted to protect her?'

'I love her. I've loved her since the day I met her, twenty years ago, at my brother's wedding.'

'So what changed your mind?'

Jasper struggled to articulate his reasoning. He said, 'I'm not sure, really. I tried to protect her because I loved her. I knew I couldn't have her, not if I was going to end up in here. But to find out she had a boyfriend all along . . . I thought she was alone, you see. That she needed me. Had no one else.'

'Why were you so sure that she killed Alan?'

The question penetrated the daze. He said in a sharper tone, 'I am *not* sure! But you seemed ready to hang her.'

'Do you know anything that made you suspect that she'd done it?'

'Where the smoking gun is, you mean? Look, I've decided I don't want to swing for Chelsea. Her boyfriend can do that if he wants. But that does not mean I plan to help you hang her!'

This flash of spirit quickly died down and Jasper slumped back into his chair. He said, 'What now?'

'I guess we let you go,' said Inspector Mohammad. 'But don't go too far.'

Singh tapped the Malay policeman on the shoulder and nodded in the direction of the door. 'I need a quick word,' he said.

The two men walked out and Mohammad said impatiently, 'What is it? Do you want me to thank you?'

'No, no. Don't let him go yet.'

'What?'

'Don't let him go yet!'

'Why not? Weren't you the one who couldn't bear Chelsea Liew spending one hour more than she had to in prison?'

Inspector Singh brushed aside his previous position with a quick gesture. 'Look, you don't think Chelsea did it, do you?'

'I wouldn't say that,' said Mohammad cautiously.

'At least you agree that there are a few

250

suspects floating around?' He ticked them off on his fingers — 'Kian Min, Marcus Lee, Ravi, that woman who might have been scorned.'

'And Chelsea Liew.'

'All right, and Chelsea.'

Mohammad said, 'I am willing to accept that we have a few suspects, yes. So what?'

'Let's keep Jasper here. The murderer, whichever one he is, will think he's home and dry. He might make a mistake.'

If Mohammad noticed the masculine pronoun for the murderer, he didn't show it. Instead, he nodded. 'That's actually not a bad idea. We'll try it.'

The policemen walked back in to inform Jasper Lee that he would have to wait a little bit longer to get out. He didn't seem to care.

Sharifah looked out of the window. The day was so hot a shimmering haze was visible, as if the heat had warped the air. She was devastated by Chelsea's visit. It was a terrible thing to have a conversation with the woman whose husband she had slept with. It was no use telling herself that if it was not her, it would have been somebody else. Because it hadn't been someone else — it had been her. She thought of her parents, who had worked hard to bring her up to know right from wrong. She thought of Marcus, who had loved her and been completely destroyed by her betrayal of him, not just with anyone, but with the father he hated. She felt very, very ashamed. She wondered if she dared call Marcus. She looked at her mobile phone on the dining table. No, she could not call him. Not after what she had done. Thank God the uncle had killed Alan. If she had provoked Marcus to murder, she could not have lived with herself. Sharifah made up her mind. She would make amends as best as she could. The past was inviolable. But she would sell the flat bought in her name, as well as all the jewellery, and return the money to the Lee family — anonymously. She was not looking for public forgiveness, just personal redemption.

The doorbell rang and she went to answer it nervously. She really hoped it was not Chelsea again.

A Sikh man said, 'We are the police. We want to ask you some questions about Alan Lee.'

She let them in reluctantly, the fat man and his handsome Malay sidekick.

Singh did not beat around the bush. He had decided early to be aggressive to the adulteress, convinced that only tough questioning would have an impact on a woman so bold as to have an affair with Alan Lee. When Sharifah opened the door and peered out fearfully, he realised at once she was not the scheming woman of his imagination but a pretty, young thing — a victim of Alan Lee. Despite this, he felt a sudden anger at the woman who had added to the misery facing Chelsea Liew as she tried to escape her abusive marriage and rescue her children from their father's unhappy influence.

He said abruptly, 'We have good reason to suspect you killed Alan Lee.'

'We were going to get married! Why would I kill him?'

Sharifah was angry and frightened. Just as the door to the past was closing, this fat policeman had stuck his great foot in its dirty white shoe in the crack.

Inspector Singh asked rudely, still infuriated at the role the young woman had played in the unfolding drama surrounding Alan Lee's life and death, 'Why in the world would a man like Alan Lee marry *you*? Here's what really happened. He showered you with attention, got you into bed and then dumped you as he had done all the women before you. You got upset, got a gun, found a quiet moment and killed him.'

Sharifah's eyes were wide with shock. She

was young and had never been confronted so aggressively before. Even Chelsea, who had better reason than most to hate her, had not raised her voice. She felt tears fill her eyes. 'But he converted to Islam — he did that for me!'

'You might have given him the idea, but he converted to get custody of the kids and spite his ex-wife.'

'I don't believe you!'

Singh said in genuine disgust, 'It's naïve, stupid young women like you who make it possible for men like Alan to exploit and ruin them.'

Sharifah said quietly, 'I know I made a mistake, I see that now. But I didn't kill him. At the time when he died, I still thought I loved him.'

'I still thought I loved him,' imitated Singh in an irritated tone. 'If you were my daughter, I'd lock you in a room and not let you out until you developed some common sense.'

'I've told you I didn't kill him. Is there anything else I can help you with?' asked Sharifah.

Singh noted with approval that the young woman had some gumption. He wondered at Alan Lee. He had been attracted to strong, beautiful women, if Chelsea and

Sharifah were anything to go by, but then was not content until he had beaten the spirit out of them.

'Did Alan beat you?' he asked abruptly.

She flinched at the sudden change of tack but she said firmly, 'No, of course not. Why would he do that? I told you — he loved me. He loved me very much. We were going to get married.'

Singh knew she was lying. She was protesting too much. Rehearsing the arguments she had used to explain away the violence.

'How often did he hit you?'

'I've just told you, he didn't!'

'Just once, twice? Was it all flowers and apologies after that? What did he tell you — he was under pressure at work? The custody battle was going badly that day? He loved you so much he got jealous because you were talking to the postman? I bet you thought it was a compliment that he gave you a black eye!'

Sharifah said in a subdued tone, 'It was only the once. He slapped me. But he was really sorry about it.'

'And you believed him?' asked Shukor, speaking for the first time during the interview.

She looked at him defiantly. 'Yes.'

'So let me get this straight,' said the

inspector. 'He was much, much older than you, was going through a divorce where he was accused of adultery and brutality and was locked in a bitter custody battle for his kids. He had started to hit you — and yet you thought you were going to marry him and live happily ever after?'

She nodded and said, 'I guess it sounds unlikely.'

Singh said, 'All right then, let's suppose I believe you . . . maybe you didn't kill him.'

Sharifah looked up at him quickly, hope dawning in her eyes. Was the door to the past to be allowed to close after all?

'Why don't you tell us how you drove Marcus Lee to kill his own father?'

SIXTEEN

Mr Chan, the private investigator, had given a copy of the disc to the police. Chelsea Liew, he thought, would think twice about not paying up for work done in the future. And he was quite sure he had found a way to recoup the losses that he had made on the Lee investigation. He neatly arranged his hair, changed into a fresh shirt and approached the newspapers with an exclusive. The tape in exchange for two thousand ringgit. When he explained, in lascivious detail, what was on the tape, he started a bidding war. In the end he walked away with five thousand ringgit. Not bad, he thought smugly. His cunning had resulted in a much better outcome than he could have predicted when that woman had not paid him. It was only when he got to the car that he experienced a pang of regret that caused his stomach juices to wash over his ulcers. Doubled over and gasping with pain, one hand on the door of his car to keep from ending up on his knees in the dust, gravel and dog shit that characterised the open plots of city land doubling as car parks, Mr Chan was really cross with himself. He should have approached the Singapore newspapers too. They would have paid double at least and in a more valuable currency.

The newspaper that won the tape watched it, cut stills from it, consulted their lawyers and prepared the morning edition with an enthusiasm that had not been seen on the newsroom floor for many years. They had the Malaysian scoop of the year.

Chelsea had persuaded Marcus to sit down with her for a coffee. It had not been easy. He had insisted he was busy, he had schoolwork, he was just popping out for a moment — they could do it later. But she had insisted, finally she had begged and he had agreed to join her for a quick drink. They sat at the dining table, a heavy, rectangular table with sixteen chairs around it, sipping hot coffee. The two younger boys had gone to the park with their nanny. They would not be interrupted — not for a while anyway.

Chelsea broke the silence that was becoming oppressive. 'I'm worried about you, Marcus.'

'Why?' asked Marcus. 'I'm fine.'

'I don't think you're fine. You're hardly at home. You don't speak to me or the boys any more. Your clothes stink of alcohol and cigarettes. I checked with the school — you've not been turning up there.'

'I don't like you spying on me!'

'I'm not spying on you. I'm your mother, I'm worried about you.'

'Yeah, you're a great mother . . .'

'What's that supposed to mean?'

'Nothing!'

'Marcus, I did my best for you. I'm doing my best for all you kids. Things haven't been easy — you know that.'

Marcus fidgeted in his chair. 'Can I go now?'

Chelsea said quietly, 'I know about Sharifah.'

His skinny body grew stock still. He looked up at his mother and saw the sympathy and pity on her face.

Images of Sharifah flitted through his mind like a series of photos on a screen saver. And then the last time he had seen her — at that club. Standing there, all dressed up like he had never seen her — looking so much older than she had ever done before. Wearing clothes his father had bought her, wearing jewellery his father had bought her, selling herself to a rich man. He had begged her to come away with him. Promised her that he loved her. Tried to explain the sort of man his father was. He had thought, for a moment, that he was getting through to her. Her face had softened, she had looked younger. More like the girl he had known at school. And then he had realised that she was looking at him with sympathy, with pity. That same expression she had worn he now saw on his mother's face.

Marcus put his head down on his folded arms. His mother reached out and put an arm around him. He did not shake it off. For a long time they stayed in the same position until at last Marcus sat up.

He looked at his mother with red-rimmed eyes and said, 'How do you know about Sharifah?'

'That's not important.'

'You know about Dad too? What he did?'

She nodded, not trusting herself to speak. Her anger at her dead husband burned so hot she felt as if she could set fire to things simply by touching them.

'I hated him. I'm so glad he's dead,' said the boy bitterly.

'Marcus, I need to ask you an important question. And whatever you tell me, I will protect you. But I need to know the truth.'

Marcus looked at her, his face twisted with sadness.

She asked softly, 'Did you kill your father?'

'Marcus did not kill his father.' Sharifah spoke emphatically, complete conviction in her voice.

'How would you know that for a fact?' asked Singh.

'I know Marcus. He would never do a thing like that!'

'I can just see the court taking your word for it,' said Singh snidely. 'You'd make a wonderful character witness — your behaviour in this matter has been so upstanding.'

Sharifah winced at the sarcasm but would not budge from her position. 'Marcus Lee is a very gentle boy.'

'A gentle boy, not like that big strong man, his father, eh? If that's how you spoke to him — and not just about him — no wonder he was provoked to kill his father.'

'He did not kill his father!'

'Somebody did.'

'I thought it was the uncle.'

'I bet that made you feel better,' remarked Inspector Singh with his usual intuitive insight. 'You must have been very worried, when you heard Alan Lee was dead, that you had driven Marcus to do it.'

'I was not worried at all,' she said firmly.

'Look, the only way you could know for sure Marcus Lee did not murder his father is if you killed Alan yourself.'

'No, I know Marcus didn't do it . . . because I was with him at the time of the murder.'

Singh looked at her disbelievingly. 'That's your story?'

She nodded, pale but determined.

'So what was this? The grand reunion?'

She thought about her answer.

Trying to remember exactly what she had said earlier so that she would not contradict herself, guessed the inspector. It would be almost amusing if it wasn't an effort to mislead them in a murder investigation.

Sharifah said, 'No . . . I hadn't broken up with Alan. We were still getting married. But I wanted to apologise to Marcus — make him understand.'

'I struggle to see a situation in which Marcus would be willing to listen to an apology from you.'

'I thought I had to try.'

'So when was this grand reconciliation and forgiveness fest?'

'I told you — the day Alan was murdered.'

'And which day was that?'

'I don't remember.'

'You don't remember the day your fiancé was killed?'

'Of course I remember. I mean I don't remember the exact date!'

'Do you remember what time this reunion with Marcus was?'

'Not exactly. But we were together quite a while.'

'I can see why that would be — you had a lot to talk about, after all.'

Shukor wondered why the inspector was being so unpleasant to Sharifah. He had not seen him, until that moment, be so harsh and sarcastic with a witness. She was very young, this girl. She had made some pretty awful mistakes — but that was what young people did. She was unlucky in the unintended consequences that had flowed from them, that was all.

Singh had not finished. He said abruptly, 'Morning or afternoon?'

She was confused. 'I don't understand.'

'Were you with him in the morning or the afternoon?'

'I don't know, I don't remember. Both!'

Singh laughed out loud. He said, 'I feel sorry for you, spouting these lies in front of

263

the prosecution at Marcus Lee's trial for murder.'

'What are you going to do?'

The inspector didn't answer her question. Instead, he turned to Shukor and said, 'Come on — let's go. We've got work to do.'

Shukor nodded to Sharifah almost apologetically and trailed after his superior officer. He had no idea why Singh had been so aggressive with Sharifah and he certainly wasn't going to ask. He didn't relish feeling the rough edge of the inspector's tongue. It was bad enough to be a witness to it. Still, it had produced results. The young woman — he felt another pang of sympathy as he remembered her wide, frightened eyes — had tied herself in knots with her hastily concocted version of events, desperate to provide her ex-boyfriend an alibi. Shukor could not decide whether her attempts had been provoked by guilt or a residual affection for Marcus.

The two men took the lift to the ground floor and got into the car. They drove quietly for a couple of minutes.

At last Shukor asked, 'Are we on the way to arrest Marcus?'

'No. In fact, just pull over here.'

Shukor stopped by the side of the road. 'What now, sir?'

'I want you to go back.'

'Back?'

'Yes, to the apartment building. Find a convenient bush, hide behind it. Wait for Sharifah to come out and stay on her tail. *Don't* let her see you.'

'Yes, sir. But what are you hoping she'll do?'

'Run to Marcus and warn him.'

'Won't she just call him?'

'I suspect she'll want to see him face to face. Try and get this alibi straight. Besides' — Singh fished in his pocket — 'I nicked her mobile phone.'

Shukor looked shocked at this petty theft but did not protest. He said, 'You don't believe she was with him?'

'No!'

'Me neither,' said Shukor ruefully, climbing out of the car.

Inspector Singh got out too and walked around to the other side, sliding into the driver's seat with difficulty and moving the seat back so his stomach had more space.

Shukor put a hand on the door and leaned forward earnestly. He asked, 'Do you think she did it, sir? Or him?'

'Don't know. But both scenarios are quite possible. Alan Lee might have dumped her. She could have killed him for revenge. Marcus was certainly angry enough. They might even have done it together.'

'What do you mean?'

'Marcus would have inherited a stack of money — and Sharifah could have married a *young,* rich man.'

'I don't think she did it.'

Singh laughed. 'You're never going to be a successful policeman if you don't believe a beautiful woman can commit murder!'

'Isn't that why you believe Chelsea is innocent?'

Singh's laughter dried up. There was more than a hint of truth in what the young policeman had said. He snapped, 'Get on with the job.'

'What are you going to do, sir?'

'Get lost on the way back to the office.'

Singh accelerated away, spitting dust and pebbles at the policeman standing by the road.

Shukor dusted himself off and headed back in the direction he had come.

Inspector Singh was as good as his word. In a very short time, he was completely lost. He regretted not taking a taxi. The traffic was heavy, the drivers aggressive and many of the cars looked like they were on the verge of a breakdown. In Singapore, by contrast, remembered Singh wistfully, the vast majority of cars were less than ten years old. The tax system worked such that it was usually better to scrap a car or export it and buy a new one than hang on to an old jalopy. A tiny island, the government was desperate that Singapore should not turn into a parking lot, so it invested in public transport and kept cars expensive. As a result, cars had real value and owners looked after them. A dirty car was a rarity in Singapore, let alone an old one. In Malaysia, Singh guessed, there were no such incentives. So old men ferried their extended families around in beat-up vans with six or seven kids hanging out of the windows and waving to the other cars. Salesmen drove ancient run-arounds. Thirty-year-old Mercedes Benz doubled up as taxis. Motorbikes weaved in and out of traffic. Small cars with 500cc engines, basically motorbikes with a body, raced along the fast lane at murderous speeds. Four-wheel drives, raised high with extra-large tyres, sped by. Mysterious limousines with dark, tinted windows went about their shady business. It was all too challenging for a policeman from Singapore who was unfamiliar with the road network.

Singh wondered whether his wandering

around Kuala Lumpur, taking wrong turns and making u-turns, was supposed to be some sort of metaphor for the way the case was shaping up. There had certainly been enough confusion to go around.

First, was the arrest of Chelsea. He wriggled in his seat, trying to get his shirt, adhering to his back with sweat, to unstick. It was quite revealing, the sergeant's comment, that he was so convinced about Chelsea's innocence because he had been bowled over by her looks. Singh, who loved cricket and had once, in his youth, opened the batting for Singapore, loved his cricketing analogies. It was possible, of course. What was it that they said? There was no fool like an old fool.

Singh swerved suddenly to avoid a motorbike which had raced up to overtake him on the left just as he considered changing lane. He almost hit a Mercedes Benz, a big, ugly, inflated beast of a car. The driver horned and the man in the back looked up briefly and then returned to his papers. The inspector went back to his circuitous musings and turned his attention to Jasper. His doubts as to Chelsea's guilt had been so spectacularly vindicated. Jasper Lee had walked in of his own accord, and confessed. Singh searched his mind. Had he doubted the confession? He had to admit he had not. Not until Chelsea had insisted that Jasper did not kill Alan Lee. Even then, he was humouring her more than anything else. Further evidence of his partiality for Chelsea? Shukor would certainly think so. Singh was not convinced the young man was wrong.

He was passing the Twin Towers now — two massive rockets in geometric designs brushing against the sky. He remembered the rumours, constantly circulating, that the towers were leaning this way or that way. They looked steady enough to him. Apparently, the task of building them had been given to two different contractors, so that they would work as quickly as possible in the race to touch the heavens first. Singh hoped it was not true. It sounded like a recipe for short cuts and shoddy work.

And what of the other brother? Kian Min had a lot in common with Alan, his dead brother. It was just that Alan's lusts were of the flesh, Kian Min's were for power and wealth.

Lust. Was it at the root of this case? Had Kian Min's lust for power finally led him to kill his brother? Kian Min, Singh guessed, would have been more than happy to have his brother out of the way. But this was a man who paid people to do his dirty work for him. That was his *modus operandi.* He paid people to chase the Penan off their land in Borneo. He paid policemen and government employees to turn a blind eye. Surely, if he wanted his brother dead, he would have paid someone to do it. But the death of Alan Lee had not looked like a professional hit. Singh was convinced that Alan had known his assailant. He would be quite content if Kian Min turned out to be the murderer. But he was not convinced it was the right solution.

What about Alan then? Was it *his* lusts that had led directly to his death? Had that girl, Sharifah, killed him when she woke up to the fact that she was just his latest conquest of the flesh, bought and paid for in cash and kind? He had been tough with the girl during her interview. He suspected Shukor had noticed. Why had he done that when it became apparent that she was not the painted tart he had anticipated? Was it because he thought she had killed Alan Lee and that he was face to face with a cold-blooded killer? He pictured her young face, shorn of make-up. Singh had not spent a lifetime as a policeman to leap to conclusions based on appearances. Except, he reminded himself, that was precisely what his sergeant had accused him of doing in the case of Chelsea.

It was a pity that he was above framing likely suspects, Singh thought ruefully — at least not unless he was absolutely sure they had committed the crime. Otherwise, he would have loved to pin the murder of the loathsome Alan Lee on that equally unattractive character, Ravi. There would be a wonderful symmetry in the removal of both the exploitative men in Chelsea Liew's life. But sadly, wishful thinking did not translate into hard evidence.

Singh saw a sign that read 'Bangsar' and turned the car in that direction. At least he was familiar with the area. The petrol gauge inched towards empty. And so did his bag of suspects. There was only Marcus Lee left. God knows he had motives in spades. The regular abuse of his mother. The stolen girlfriend. He was very young, Marcus — young enough that a surge of testosterone might have given him the courage to carry out the murder. And young enough to believe he could get away with it.

He had reached Bangsar but could not for the life of him find his way out. There was only one thing to do. He parked the car neatly by the side of the road, ignoring the double yellow lines. A troop of monkeys from a nearby nature reserve screamed at him from the telephone wires. He glowered back at them but decided not to indulge in a shouting match. The monkeys moved on to a nearby bin and started methodically emptying it, chattering with excitement every time they found something tasty. They glared at the inspector from time to time in case he should be considering making a grab for the food. Singh flagged down a taxi and headed for the station.

Inspector Mohammad was not at the station. He was at the Lee Building talking to Lee Kian Min. Kian Min was not amused to be at the receiving end of two visits from the police in as many days. He calmed down a little when Mohammad told him that he was just there to apologise for Sergeant Shukor's behaviour and to assure him that the policeman had been disciplined.

'He should be sacked,' asserted Kian Min, daring the inspector to contradict him.

Mohammad chose discretion. 'It was not my decision,' he said, hinting that if he was in charge, Shukor would have come out of it much the worse. 'The higher-ups thought that he should have a second chance since he is so young and had an unblemished record until the regrettable incident with you.'

'It better not happen again.'

'It won't, Mr Lee.'

Kian Min looked at the inspector expectantly. 'You want something else? I need to carry on with my work.'

'There is something you could help me with, sir.'

Kian Min did not see anything incongruous about the dignified policeman addressing someone his junior as 'sir'. If he had thought about it, he would have found it entirely appropriate.

'I'm a busy man. I don't know why you policemen don't understand that.'

'I won't take much time, sir.'

Kian Min nodded and looked at his watch. 'All right, what do you want?'

'Did you kill Alan Lee?'

'What?'

'I asked you if you killed your brother, Alan Lee?'

'What for I would do that?'

'For this!' said Mohammad, waving a careless hand at the businessman's surroundings.

'I no need to kill him to get this. I was boss of the company already.'

'That's not what I hear. My sources tell

me that Alan Lee was the brains behind the success of the company.'

'Alan? The brains?' Kian Min barked with loud, angry laughter. 'Who told you that?' He jabbed his finger at the inspector to emphasise his point. 'They know nothing about Lee Timber. I have been the boss of this company since my father died. Alan was a figurehead only.'

'But what about that decision to switch to growing oil palm for bio-fuels? I read in the papers that it was Alan's last decision in charge before he was killed and the analysts think it's a stroke of genius.'

'Of course it is genius — my genius!' Kian Min was almost shouting now.

'But the newspapers . . .'

Kian Min interrupted him. 'I tell you it was my idea! Alan did not even understand the business.'

Mohammad shook his head, like a man struggling to understand what he was being told.

Kian Min said, 'I thought Jasper killed Alan anyway.'

'We have reason to doubt his story,' said Mohammad stolidly.

'Really? That's a pity. But, for your information, I have nothing to do with it.'

'You think Jasper Lee did it?'

'I don't know and I don't care who killed Alan. He was useless, a piece of nothing his whole life.' There was a small speck of saliva at the corner of Kian Min's mouth.

'But you testified at the custody trial that he was a fine man, a good father and a brilliant businessman.'

'Maybe I did, I suppose . . . family must stick together.'

'You've been sitting there telling me you don't care who killed your brother but it was most likely your other brother and then you expect me to believe that you felt a *family* obligation?'

Kian Min maintained a sullen reticence for a few seconds and then said, 'Well, murder not the same, right?'

'Perhaps, but perjury — giving false testimony under oath in court — is an offence.'

'I not committed perjury.'

'You lied about your brother's character. I could arrest you right now and drag you down to the police station in shackles.'

Kian Min turned pale. He said, 'How can I change your mind?'

'What are you offering?' asked Inspector Mohammad carefully.

'Some contribution to your retirement fund?'

Mohammad looked at the man across the table with an unreadable expression. 'How much?' he asked bluntly.

'A hundred thousand.'

Mohammad shook his head.

'Five hundred thousand? That should be enough. You can retire in style!'

'That's a lot of money,' said Mohammad thoughtfully.

Sharifah left her apartment hurriedly, jumped into a small Toyota sports car, no doubt another gift from Alan, and set off at top speed. Shukor, waiting in a taxi, had no difficulty following her. But when she reached the neighbourhood where Alan Lee had his mansion, she drove past the house slowly, turned around, parked the car at the bottom of the street and waited. Shukor disembarked from the taxi some way up the street, paid off the driver and sat at a bus stop. He did not think she would spot him. Her whole concentration was on the street, watching cars and people with a fierce intensity. He was obscured by bushes and passers-by and had a newspaper for verisimilitude. But how long were they going to sit there? If she was planning to warn Marcus, she needed to be quicker about it.

The gates to the Lee residence opened. A

Mercedes Benz purred out. Shukor, watching Sharifah, saw her duck down silently so the car she was in looked driverless. He wondered at this until he glimpsed the passenger in the back seat. It was Chelsea, her face partially obscured by a very large pair of sunglasses. Shukor realised that Sharifah must have been waiting for her to go out — unable to face the wife.

Sharifah waited a few minutes and then got out of the car. She walked slowly up the hill, each step laboured and reluctant. Shukor stayed a safe distance away but there was no danger of Sharifah turning around. All her attention was on the shiny gold gates of Marcus's home. She reached the entrance, looked around for the bell, found it and gave it a good, long ring. She spoke a few words into the mike and the gates swung open mysteriously. Sharifah took a few tentative steps forward. The gates shut behind her.

Shukor found a shady spot under an acacia tree, and waited for her to come out, whiling away the time by weaving a flower out of the crescent-shaped leaves as his sisters had done when they were young.

Sharifah was terrified. She tried to remember when she had ever been so scared.

Perhaps it was the time when she had fallen into the swimming pool and her father had rescued her — but only after she had gone under a couple of times and experienced the raw panic of a four-year-old unable to breathe or swim. It was a not dissimilar sensation she felt now, she thought. Her chest was constricted, her movements slow and uncoordinated, her skin tingling with nerves. The housemaid was at the door as she walked up the long drive. She was ushered in, led to a sitting room, invited to sit down on a comfortable sofa and offered a drink which she declined. Sharifah explained she was a schoolfriend of Marcus.

The maid said, 'I will fetch Master Marcus. May I know your name, please.'

She said, 'I'm Sharifah. But please don't tell him. Just say it's someone from school. I want to surprise him.'

The maid nodded. She was pleased to be part of a conspiracy to cheer up the young master. He had been so miserable for so long now. It was like her mother had always said, wealth didn't make you happy. The young Filipina, leaving her farm in Mindanao to seek employment abroad, had never believed her. Surely the worst state of existence was to be poor, to never be sure that there would be enough money to feed a sprawling, hungry family. She knew better now. Since her job with the Lee family, she had truly understood how lucky she was to belong to a big loving family where everyone looked out for each other. She smiled again at the young, beautiful visitor. She noticed that the girl looked pale. Perhaps there was something more here than met the eye. This could be a girlfriend. She could not fail to cheer Marcus up.

Marcus was slumped in bed playing with a portable Gameboy. He wore the same clothes he had gone to bed in. He smelt, not just of alcohol and cigarettes, but also rancid and unwashed. The maid hoped the girlfriend was the tolerant sort. Marcus, however, had no inclination to drag himself out of bed and go down to his guest.

'Who is it?' he asked irritably.

'I did not ask,' said the maid.

'You know you're always supposed to ask.'

'Yes, Master Marcus. I just forgot.'

'Well, just find out who it is and send him away.'

'Why don't you just come down and say "hello"? Maybe it will make you in a good mood?'

Marcus snorted and then remembered that one of his schoolmates owed him some money. That must be who it was. And he wanted to ask Charlie Hua whether he could get him something to smoke that would help him forget his profound misery. This would be a good time to do it. Charlie was plugged in to all the pushers who hung around the school. And he owed Marcus a favour for lending him money when he had been a bit short. He had said at the time that the loan would save him from a good beating, or worse. Marcus got to his feet.

'All right, I'll see him.'

The maid did not think this was a good time to mention that the visitor was female.

'What are you doing here?' Marcus didn't shout. His voice was barely audible. But anger ran through the words like a major artery. 'Get out of my house!'

She cowered, as if his words were physical blows. Her shoulders shook and she wrapped her arms around herself — part defensive gesture, part an attempt to stop the trembling.

She tried to speak. 'Marcus . . .'

He screamed this time. 'No, I don't want to know. Get out!'

She didn't know how to break through his wall of anger. It had an almost physical quality. It was an impenetrable barrier between them. She tried again. 'I wouldn't be here if it wasn't important.'

She rushed the words, got them out, but he did not appear to have heard them. He was still staring at her as if she was some sort of apparition. One small part of his brain noticed her pallor. She had lost weight and was not wearing make-up as she had done in those last days with his father.

She said again, 'You have to listen to me, Marcus. This is important or I wouldn't be here.'

Somehow that got through. 'You have something important to tell me? That's a change, isn't it? The last time you had something *important* that you should have told me, you didn't bother, did you? But maybe — just maybe — I would have been just a little bit interested to know that my girlfriend was sleeping with my father.'

The words dripped with sarcasm, but the voice was still pure, undiluted anger.

Sharifah thought she had known, had guessed, how much she must have hurt him. But now she looked at the thin, young boy in front of her and realised that she had no idea what he must have gone through. She lacked the imagination to comprehend what a betrayal like hers could have done to a sensitive character like Marcus.

She said, 'God, Marcus. I am so sorry. I

could not have been worse or done worse and I will never forgive myself as I know you will never forgive me.'

He shook his head, as if her words were like a mosquito buzzing in his ear at night time.

'But I must talk to you. You must listen to me.'

Marcus stared at her fixedly, unblinkingly.

Sharifah was beginning to worry for his sanity. She said in a determined voice, 'The police have been to see me. They know about us. And about me . . . and Alan.'

He did not respond or appear to have heard her.

'Marcus, the police think you killed your father!'

'Well, was it the girlfriend? Or the son?' The Malaysian inspector's tone was flippant but Singh ignored it. He did not know why Mohammad was in such a good mood but he did not plan to match it. Not after having driven around Kuala Lumpur for two hours.

Singh said, 'Hard to say. The girl claims that she and Alan were still an item when he was killed and so she was not the woman scorned. And also that he converted to Islam to marry her.'

'Really? Did you believe that?'

'No. I think she gave him the idea and he realised it would be a powerful weapon in the custody hearings. But I doubt he would have married her.'

'What was she like, this girl?'

'Pretty, dangerously naïve.'

'A killer?'

Singh said reluctantly, 'I don't see it. But I've been wrong before.'

'Wrong? Not our infallible inspector from Singapore!'

Singh scowled at his counterpart. 'Why are you in such a good mood, anyway?'

Mohammad ignored the question and said instead, 'It must be the son, then . . . Marcus Lee.'

'She claims to have been with him at the time of the murder.'

'Who does?'

'The girlfriend, Sharifah.'

'She's sleeping with the father but hanging out with the son? One big happy family?'

'It was a fairly shaky alibi. She had no idea when Alan was killed so was trying for a fairly broad-brush approach.'

Mohammad laughed. 'What prompted it?'

'Guilt, probably. She knows the only reason we suspect Marcus is because, thanks to her, he has a powerful motive.'

'You should have followed her. Presumably she'll rush off and warn the young man now.'

'I sent Shukor.'

'Good thinking,' said Mohammad approvingly.

'So, what's been happening around here?' asked Singh.

'Chelsea Liew came to see Jasper but was turned away.'

'By us?'

'No, by him. He's not ready to tell her that she's back on the list of suspects, I guess.'

'Which brings us to the original question. Why do you look like the cat that's swallowed the cream?'

Mohammad said, as nonchalantly as he could, 'I dropped in to see Lee Kian Min.'

'He agreed to see you? I would have thought he'd be reluctant to expose his person to a policeman for a while.'

'He was. I said I was the official delegation to apologise to a leading member of the business community.'

'I bet he lapped that up.'

Mohammad nodded. 'He was fine until I asked him if he had killed his brother — then he got a little bit agitated.'

'What did he say?' asked Singh.

'Well, he denied everything, of course, said

that it was probably Jasper.' Mohammad shook his head at the willingness of the Lee brothers to point the finger at each other.

'No love lost between the brothers, eh?' remarked Inspector Singh, unconsciously echoing the other policeman's thoughts.

'No. It made it very difficult for him to explain why he had testified at the custody hearings that Alan was such a fine fellow.'

'Good point. We can threaten him with . . .'

Mohammad interrupted him, determined that no one was going to steal his lines. 'Perjury! Yes, I did point out to him that we could make his life miserable.'

'What did he say?'

'He tried to bribe me,' said the Malaysian policeman.

Singh refrained from saying that Kian Min must have felt on pretty safe ground if the reputation of the Malaysian police force was accurate.

He asked instead, 'How much?'

'Five hundred thousand without bargaining . . .'

'Not bad. He must really want to stay out of trouble.'

'Well, I told him money wouldn't do the trick. I needed another credible suspect.'

'Did he have one?'

'Yup,' said Mohammad, grinning.

SEVENTEEN

'So who did Kian Min serve up to save his own skin?' asked Singh.

'A businessman from Hong Kong,' replied Mohammad evenly.

'What was his reason?'

'Quite complicated. This Chinaman from Hong Kong — Douglas Wee — fronts for some Chinese conglomerate looking for bio-fuels.'

'So?'

'Lee Timber has been considering diversi-fying into bio-fuels, partly because this syndicate, or Douglas Wee anyway, promised to buy whatever they can produce.'

'I read in the papers that they had decided to go ahead with it?'

'Yes, that's right — now that Alan Lee is dead. Apparently, he was standing in the way of the project while Kian Min was in favour of it. Alan's dying made it happen.'

'So why should this Donald or Douglas,

or whatever his name is, have killed Alan?'

'According to Lee Kian Min, he needed to land the deal for his Chinese masters or wear knee-cap protectors.'

'It's possible, I suppose,' said Singh doubtfully, scratching his nose.

Mohammad laughed. 'There's no need to be polite. I know it's farfetched. But we can get this guy in. He's in Malaysia apparently, tidying up loose ends.'

Singh nodded. 'And if it does turn out to be a load of bollocks, we'll have more to harass Lee with.'

Mohammad raised a warning finger. 'Let me make it quite clear — under no circumstances are you or Shukor to go anywhere near Lee Kian Min. He's a petty, vindictive bastard. If you annoy him again, I won't have the influence to protect you — and nobody else will give a damn.'

Singh held up a pudgy, stubby-fingered hand with only moderately clean nails. 'I hear you,' he said.

'Good,' said Mohammad.

Chelsea heard her. Back early from the jail when Jasper had refused to see her, she had walked into the house and followed the sound of voices. Marcus was talking to someone. She wondered who it could be.

He was morose and alone most of the time. He never invited friends home. It was odd that he should have a guest. The voice sounded familiar as well — a low, musical tone with that slightly lyrical cadence of the Malay. Who could it be?

To her utter amazement it was Sharifah. Chelsea was speechless with shock. Was no place sacrosanct? How dare that woman set foot in her house? Alan was dead. Did she think that she had any rights in his conjugal home? And then she heard the sentence that drove all other thoughts from her mind, 'Marcus, the police think you killed your father!'

She was at the door now, unseen by the two of them. They were engrossed in each other. It was the perfect stage entrance. There were overtones of tragedy with perhaps a hint of farce. All she knew was that she was not the main character in the unfolding play. That role now belonged to her son.

Instead of throwing Sharifah off the premises with all the raw rage she could summon, she found herself asking quietly, 'How do you know? How do you know they suspect Marcus? What about Jasper?'

She might as well have yelled. Her words fell on the silent tableau like oversized hailstones. The pair whirled to look at her. They were of different ethnicities, the pair of them, but their expressions — pale and frightened, eyes wide and mouths slightly open — gave them such a strong similarity of appearance that they might have been siblings.

Marcus spoke automatically. 'This has nothing to do with you, Mum.'

Sharifah said, 'I'm so sorry. I wouldn't have come here. But I had to warn Marcus.'

Chelsea barely heard them, barely registered their surprise to see her. She ignored the dismissal and apology with equal indifference. She said again, 'How do you know they suspect Marcus?'

Sharifah turned to Marcus for guidance but he was looking at his mother. His expression revealed how he was torn between a desperate desire to lean on her strength and a reluctance to expose her to more pain.

Sharifah said quietly, opting for full disclosure, 'The police came to see me.'

'What did they say?'

'That they were no longer certain of Jasper's guilt — they didn't say why — and their next best bet was me or Marcus.'

'Why you?'

'They thought I might have quarrelled

with Alan. That perhaps he dumped me and I was angry or jealous.'

'And were you?'

Chelsea's questions were staccato and to the point. She wanted to understand fully what they were up against. She forced the fear that welled up in volcanic waves back down through a sheer effort of will. She visualised the terror and compressed it into a small black ball and placed it neatly at the bottom of her stomach. There would be time for that later. Right now she had to question this woman until she fully understood the danger that Marcus was in. He was her eldest son. Whatever information Sharifah had, whether it was hurtful or exculpatory, she needed to know it.

Sharifah said, 'No. I still believed we were going to get married.'

'Still believed? What does that mean?'

The younger woman hung her head, unable to look at either of them in the eye as she was forced to discuss her relationship with the husband of one and the father of the other. 'I'm beginning to realise now that Alan never had any intention of marrying me. That was not the sort of man he was.'

Chelsea dismissed this as irrelevant. She tucked a tendril of hair that was escaping its pins back behind her ear and asked, 'How did the police know about your relationship with Marcus?'

Sharifah shrugged. 'I'm not sure. From the way they talked, they seemed to have some sort of tape.'

Chelsea sat down suddenly. 'My God,' she whispered to herself, completely forgetting the presence of the others. 'I forgot to send the money.'

'What are you talking about, Mum?' asked Marcus.

Chelsea's hands were shaking. She put them on the arms of the chair, trying to steady herself. Had she brought this catastrophe down on them?

'A private investigator — I hired him during the divorce and custody hearings to dig up some proof of adultery to help my case against your father. He turned up the other day with a tape. It had all three of you on it — at some club.'

From their worried faces she could tell that they knew immediately which occasion it must have been — and they both knew it would not have looked good.

'But how would the police have got a copy?' asked Sharifah, confused.

'I forgot to send the money. The investigator asked for two thousand ringgit. I came to see you.' She looked at Sharifah. 'And I just clean forgot to pay him. He must have decided to teach me a lesson.'

Marcus guessed how much his mother was suffering from the thought that she had led the police directly to him. He sat down on the arm of her chair and gave her a hug. 'They would have found out about Sharifah and me somehow. It's not your fault, Mum.'

Chelsea shook her head. 'I don't know, son.'

Sharifah interrupted them. 'I didn't finish. I said I was with you, Marcus — when your . . . when Alan was shot. But I didn't really know when that was so I wasn't very convincing. I'm not sure they believed me.'

'You alibied me?'

Sharifah nodded, a little sheepishly.

'Why?'

There was a pause while she considered her answer. Her young, fresh face was thoughtful, like a student pondering an exam question, not an adulteress considering an alibi.

At last, she said, 'They think you did it because of me. I guess that makes it my fault that you're in trouble. I just wanted to try and make things better.' She trailed off.

Chelsea guessed that she was longing to make things better, not just in the context of the suspicion the police had about Marcus, but with everything else she had done in the last few months. This was a young, smart woman who had somehow come adrift and made some truly appalling decisions. Chelsea might have found it in her heart to feel just a tiny bit sorry for her if it wasn't for the fact that the consequences of her actions were about to engulf her son.

'Do you think I did it?' The question was blurted out more stridently than Marcus intended. He was looking at her but she suspected the tension in his body was for fear of Sharifah's answer.

Chelsea said immediately and as reassuringly as she could, 'Of course not, darling. I *know* you had nothing to do with it. You've told me so and I believe you.'

Sharifah did not say anything and Marcus, unable to bear her non-committal silence, said almost roughly, 'What about you?'

'No,' she said quietly, 'I don't think you did it.'

Marcus sat down suddenly. He said, 'That means a lot.'

Sharifah said briskly, 'I guess it's not what we think that's important. It's what the police believe that counts. So let's get this alibi straight.'

Marcus said, 'I don't want you to have to

lie to protect me.'

Chelsea said sharply, 'Don't be ridiculous, Marcus. Sharifah is trying to help — and you're in no position to refuse.'

'But she could really get into trouble . . .'

'You could hang,' said Chelsea.

There was a silence after Chelsea had so brutally pointed out Marcus's fate if he was found guilty of murder. In their imaginations, all three could picture Marcus at dawn, a hood over his head, with only a couple of policemen and a doctor for company, waiting to drop through the trapdoor with the thick, rough rope wound around his neck.

Sharifah realised that her instinctive attempt to protect Marcus would have to be carried through in earnest. This could not be limited to a lie told under the pressure of circumstances.

She said, 'Your mother is right, Marcus.'

He was white faced but resolute. 'I still don't like it.'

Chelsea brushed a greasy strand of hair away from his forehead and said gently, 'We understand that, Marcus. I don't think we're looking at Sharifah testifying in court or anything like that. But if you have an alibi, the police will keep looking for the murderer and not stop with you. Once they've found someone else, we won't have to pretend any more.'

'I wonder why they don't think Uncle Jasper killed Dad? Why haven't they released him if he didn't do it?'

Chelsea shook her head ruefully. 'That may be my fault as well. I persuaded the policeman from Singapore to keep looking into things. I just didn't believe Jasper murdered Alan. I had no idea there was evidence out there that would implicate you.'

'It was a Sikh policeman who came to see me,' said Sharifah. 'He was pretty unpleasant — really aggressive and accusing.'

'It could be that they still think Jasper did it. But thanks to my kicking up a fuss, they're looking around a bit as well.' Chelsea turned to her son and said with something approaching bleakness, 'I'm so sorry, Marcus. Everything I've done seems to have gotten you into more trouble — it was the last thing I intended.'

Marcus shrugged. 'Let's not concentrate on what we could have done different, Mum. It's water under the bridge.'

Sharifah said practically, 'Someone needs to tell me when Alan was killed. And we need a good story about where we were at the time and what we were doing.'

The three sat down, wife, son and girl-friend of a murdered man, and tried to concoct an alibi.

The newspapers the next morning caught them all completely by surprise. Singh saw them first. He was up early — unable to sleep — which was very unusual for him. He normally slept, not like a baby, awake every few hours, but like a tired six-year-old, completely and utterly knocked out by a day's exertions. Contrary to what his sister suspected, he had no difficulty sleeping through his own snoring. But he had drunk too much coffee the previous night, his sister had annoyed him with a tedious nag about some wedding that he should have attended but didn't, the mattress in the room was filled with lumpy cotton and the small bedroom was either unbearably stuffy or, if he turned on the air-conditioning, an icebox. So he got out of bed just as dawn was breaking, wandered around the house looking for the source of coffee and heard the thump of the newspaper landing on the front porch.

It was a thick wad of newsprint tied up in a rubber band that snapped against his hand the minute he picked it up. Singh grimaced. It was going to be one of those days.

To his relief, his sister appeared at the door, bleary-eyed but instinctively hospitable. 'Coffee?'

He nodded curtly and sat down at the small table outside. A few potted plants provided the only hint of green to the tiled 'garden' and in the distance he could hear birdsong as well as the guttural cooing of pigeons. The day was still cool. The tropical sun was just a sliver on the horizon. Singh felt almost relaxed. He took the coffee his sister proffered with a muttered thanks and unfolded the paper.

It was the lead story on the front page. Three large, slightly grainy, but immediately recognisable faces were side by side looking out at the reader. Sharifah looked beautiful and worried, Marcus looked distraught and Alan was smug. Singh recognised the photos as being lifted from the disc. He wondered how the papers had got hold of it. The same place the police had got it, he supposed. Not content with earning brownie points with the police, the source of the disc had cashed in as well. It really didn't matter now. The cat was out of the bag and far away.

There were so many font sizes on the cover — headlines, by-lines, sub-headings — it was difficult to take in at first. 'Alan

Lee's Girlfriend', 'Night Club Rumpus', 'Father, Son and the Woman Who Came Between Them'. There was more inside. 'See pages 3–12 for more details.' Singh read the articles slowly. The newspaper had extrapolated wildly from the facts at its disposal. It was interesting that within the same newspaper, individual columnists had put a different spin on where the blame should lie for the sordid turn of events. There were articles that painted Sharifah as a *femme fatale* and others that had her as the exploited sweet young thing. Some journalists laid the blame squarely on Alan Lee — implying it was hardly surprising that he was murdered. It had only been a matter of time. Others pointed out that the Moslem girlfriend was evidence that Alan had intended his conversion to Islam and those who had suggested it was a cynical ploy to gain custody of his children had been proven wrong once and for all.

Only Marcus emerged without blame — but he was made to look like a pathetic young thing, superseded by his own father in the affections of his girlfriend. The newspaper stopped just short of suggesting that motives for murder abounded in the love triangle they had discovered. Jasper's confession was a bulwark against that particular storyline — but they would have a field day when Jasper was eventually released. Singh shook his head. An ugly case was getting uglier. His thoughts turned to Chelsea. She was going to be a very unhappy woman when she saw the papers that morning.

Mohammad ordered Jasper's release. When Singh heard, he was furious.

'Why in God's name did you do that?'

'He's innocent,' replied Mohammad patiently.

'You know and I know that has nothing to do with it. I'm not asking you why you released him, I'm asking you why you released him *now!*'

'It seemed like good timing. The other suspects more or less know that we don't think Jasper did it any more.'

'Good timing?' Singh almost exploded with rage. 'How can this be good timing? About the only thing the newspapers didn't do this morning was accuse Marcus Lee of murder. By tomorrow, even that will change.'

'That's why I did it,' confessed Mohammad unexpectedly.

'What do you mean?' Singh's patience was long gone. He snapped at his Malaysian counterpart like a bad tempered dog.

'Unlike you, I'm trying to find a murderer!' The phlegmatic Inspector Mohammad was getting annoyed.

'What's that supposed to mean?'

'*I* am trying to catch a murderer.' Mohammad enunciated each word carefully as if he was talking to someone of subnormal intelligence. '*You* are trying to protect Chelsea Liew from the "slings and arrows of outrageous fortune".'

Singh did not know it but it was a sign of how angry Mohammad was when he started quoting Shakespeare. Shukor tried to catch the Singaporean's eye but to no avail. The Sikh was six inches shorter but toe to toe with Mohammad and neither was backing down.

'That's nonsense anyway,' said Singh through gritted teeth. 'She's not even a real suspect any more.'

'That's precisely what I mean. Your remit was to protect her from being hanged for a murder she didn't commit, not shield her from the harsh winds of fate. If Marcus Lee killed his father, he's going to swing for it. If we let the newspapers have a go at him, he might do something silly and give himself away. You might not have noticed but we are down to a small band of suspects with no way of narrowing the list further.'

Singh looked at the other man thoughtfully. Was he right? Had he, a policeman who prided himself on his objectivity, who prided himself on never losing sight of the endgame, so lost his sense of perspective that he was no longer looking for a murderer but just trying to protect a woman who had caught his fancy?

Mohammad sensed that he had caused at least a pinprick of doubt and was satisfied. He said, 'I'm off to bring Douglas Wee in for questioning.'

Met with blank stares from the others, he said impatiently, 'You know, Lee Kian Min's latest sacrificial lamb.' And then perhaps regretting his harsh words a little bit, he said, 'I'll call you in when I've got him — you might want to sit in.'

Singh nodded absently and the other man beckoned to Shukor and left. Inspector Singh sat down on a stool and bent over to tie a shoe-lace. He felt slightly light-headed from doubling over and squashing his huge gut. He sat up once more, waited for the dizziness to pass and pondered Mohammad's words.

It was possible, he decided, that he was not behaving as professionally as was his norm. It might be about Chelsea but he thought it was also partly because he was not in Singapore. There, constrained by superiors who distrusted him, colleagues who were suspicious of his methods, subordinates who feared him and the endless red tape that engulfed any investigation, he did not have the freedom to follow his own instincts so single-mindedly. But here he was functioning partly as a private investigator and partly as some consultant flown in for his two cents' worth of advice. It had led to a feeling of freedom from the normal constraints of police work.

After all, back in Singapore he would hardly have agreed to work freelance for an ex-murder suspect to prove someone innocent. He would never have gone to visit a suspect and then let a junior policeman rough the suspect up, not even one as deserving of a good kicking as Lee Kian Min. It was this free and easy Kuala Lumpur society with its hard edge of aggression that had sucked him insidiously into its culture. Singh shook his head. What did they put in the water in these parts? The stuff they pumped over to Singapore was a less potent blend.

Marcus woke up that morning in a good mood. Considering that he was suspected of murder, he had slept well. He got out of bed, showered quickly, brushed his teeth vigorously and dressed. Marcus did not lack self-awareness so he was perfectly aware that his good cheer was the result of Sharifah's apparent concern for his welfare. It was absurd that the goodwill of a woman who had pretty much ruined his life should have the power to raise his spirits this way. But there was no doubt — he felt great. And with the careful alibi they had worked out the previous evening, he felt safe too.

Then he saw the newspapers. Marcus was only seventeen. When he saw how public his humiliation was to be, how impossible it would be to forget the past and reconnect with Sharifah, he sat down on his bed and sobbed — big, heavy, dehydrating tears — like a child who had lost something precious.

Chelsea overslept. As a result she did not wake up to the newspapers like the other protagonists. She missed three frantic calls from her civil lawyer and two from her Syariah lawyer. When she got up it was close to eleven in the morning. She reached for her expensive wristwatch, which she took off and kept by the bedside table at night, and looked at the time in surprise. She did not feel like she had slept for twelve hours. Her eyes were dry and her head was full of what felt like clogging strands of cobwebs. Her mouth tasted like it had done after three weeks of prison food. She dragged herself out of bed and walked slowly to the bathroom.

She thought ruefully that she looked exactly like a woman who had been through a lot. Her skin was stretched taut over the bones, her irises were faded and the whites of her eyes had a hint of yellow — like the early stages of jaundice. She remembered that all three of her children had been born with jaundice, tiny things with yellow feet and eyes to match their new-born skin, lying under hospital ultra-violet lamps in little wrap-around sunglasses. She had been panic stricken when it was Marcus, only moderately worried with the second and had taken the newborn jaundice of her third child in her stride. Experience facilitated the ability to judge whether a situation was as bad as one feared — a mother's instinctive fears could be trumped by the medical certainties. Could it be that her worry about Marcus was misplaced? It was impossible to know. She liked the fat policeman from Singapore. She admired his ability to lumber towards his goal, like a short-sighted rhino making a beeline towards lunch, ignoring all distractions. She had appreciated his support when she was isolated in the physical confines of the Malaysian jail and the mental prison that Alan had created for her. But she was under no illusions — Singh was not going to ignore the truth for her. If Marcus had killed Alan, and he found some evidence, there would be no dereliction of duty on his part.

Chelsea stood under the hot shower and turned it on. She turned her face to the water and tried to wash away the worries and the wrinkles. One of the true advantages of wealth, she decided, was a high-powered shower. She remembered the bathroom in the small house where she grew up. There was no hot water, of course. The whole household bathed using a plastic bucket to pour cold water from a large, tiled receptacle in one corner of the bathroom. Floors were cement, slippery and always wet. Soap was very pink and harsh on the skin. And the towels — Chelsea smiled when she remembered the threadbare towels, thin, cotton rectangles with hardly any water-absorbing qualities.

She dried herself quickly on a carpet-sized, fluffy towel. She considered make-up and jewellery but eschewed both. She understood public opinion. This was not the time to appear too much in control. She debated what her first step of the day should be. Perhaps she should contact Inspector Singh and somehow convince him that her son was innocent. She paused in the middle of the thought. Could she be convincing? She admitted to herself that she was not sure that Marcus had not killed Alan. At any time when he was growing up she would have sworn that her gentle son, who would weep over a dead kitten or spend hours digging in the garden for worms to feed a small mynah bird that had fallen from its nest, was incapable of harming anyone. But the perfect storm of events that he had encountered would have left him completely off balance.

Chelsea almost wished that she had not insisted to Singh that Jasper was innocent. Did she really mean that? she wondered. Would she prefer that an innocent man was hanged in place of her son? She acknowledged that, while her conscience spoke out firmly against leaving Jasper unaided, her heart was much less certain.

Chelsea heard the doorbell and grimaced. The last thing she wanted was a visitor right now. She peeked out from behind the curtain and saw to her surprise that it was Jasper. Her brief pleasure was immediately swamped by the confirmation of her fears. If the police had released Jasper, they must be on the trail of her son.

EIGHTEEN

Jasper was dressed in civilian clothes that were too big for him. His blue jeans and white shirt were clean but not pressed. He was not wearing socks. His hair was a little too long and he had a furtive air that would have seemed appropriate in prison but was at odds with his luxurious surroundings in Alan Lee's home. Chelsea had run down the stairs, opened the front door and hugged him tightly. He stood stiffly in her embrace and then let her usher him into the house. She made him sit down, fussed over him, asked him what he wanted to eat or drink and whether she should have lunch cooked for him. He sat on the edge of his chair with his hands on his knees, quite still, except for a finger and thumb that picked nervously at a loose thread on his jeans.

She realised that there was something wrong, sat down in a chair opposite him and said in a gentle tone, 'What is it, Jasper?'

He did not answer and she did not press him immediately. She understood the first feeling of freedom. There was relief, of course, but also a sense of spaces that were too big and contained too much nothing-ness. Choice was oppressive on the outside. Chelsea had found it difficult to decide what to wear and what to eat when she was first released. But it had passed quickly, and it would be the same for Jasper. Neither of them had been inside for that long.

She asked, 'Did you get out yesterday?'

He shook his head. 'No, this morning.'

'And you came straight to see me? That's very kind of you, Jasper.'

He looked up at her when she said this but then turned his glance to the floor again, blinking slightly as if she was too bright a light that he had looked at directly.

Chelsea opted for a conversational tone. 'As you can see, I'm bearing up.'

He spoke in a half whisper, 'I'm glad of that, of course.'

Jasper did not sound glad, he sounded worried and tired. She wondered again why he had come to her almost as soon as he was released.

'Why did they let you go? Did you change your mind about the confession?'

Jasper nodded once.

She said, unconsciously echoing his words, 'Well, *I'm* glad of that!' She continued, 'Although I'll never understand why you confessed in the first place . . .'

This provoked a response. He spoke quietly. 'I did it for you.'

Marcus made up his mind. He got into the small Mercedes SLK that his father had bought him when he had obtained his driving licence. His mother was furious but he, Marcus, had been so smug. He knew·he was just a spoilt, rich kid — but damn, it had its moments. Marcus did not see himself as exceptionally wasteful or lazy. He was not dishonest. Having too much money hadn't ruined him. It was having a father who had engineered a public humiliation from the grave that had destroyed him. Marcus thought to himself that although he felt like the wronged party, he had not done Sharifah any favours by introducing her to his father. She had been a joyful, engaged teenager looking forward to a bright future as a scientist. He'd never understood that ambition — he hated chemistry and physics and all the other impossible subjects. He'd probably have gone to a third-rate university, got some sort of degree in marketing or business administration and joined the family business. His mother would not have been happy about that but what choice did he have? He wasn't brimming with any particular talent. Marcus realised that he was thinking about his future plans in the past tense. So be it, his subconscious had raced ahead of him.

He pulled up at traffic lights turning red. The car was so silent he wondered for a second if it had stalled. It would be a mundane way to have his plans thwarted. But no, he could hear the faint purring of the powerful engine. The light turned green and he accelerated out of the blocks, leaving the other cars far behind. He rarely put the car through its paces — he was content just to have it — and had never felt a strong desire to treat the highways as his own personal racetrack.

But today was different. His personal misery had become a public ordeal. The newspapers had not even latched on to the possibility that he might have killed his father — that would be tomorrow's news. He thought about school. How would he ever be able to go back? And it was not just school. Wherever he went, restaurants, bookshops, the guy under the umbrella at the bottom of the road who sold news-papers . . . all of them would know him, not just as the son of that larger-than-life, even in death, figure — Alan Lee — but also as the poor sap who had not been able to keep his girlfriend away from a man thirty years older than him, and his own father to boot.

As he drove down the street, weaving in and out of traffic, he saw a beautiful Chinese woman with a long, easy stride and was reminded of his mother. It had been really embarrassing at first, having a former model for a mother. All the kids had teased him and asked him to strut his stuff down the school aisles. But it was good-natured fun. It was not their fault that he was not particularly good looking — pleasant-faced in a forgettable way — unlike his striking mother. There were times when he was growing up when he had almost hated her — had not been able to understand why she let his father mistreat her so much. He had even wondered what she had done to deserve it. He knew better now. He remembered her fierce insistence that she believed him, knew he could not have killed anyone, let alone one of his parents. He had known she was lying. How could she know?

Marcus realised that he was being cowardly compared to her. After all, she knew the sheer, bloody awfulness of being gossiped about by strangers and shunned by

313

friends. But she had never taken the easy way out. She was still fighting for her children. Marcus wondered whether he would have had more courage if he had kids. Or was he a fatally flawed character like his own father? After all, he must have some imprint of his father's genes, it was only natural. He wished that he had not thought about children. There was no space in his small two-seater car for regret.

He reached the spot he wanted. A wide, high curve of highway, elevated over one of the rivers that ran through Kuala Lumpur. He accelerated until the car was almost flying. When he had reached the apex of the bridge he wrenched the wheel. In a shard of time, he had ploughed through the barriers and was airborne. The car was propelled through the air until the laws of physics dictated that it slow down. Under the influence of gravity's insistent pull, Marcus was dragged back to earth.

Douglas Wee was a rat. That was Singh's opinion. It was the large front teeth that stuck out and the reddened nostrils — perhaps he was recovering from a cold. His hair was short and somehow furry. The eyes were close set in a pointy face and scanned his surroundings furtively.

'Of course I no kill Alan Lee. What for I want to do that?'

'You tell me,' said Inspector Mohammad, looking at the specimen in front of him with some disgust. He was not yet privy to Singh's theory about the relationship of this man to rats, but he would have been in agreement.

'Why you say I kill Alan Lee? He very big business for my company. Better for me when he alive.'

'So you say, but we have credible evidence that your business interests were best served by his demise,' said Mohammad. The other man's dialect was bringing out the policeman's most idiosyncratic turn of speech. It was hopelessly lost on Douglas Wee.

He merely looked at the tall, dignified Malaysian with genuine bafflement.

Singh stepped in. 'He said better for you if Alan Lee is dead.'

'That not true,' whined the rat.

'Lee Kian Min says you killed Alan,' said Inspector Singh, throwing caution to the winds.

Douglas Wee spat angrily and they all looked at the slimy, bubbly gob of saliva on the interview-room floor.

Singh was unexpectedly reminded of the froth on beer. He scratched his beard, which

315

always itched when he was repulsed by humankind. It was the last two things in the world he wanted associated in his mind, a long cold beer and typhoid.

'Why he say that?'

'We don't know, you tell us!'

Wee looked as if he was gearing up to spit again. A flinty glare from Inspector Mohammad caused him to swallow instead and his Adam's apple bobbed up and down furiously.

'He not like me, one,' said Wee at last, by way of explanation.

'I don't like you either but I'm not accusing you of murder,' pointed out Singh.

Wee reached into his breast pocket, took out a red, silk handkerchief, patted his brow, wiped the beads of sweat, glistening like diamonds on a river bed, off his upper lip, blew his nose hard and said, 'It's business.'

'You're going to have to explain that,' said Mohammad.

'Is very complicated,' said Wee, implying that the police might not have the wit to follow the cut and thrust of his commercial dealings.

'Try us,' said Mohammad ironically.

Wee looked confused again — but decided it was an invitation to speak.

'Lee Timber wants to go into bio-fuels

business . . .'

The policemen around him nodded their awareness of this.

'Got two companies want to buy the oil — sign contract for future oil production. My boss in China very keen. But also another Hong Kong businessman.'

'And Alan didn't want to grow oil palm so you killed him,' stated Singh.

'No, no! At first, Alan no want to grow oil palm but later he change mind.'

'That's not what Kian Min said,' pointed out Inspector Mohammad.

Wee looked cross. 'You want to hear my story or you just want to say I wrong about everything?'

Singh waved him on apologetically and Douglas looked mollified.

'At first, Alan not agree to bio-fuels. But then he make deal with his brother — he want him say that he was a good man in the court — Alan was fighting with his wife.'

Singh's ears, large, sticking out and hairy, pricked up.

'Are you saying that Alan and Kian Min made a deal — favourable character testimony in exchange for agreeing to the new business strategy?' asked Inspector Mohammad.

Wee looked doubtful. 'I think that's what

I'm also saying.' He continued more confidently, he sensed he had their attention now, 'But Alan like my company to sign contract, Kian Min prefer other Hong Kong one. But Alan sign contract with me. Kian Min did not know about it.' He was triumphant. Even in a police station his having landed a deal against fierce competition was a source of pride.

'So what happened after that?'

'Alan got killed,' said Wee in a depressed voice. 'And Kian Min want to get out of contract. But I say "no". He very angry with me. He say contract not legal. I say if he tries to get out I . . . I sue him.'

The hesitation probably indicated that more direct methods of dissuasion had been threatened. The policemen did not care. Douglas Wee was turning out to be a very useful source of information.

'And now he's trying to get you out of the way by telling us you had something to do with Alan Lee's death?'

Wee understood this. He said clearly, 'I think so, yes.'

Singh asked Mohammad, 'But why would Kian Min have led us to this guy when he's just landed him in more trouble?'

Mohammad looked thoughtful. 'I would assume that he didn't know this fellow was on sufficiently good terms with Alan to know so much about their private arrangements.'

'You could be right,' said Singh.

Chelsea did not respond except to look at him, eyes wide with disbelief and, he sensed, an instinctive rejection of what he was asserting. He said again, 'I did it for you.'

She asked, in a quiet voice, her tone suggesting that she dreaded his answer, 'What do you mean?'

His nerves were taut, like the strings of a badminton racquet, and his answer was whipped back. 'What do you think I mean?'

She said, probably untruthfully, 'I really have no idea what you're getting at.'

Jasper went to stand by a window. It was an overdressed piece of glass. There were flimsy day curtains and night curtains of heavy brocade, frills along the top and more brushing the floor. The curtains were tied back with a thick cord, a knot and tassels at the end. He looked out over the well-tended grounds and could see the glint of a pool under the shade of a rain tree. This was what Alan had given the woman he loved and then some — material possessions that reeked of wealth and ostentation. But he had also hit her and tried to take her children away. And in the end he had died — and very few tears were shed by anyone.

Without looking at her, Jasper said, 'I love you.'

She did not respond and he dared not turn around to see her face. He could not bear to see rejection or dismay or even amusement. The silence in the room grew until it was bigger than both of them, a thick fog of unuttered words.

It was Jasper who spoke again, the quiet oppressed him more than her. It had always been the way that the first to declare love was the most vulnerable. He was no different.

He said, 'I guess you've never known that.'

The impulse to speak did not come with the discipline to stop. Jasper was explaining now, begging for understanding, for sympathy, for forgiveness. But he did not beg for his love to be reciprocated because he knew about Ravi, thanks to the policeman from Singapore who had taken such unholy pleasure in breaking the news to him.

Jasper said, 'Since your wedding day. Can you believe it? It was the first time I saw you. I couldn't believe that you were marrying my brother. Not Alan. I knew what he was like — selfish, unfaithful, violent. Do you know, I almost spoke up — when they

320

asked if anyone had objections . . . Can you imagine the scandal if I'd done it?'

She said, 'I wish you had.'

He turned to look at her for the first time and the pain in his heart was intensely physical. He relished it. It made him feel human. This capacity for suffering, for *feeling*, was what distinguished him from his brothers. He could not have this woman but she had given him the most intense emotions he had ever experienced.

Jasper chuckled. 'You might not have thought so at the time.'

She smiled in return but only with her lips and not with her eyes, which remained wary. 'I am really so sorry, Jasper. I had no idea.'

'It's all right. I was probably a bit subtle. I had nothing to offer you, you see. Not compared to this.' His glance took in their opulent surroundings.

Chelsea said, 'I still don't understand why you confessed?' She made the statement a question.

Jasper could see that there was real confusion on her face. She suspected him of having a youthful crush, the remnants of which had lasted for a bit longer than usual. No doubt she believed that his coming over and telling her he loved her was some by-product of his being in prison. He had feared for his life so now he was leaving no stone unturned in his search for emotional catharsis.

'I confessed,' he said slowly, 'because I wanted to save you from prison, from dying. I couldn't bear you to suffer.'

'But . . . but . . .' Chelsea didn't finish the sentence.

He made a clean breast of it. 'I knew I could never be with you, never have you . . . It seemed the best thing I could do was save you. I imagined you having a life with your children . . . without Alan. It was what you deserved — the very least you deserved after what Alan put you through.' He stopped. He had reached the point where he had to explain why he stood on her thick carpet, free. He turned away. He was ashamed of his weakness, but more ashamed of hers. He said, 'But then I found out about . . . Ravi.'

'What?' It was a single word, like the explosion of a firecracker, loud, sudden and echoing.

Jasper said patiently, 'I found out about your boyfriend.'

Chelsea gripped the arms of her chair until her knuckles showed white.

She said, 'Who told you about . . . him?'

'That fat policeman from Singapore. He said you were happy and that you'd had him on the side for a long time. He suggested I was a bit of a fool.' He continued and there was a wealth of bitterness in his voice. 'I felt a bit of a fool . . . There was I imagining that you were alone — that you really needed me, needed my help. But you already had someone.'

Chelsea was silent for so long that Jasper walked over to her chair, willing her to say something, to explain how it was that while he was standing by, ready to offer her all the protection he was capable of, she had turned to someone else.

At last she said, 'I suppose I'm glad — I have to be glad. I never wanted an innocent man — I never wanted *you* — to die trying to protect me. But the inspector was not entirely truthful, I'm afraid.'

She saw hope dawn on his face and knew that she had misled him. She said hurriedly, 'I did have an affair — it was brief, physical and meaningless. I ended it the minute divorce proceedings began. I've not seen Ravi since and I have no intention or desire to do so.'

Jasper sat down so suddenly she thought he might have fallen. He was ashen, defeated.

Chelsea said, 'I'm sorry, Jasper.'

He found a vein of strength and humour he had never suspected he possessed. 'I don't suppose they'll believe me if I confess again?'

Jasper left and Chelsea sat in her chair lost in thought for a few minutes. Jasper's revelations were extraordinary. She knew at the back of her mind that his release put her back in the frame for the murder. But she tried not to think about it. Marcus was also in trouble. That would have to be her first priority. Chelsea tracked down her mobile phone and looked at the missed calls from her lawyers in disgust. What did the vultures want? More fees? She debated whether to ring the Syariah lawyer or the civil lawyer first. She thought the Moslem lawyer shaded the integrity test. Subhas Chandra's primary motive in taking her case was to raise his own profile by being associated with the 'Malaysian divorce of the century', as the press called it at the time. Now that things were not going her way his enthusiasm had waned markedly, although he was still doing a reasonably conscientious, if despairing, job.

The choice, such as it was, was taken out of her hands. The phone vibrated and then its old-fashioned peal filled the room. The number was that of Subhas Chandra, her civil lawyer.

She picked up, feeling a tiny frisson of dread. 'Hello?'

'Mrs Lee, is that you?' The lawyer's great booming voice hurt her eardrum. She moved the phone away and said, 'Yes — I'm sorry I missed your calls. Have there been any developments?'

His voice exploded like a cannon. 'Developments? What do you think? Of course the revelations will have an impact on your case.'

Chelsea was confused and her tone reflected it. 'What revelations?'

There was complete silence at the other end. She said, 'Hello, are you there?'

In a completely normal tone — Subhas Chandra had forgotten to put on his lawyer voice — he said tentatively, 'Today's newspapers? Have you seen them?'

Chelsea shook her head, remembered she was on the phone, and said, 'Not yet. I've been busy this morning.'

'You should take a look.' His voice was still quiet. 'But I'm afraid it's not good news.'

Chelsea told him to hang on and she walked to the dining table where the newspapers were usually placed so she could read them with breakfast if she so chose. It was her usual routine on days when she was not interrupted first thing in the morning by a lover's declaration.

She had never understood the expression 'blood running cold' prior to that moment. It had seemed theatrical, impossible. Now, as she stood there and shivered, she knew precisely what it meant.

Subhas Chandra asked, 'Are you there?'

'Yes,' she whispered.

'Have you got the papers?'

'Yes.'

'It's not good news, I'm afraid.'

Chelsea realised dimly that he was not talking about the shame her son must feel that his father's exploits were front page news. The lawyer would not even know that Jasper was out. This was bad news in some way that she could not even fathom — as if the immediate horror was not enough.

'What do you mean exactly?' Her voice was constricted by the bands of fear around her throat. She doubted the lawyer had heard her.

He must have guessed what she was saying though because he said, 'Custody!'

'What do you mean?'

'Alan had a Moslem girlfriend . . .'

'So?'

'His conversion may have been genuine.'

'Don't be ridiculous! He didn't convert to marry some teenager.'

'All right — you and I know what Alan was like. But the fact is that this will have an impact on the case, civil and Syariah.'

'Spell it out,' Chelsea said curtly. She needed to completely understand what she was up against.

'We've been arguing that the civil courts should determine whether the conversion was genuine. The reason we had a shot at persuading them to look at Alan's sudden religious awakening was because of the *prima facie* injustice of the case. It was difficult to leave you with no remedy. The court of public opinion was on your side and judges don't like to look heartless. But now that there is a small chance Alan was genuine, they are not going to feel the same pressure to help you.'

'OK.'

'That's not all. Even if by some chance they still agree to look at the matter, there's now evidence that the conversion to Islam might have been for real and not just to get the kids — so we could lose.'

'I understand.' Her voice grew harsh. 'You're saying that just because the last of

Alan's numerous infidelities happened to be with a Moslem, I could lose the kids?'

Subhas Chandra said, 'Yes.'

'I assume that my Syariah lawyer, who has also been trying to call me this morning, will have the same view of the matter — that the Syariah courts might use his relationship with Sharifah as evidence that the conversion to Islam was genuine.'

'I would think so. This gives the courts a loophole. It means they don't have to rule on the issue as a matter of principle. To be frank, I think they'd jump at the chance.'

Chelsea looked at her phone — a poisonous piece of plastic and circuitry that could bring her news like this.

The lawyer said, trying to be reassuring, 'At least, with Jasper Lee in jail for Alan's murder, there's no further danger to your son. Otherwise, this evidence — the newspaper story — would raise eyebrows with the police.'

She said automatically, 'Jasper's been released.'

'I beg your pardon?'

Chelsea repeated, 'Jasper's been released. He didn't kill Alan.' She rang off leaving the lawyer at the other end more shocked than he had ever been in his illustrious career.

She debated calling her Syariah lawyer

and decided against it. She would have to speak to him soon, but there was no doubt he would say the same thing — that the judges would use the evidence that the conversion might have been genuine to wash their hands of her. Chelsea hurried up the stairs. She'd better find Marcus and prepare him for the morning papers. Unless he had seen them, in which case she would just have to try and reassure him. Clichés popped into her head — it was always darkest before dawn, even this cloud probably had a silver lining, that which did not break them would make them stronger. Marcus would not be easily convinced.

But he was not in his room. The bed was made, he had showered and changed, but he was not there. She looked out of the window. His car was gone. She reminded herself that she would have to confiscate his sports car now that Alan was not there to stand in her way and then wondered how her mind still had time for the mundane in the face of the unfolding crisis. She guessed that Marcus had gone to see Sharifah.

The doorbell clanged, its electronic sound reverberating around the house. Chelsea hoped it was not Jasper back again. She could not cope with any further emotional outpourings.

She went down and saw the maid let two policemen into the house — Inspectors Singh and Mohammad. She could not believe it. Surely they were not here to rearrest her or arrest Marcus. Both men looked solemn, worried.

Chelsea mentally girded herself. They watched her with deliberately impassive faces. Despite that, she sensed sympathy from them — and it annoyed her. No doubt they had seen the morning papers too. She didn't need their commiserations. She needed them to find the murderer and stop hounding her family.

She asked brusquely, 'What do you want?'

Singh said, 'We have bad news. There's been an accident.'

NINETEEN

Rupert Winfield checked into the Mandarin
Oriental. It was not his usual sort of hotel.
He much preferred backpacker hangouts.
On the other hand, this was not his usual
sort of visit to the city. His plan required
that he reinvent himself, albeit briefly, as
the sort of man who stayed at luxury hotels
and wore expensive, tailored suits. Rupert
pulled back the curtains and gazed at the
Twin Towers. They were so close he felt that
he could lean out of the window and touch
them. The glass pane was reinforced,
though, and there was no way of opening it.
He knew the proximity was an illusion created by the sheer size of the buildings opposite. He supposed they were beautiful,
these immense monuments to man's ability
to dominate nature. There was an appeal in
feeling separate and powerful, almost God-
like in talent and achievement, when compared with the other creatures on earth.

But Rupert had become accustomed to the Penan way. For them, nature was all powerful. Their ability to survive depended on a symbiotic relationship with the jungle around them — not a parasitic one. Rupert wondered why the parasites who lived in cities did not understand the most fundamental tenet of nature — that a parasite eventually kills its host. Did these people not know that if they continued to feed and spread and grow, with the tendrils of their greed wrapping themselves around their host, the day would come when it could no longer sustain them and when it died they would too? How much better was the Penan way that posed no threat to its surroundings? Their practice of *molong* — never taking more than they needed — was in such desperate contrast to the people he could see far below, scurrying about their acquisitive businesses, never content with what they had, always wanting more.

He had never dreamed that the quiet nomadic jungle folk would appeal to some emptiness in his heart and draw him into their culture and traditions. Rupert remembered that they had bestowed on him the honorific title *laki Penan,* which meant 'Penan man'. It was intended as an honour and received by him as such. But these quiet people, in their animal skin clothes with their diet of sago, were not to be left alone to wander through the lush jungles, living off the land, leaving no mark when they moved on, teaching their children the secrets of the forests. The greed of others could not coexist with the selflessness of the Penan with their gentle humour and generous hearts.

Rupert wondered whether it was really necessary for the timber companies to log their way through the Penan's tramping grounds. He suspected they did it not just because of their voracious appetite for hardwoods and the money it brought in, but because of a visceral fear that someday they might have to acknowledge that they were wrong. Everything they had sought and bought had not brought them happiness, let alone contentment. A jungle people dressed in loincloths had known best. It was better to destroy the potential source of such unpalatable truths than have them live to witness the lives of quiet desperation of their tormentors.

He wandered into the luxurious bathroom, almost tripping over the bedding on the floor. He had been forced to sleep on the carpeted floor because the bed was too soft for someone accustomed to hard earth beds or the wooden planks of a native long-house floor. Not that he was sleeping much anyway. Recent events weighed on him too much. It reminded him of the times he had played with the Penan children and they had wrestled with him and sat on his chest until he was short of breath, laughing and giggling with their *laki Penan,* secretly proud that they were brave enough to take such liberties with someone from the outside world.

Rupert had a long bath and a close shave. He looked at himself in the vast mirror. His body was thin and wiry, without a spare ounce of flesh. There was a random collection of scar tissue of many shapes and sizes. The jungle was dangerous for the uninitiated. Still, he had learnt the tricks of survival and there were fewer recent scars than old marks. His learning curve was etched on his body. He cupped his smooth chin in one hand. It looked peculiar. His jaw was several shades lighter than the rest of his weather-beaten face. It was the best he could do. Rupert shrugged. He had learnt from the Penan not to sweat the things he could not change.

The doorbell rang and he slipped on a dressing gown and went to answer it. It was the hairdresser he had asked to be sent up.

He slipped the newspapers out of the cloth bag hanging on the door and sat down to read the latest details on the Lee family scandals while his hair was neatly trimmed for him. It served to keep him abreast of developments but also indicated to the stylist that he was not in the mood for small talk. A second ring was the delivery of the suit he had ordered. He had been fitted for it the previous day and it was ready, as had been promised, within twenty-four hours. Amazing what efficiencies the pursuit of material wealth could engender, thought Rupert while smiling at the man and paying him.

Singh despised himself for his choice of words. 'We have bad news. There's been an accident.'

He had used them before, stood at other doorsteps with information that would crush the recipient and been unable to forewarn or to prepare the ground for what he needed to disclose, except with such triteness.

Watching Chelsea's face drain of blood was like watching the tide go out in fast forward. She at least understood that this was the opening line in a tragedy. She could not speak. She opened her mouth but no words came out. Singh knew he had to break the news to her — but he could not bring himself to do it. This was not one of those instances where knowing was better than not knowing. Ignorance was the last scintilla of protection this woman had.

It was Mohammad who stepped in. He said, reaching out to her and then letting his hand fall to his side, 'It's about Marcus. He's been in an accident . . . a car accident.'

'Is . . . is he . . . dead?'

Singh took hold of Chelsea by her upper arm. She did not seem to notice. Her eyes were fixed on Mohammad's face, trying to read his answer, to anticipate it in that second before he spoke again.

He said, 'No, he's still alive. But it doesn't look good.'

Mohammad had said enough to spur Chelsea into action. She had only taken in the first part. Marcus was still alive. If he was alive, he needed his mother and she needed to get to him.

She said frantically, 'Where is he?'

Singh said, 'Come, we'll take you.'

Shukor was waiting with the car. Mohammad climbed in the front and Chelsea and Singh slid in the back. Shukor set off immediately, slipping the siren onto the roof and weaving through traffic.

Chelsea asked, unnaturally calm, only the fingernails digging into her palms giving away her anxiety, 'What happened?'

Singh said, 'The details are sketchy. He went off a bridge and ended up in a river. He was rescued by people on the banks, just before the car was submerged entirely, and taken to hospital.'

He did not say, there was no need to add to her pain, that eyewitnesses had insisted that the car had accelerated and swerved towards the barriers intentionally.

But Chelsea Liew was no fool. She asked, 'Did he do it on purpose?'

Mohammad interjected from the front, 'Why would you think that?' He was still the policeman on the trail of a murderer.

She was not in the mood for mind games with the police. 'You must have seen the newspapers,' she said tiredly.

Singh answered her original question quietly. 'There's some evidence that it wasn't an accident.'

Chelsea shielded her eyes with a hand and leaned her head against the window.

In twenty minutes they were at the hospital. Shukor dropped them at the main entrance and the small, ill-assorted group of people hurried in. Mohammad, familiar with the layout of the hospital from previous visits in the line of duty, took them directly to the intensive care unit. Chelsea looked around desperately, trying to distinguish her son amongst the patients lying in the ward, all bristling with tubes and wires and bandages and completely unrecognisable.

Mohammad showed his police ID to the nurse at the reception, a matronly figure with iron-grey hair and an air of hard competence, and asked in a low voice, 'Marcus Lee?'

She looked down at the chart on her desk, running a neatly trimmed, unvarnished nail down the list of patients. Chelsea looked at her in agony.

The nurse said, 'He's not here. He's been taken downstairs for emergency surgery. There's a lot to do. They won't be out for a while yet.' And then she glanced at Chelsea and her face softened. She had children of her own. She said, 'There's a waiting room outside the OT — the operating theatre. You can wait there. I'm sure the doctors will be out to tell you how it is going as soon as possible. I will send word down that the family is here.'

Chelsea nodded, her eyes revealing her gratitude.

They turned to leave and the nurse asked,

'Will there be other family arriving? The father?'

Singh wondered if the nurse was the only person in Kuala Lumpur who did not recognise the woman in front of her nor know who the boy on the operating table was.

Chelsea shook her head — she was not expecting anyone else — and went to look for her son.

Kian Min felt pleased with himself. He had heard that Douglas Wee had been picked up by the police. That should act as a warning to him not to mess with the new boss of Lee Timber. Bloody Alan, though — he had not expected that the bastard would sign a contract with the Chinese conglomerate. It was annoying that even from the grave he could ruin well-laid plans for the expansion of the business. Kian Min preferred the Hong Kong company as a partner in the bio-fuels venture purely on commercial grounds. He suspected that Alan had probably been swayed not by Douglas Wee's business acumen but by the combination of prostitutes and alcohol that he wielded so well. Douglas had offered the same entertainment to Kian Min, but he was not interested. Kian Min did not seek the pleasures of the flesh. His thrills were derived from a deal executed, a rival trampled or an opportunity spotted. Women were trouble and not much else. One only had to look at what had happened to Alan — and see his weaknesses manifest in the next generation, if there was any truth in these newspaper reports about Marcus. Kian Min remembered that Marcus, under the Lee patriarch's trust, would inherit the company when he died and felt a flash of irritation. The boy seemed as feckless as his father.

His secretary walked in quietly. He looked up, inquiring but also impatient.

She said, 'I've just had a call, sir. Your nephew, Marcus Lee, has been in an accident. He might not survive.'

She watched him carefully but he gave no outward sign of having heard. She continued uncertainly, 'I'm so sorry, sir. Is there anything you would like me to do?'

'Do? No, you can go. Unless there's anything else.'

She shook her head and walked out, closing the door with the faintest of clicks behind her. He really was a bastard.

Kian Min looked pleased. It looked like Marcus might not live to inherit after all. Perhaps one of Alan's other sons was made of sterner stuff.

Chelsea was alone. The policemen had left. Singh had been reluctant to leave but unable to think of an excuse to hang around. Chelsea called home and explained to the other two boys that she would be late getting back. She sounded normal, cheerful. It was only after she hung up that she allowed herself the luxury of tears. But she quickly dried them. While Marcus was alive she would continue to be strong, even if the foundations of her strength were crumbling under the weight of events.

A shadow fell across her and she looked up. It was Sharifah. Her eyes were bloodshot and her hair was tied up under a scarf. She was dressed in a *baju kurung* but the top half and the bottom were from different pairs. Chelsea thought cynically that if she had set out to look as different as possible from the young woman in the morning's papers she could not have succeeded better.

But then she saw the apprehension in the girl's eyes and felt a wave of compassion wash over her. It had a cleansing effect. It soaked away the last of the ill feeling Chelsea had for this foolish girl.

Sharifah asked, 'I heard on the radio. Is there any news?'

Chelsea shook her head. 'He's still in surgery. I haven't spoken to a doctor yet.'

As if on cue, a doctor in green scrubs and a face mask walked out of the swing doors leading to the operating theatre.

He looked at the two women and inquired politely, as if they were acquaintances who had bumped into each other at an airport somewhere, 'Marcus Lee's family?'

Chelsea said, 'I'm his mother. How is he? Tell me please!'

The doctor sighed, his thick glasses reflecting the bright lights and obscuring his eyes. 'Well, he survived the surgery. It was touch and go.'

Again, Chelsea sifted through the words and latched on to those she wanted to hear. 'He survived? He's going to be all right?'

The surgeon shifted uncomfortably. He had been standing for a long time, bending over the broken body of a young man, trying to fix and rearrange, stitch and join. It was exhausting. His lower back ached, and his neck too, from the strain of the surgery. But he would rather have gone through the whole thing again than discuss a critical case with family.

He said, 'It's too early to tell. He has a lot of impact injuries, a ruptured spleen, collapsed lung, dislocated shoulder, a few broken bones, including all the fingers in his right hand.'

'My God,' said Sharifah in a hushed tone, the magnitude of Marcus's injuries overwhelming her for a moment.

The doctor continued, 'The only reason he survived the accident is that all the airbags in the car deployed on contact with the water. It just cushioned him enough — or the impact would have killed him on the spot.'

Chelsea looked at the blood on the green overalls of the surgeon and felt sick to the stomach. That was Marcus's blood, all over this man. She could taste the bile in the back of her throat and it reminded her of the terrible morning sickness she had suffered when pregnant with Marcus. She had been so ill and yet so proud when he was born.

Chelsea looked up at the doctor and said, 'There's more, isn't there?'

The doctor could not meet her eyes. He tried to look at her but then found himself gazing down at his blood-splattered shoes. He said, 'There was also a blood clot in the front of his brain. We've removed it successfully. But I'm afraid, even if Marcus makes it through post-op, there might be . . . brain damage. It's not unusual in this sort of case.'

'When will you know?'

'Not until he wakes up — which won't be for several days, I'm afraid. We need to keep him heavily sedated or the shock will be too much for his body to handle.'

'Where is he now?'

'Still in there.' The doctor jerked his head backwards towards the operating theatre doors. 'He'll be back in the ICU, the intensive care unit, in a couple of hours if you want to see him.'

Sharifah bit her bottom lip to keep from screaming with the black, spinning horror of it all.

The doctor said warningly, 'He'll be unconscious and won't look good. Don't be too surprised and upset by that.' And then perhaps recognising how facile it was to warn the mother of a probably brain-damaged kid that he might look a bit beat up, he raised a hand in a gesture of nervous leave taking and disappeared into the inner recesses of the hospital.

The three men were in the car on the way back to the police station. Each was lost in his own thoughts. There was complete quiet in the car except for the crackling of the police radio. Mohammad and Singh had been policemen for more than thirty years.

Shukor was a rookie. But none of them had grown callous despite years of exposure to the least attractive aspects of human nature. It was both their strength and, at moments like these, when their judgement was clouded with sympathy, their weakness.

It was Singh who gave some expression to the conflict within. He said, 'I really, really hope we can pin the murder on Kian Min . . . or Ravi.'

There were nods of agreement from the rest. They could relate to that.

It was Mohammad who acted the spoiler this time round. 'It could be the kid.'

'Because he tried to kill himself?' Shukor was the one who asked the question, glancing into his rearview mirror to see how Inspector Singh reacted to the suggestion.

Singh said in a depressed tone, low and gravelly and barely audible, 'It is suggestive. We let Jasper go. Marcus drives his car off a bridge.'

Shukor was the unexpected source of adamant disagreement with his superiors. 'That need not be the reason, sir. He could have been driven to it by today's papers.'

'Really?' asked Inspector Mohammad sceptically. 'He gets a bit embarrassed and he tries to kill himself? Would you do that?'

Shukor was defensive but firm. 'I might if

I were seventeen, sir.'

He could see the other two men consciously try and remember what it was like to be seventeen. It was not such a long journey for Shukor. He could easily recall the sensitivity and the insecurity of a seventeen-year-old. For sure, he thought, he might have tried to kill himself — been at least tempted — if he had found himself in such a public mess as Marcus had done.

Singh had managed the act of travelling back into his own past. He remembered the thin, young cricket player who had been humiliated because he'd been wrongly accused of ball tampering once. He had felt ready to die, his embarrassment was so overwhelming. Perhaps it was unfair to assume that Marcus had killed his father on the evidence of one attempted suicide only.

Mohammad's time machine was working less well. He said doubtfully, 'You might have a point. But I think there was every chance that he guessed we'd come looking for him once we released Jasper — and tried to find a way out.'

TWENTY

When he saw on the news that Jasper had been released, Rupert called him. They agreed to meet at the hotel lobby. They almost didn't recognise each other although it was no more than a week since Rupert had visited Jasper in prison. Jasper, who had been cheerful and relaxed, was crushed and tired, still wearing the same clothes he had gone to see Chelsea in the previous day. Rupert Winfield, who had spent a good part of the last five years living the life of a nomad in the jungle, was conspicuously well-kempt, only his golden brown tan looked too deep to be of the sun-bed variety.

The men shook hands and sat down. They ordered coffees, black for Jasper and a cappuccino for Rupert.

The latter said, as he sipped his frothy hot drink with the slowly melting sprinkle of chocolate, 'I swear, Jasper, the only thing between me and perfect happiness in the jungle was a coffee machine.'

Jasper said ruefully, 'I felt the same way about prison.'

'What was that about, anyway?'

'If it's all right with you, Rupert, I'd prefer not to talk about it.'

Rupert nodded his understanding.

He changed the subject with a forced casualness that would not have fooled most people. But he was talking to a man so lost in a mental maze of his own creation, it passed unnoticed. 'I was just wondering about the office set-up at Lee Timber,' he said.

'Oh? Why?'

'You remember you mentioned that Alan had never been the brains behind the company — it was your dad and, when he died, your other brother, Kian Min?'

'Yes, Alan was just a figurehead — he was too busy playing around and beating his wife to have time for business.'

It was Jasper's turn to ask, 'Are you still disappointed that Alan is dead?'

'It sounds like he deserved a bullet,' said Rupert and then glanced quickly at Jasper to see if he found such strong sentiment misplaced. Rupert was finding it harder to control his emotions than he had expected.

He was making mistakes.

Jasper shrugged. 'That's why the police are having such a tough time. People were queuing up to have a go at him.'

'Well, you know why I was so upset. I wanted to make sure he paid for what he did — evicting the Penan, causing the death of that woman. I had big plans to confront him, force him to acknowledge what he had done.'

'I suppose he did pay for what he did,' said Jasper.

Rupert nodded a half-hearted acknowledgement of the correctness of what Jasper had said. Alan had, after all, been gunned down on the street where he lived.

Jasper grinned at the other man, affectionate but mocking. 'I know, I know — it's not the same unless you get to shoot him yourself!'

He was surprised to see how badly Rupert took his attempt at humour.

'That's not right, Jasper.' He was stuttering. 'Th-that's not r-right. Why would you say such a thing?'

'Damn it! Give me a break, Rupert. I've been in jail for ages. I was just trying to be funny. God knows, I don't feel like being funny. My brother is dead, his wife thinks I'm a fool, my nephew is in hospital, Kian

349

Min is making sure that the Lee legacy is safe, Lee Timber continues to destroy everything I've sought to preserve . . .'

He buried his face in his hands and Rupert patted him awkwardly on the shoulder.

'I'm sorry, mate. I'm just a bit touchy myself.'

There was no response from Jasper, so he continued hesitantly, 'I'm going to see Kian Min. I've an appointment next week.'

Jasper looked up, sipped his coffee and grimaced. 'I need something much stronger than that.' He waved a waitress over and ordered whiskies for both of them. He looked at his companion and said, 'What are you hoping to achieve?'

Rupert shook his head. 'I have no idea. I just want to explain what's going on in Borneo.'

'You think he doesn't know? He'd have ordered the attacks himself.'

Rupert looked at Jasper, his blue eyes glowing with a curious intensity. 'You really believe that?'

'Of course! But how are you going to get in anyway? Kian Min is not stupid enough to let a Penan sympathiser into his office to harangue him.'

Rupert fingered his suit. 'What do you

think this is? I'm not *laki Penan* any more, I'm Jonathan Hayward, representing the European Commission. I want to buy bio-fuels to meet European Union emissions targets.'

'I wondered at the new look. Jungle metro-sexual, I thought of calling it.'

Rupert laughed but then asked with sudden, absolute seriousness, 'But can it work?'

'It's a good plan,' acknowledged Jasper reluctantly. 'Kian Min's greatest weakness is his greed. I like it. You give him hell!'

'I plan to,' said Rupert. 'I certainly plan to.'

He drained his whisky in one gulp, feeling the warmth descend until he had a literal fire in his belly.

'There's one more thing . . .' Rupert reached into his pocket and took out a sealed envelope. 'Can you hang on to this? Open it if . . . you'll know when to open it if it becomes necessary.'

Jasper looked at him quizzically. 'What is this? Your last will and testament? Kian Min is not going to shoot you in the middle of his office in downtown Kuala Lumpur!'

Rupert leaned back in his chair. 'Better safe than sorry and all that.'

Chelsea Liew developed a routine. Get the

boys ready for school and send them on their way with cheery smiles and re-assurances about the condition of their older brother. Have a quick breakfast, or perhaps a sandwich in the car, and head for the intensive care unit. Sit down in the chair next to her son, talk to him, read to him or be lost in her own scattered thoughts. Head back in time to meet the younger boys when they got home from school. Spend the afternoon with them while Jasper or Shari-fah took over at the hospital. It tore her apart to be away from Marcus but she felt that she had to provide the younger kids with a semblance of normality. If she dis-appeared from their lives again, it might be too much for them so soon after the death of their father, her incarceration in jail and the hospitalisation of Marcus. So she played Lego and did puzzles and listened to their tales of school and helped them on the monkey bars and with their homework — and all the while she hung on to her mobile with a sweaty palm and worried about Mar-cus.

When the boys sat down to dinner she would go back to the hospital and spend a fitful night in a hard chair — mostly awake but occasionally chased across a dreamscape by her worst nightmares. In the morning, she would make sure she was home again before the boys realised she had spent the night away.

That was the routine. It was punctuated with hushed telephone confrontations with lawyers, her eyes restlessly peering back into the ward, as her legal team warned her that developments were not good, she was not getting anywhere in the courts. She had urgent, difficult conversations with all the specialists that she brought in for second and third and fourth opinions of Marcus's case — elderly types proceeding on instinct born of experience and young swots quoting the latest medical research. None of them could reassure her that Marcus would be all right. None of them, despite much humming and hawing, could suggest a different or better course of treatment than to keep him asleep, let his body rest and recover from the trauma of his injuries and cross their fingers that there would be no permanent brain damage. Her schedule was interrupted by the moments of blind panic when a machine would bleep or she would suddenly fear that Marcus's deep sleep had slipped over the border into perpetual night without her noticing.

The sight of him no longer upset her as much as it had. She was accustomed to the bandages and the tubes to help him breathe, to collect his urine, to intravenously feed him drugs and food and whatever else the nurses in their starched white uniforms took into their heads to add to those soft clear plastic bags of liquid hanging from metal poles. The bruises peeking out from behind bandages, like a canvas of modern art, were slowly moving through the colour charts, red and raw, then blue and purple and, eventually, orange like the rising sun. Some of the swelling had gone down too — she could see that when dressings were changed. The long centipedes of stitches crawling across Marcus's body were no longer traversing their individual fleshy hills of swollen tissue. He was actually getting better. His young body was fighting for his life — ignoring the desire for death that had caused him to drive his car off a bridge in the first place.

But Chelsea still had to worry about the state of his mind. Although she dreaded his waking up still resolute in his desire to put an end to his troubled existence, she was much more afraid that he would recover consciousness and be unable to form a desire whether to live or to die, a human vegetable, with no capacity for decision making.

Through it all, Sharifah was her companion and Jasper was her support. If she had time to think thoughts that were not related to the welfare of her children she might have appreciated the irony — but her thoughts, like a candle spluttering under a ceiling fan, pulled in one direction and then another but, never straying from the wick, were tethered to a single spot.

The women grew thinner but Jasper gained weight. Chelsea and Sharifah were barely able to swallow morsels of food, their stomachs were so shrivelled and twisted with anxiety. But Jasper, who would not have admitted it to anyone in the world, was happy. He had never previously been able to be of service to the woman he loved. His big attempt had backfired. He had, in the clutches of a monster of jealousy, recanted his confession. But now, finally, he was of real use to her.

He did not see Chelsea much. Quite often when he arrived at the hospital it was time for her to go home to the boys. They would exchange a few brief words about Marcus's condition, whether the doctors had made any cryptic remarks about his state, whether his eyelids had quivered, had he seemed in pain, had the nurses topped up his sedation efficiently. She would tell him if she had spoken to the lawyers, if there were any developments in their efforts to convince the civil courts to rule that Alan was a fraud or the Syariah courts to determine that he was the least convincing Moslem they had ever come across. Sometimes Jasper would drop in and play with the boys. He always told Chelsea when he was going to do that — he did not want her to doubt his motives or to imagine that he was trying to ingratiate himself with the children to find a spot in her family.

Once, he came in and found her sobbing quietly, but with such intensity that her shoulders, wrapped in a pashmina to keep her warm in the freezing temperatures of the ICU, were visibly shaking. He put a hand on her shoulder and looked at Marcus, numb with fear. But the boy was still alive, his condition unchanged. He knelt down by the chair and wrapped his arms around her and she whispered through her heartbreak that it was Marcus's eighteenth birthday. He had come of age in a medically induced coma. But then she wiped her eyes on the corner of her wrap and squared her shoulders. Jasper got to his feet and gave her arm a quick squeeze of comfort and fellowship and she smiled at him, her eyes distant, lost in other thoughts.

It was the closest he got to providing her with emotional support instead of practical help — but Jasper was happy.

The police were at a loose end. Singh was running out of leave. They each had a different preference for the murderer. Mohammad was convinced it was Marcus. Singh was sure it was Kian Min. Shukor thought that Ravi had tried to ensure his meal ticket by murdering the wealthy husband of his lover. But despite his best efforts, Shukor had not been able to find any evidence linking Ravi to the crime. And a motive, however persuasive, was not enough for an arrest, especially when the two senior policemen were both convinced that Ravi was too protective of his own skin to risk committing a murder.

Nobody was pointing a finger at Chelsea. Singh, because he acknowledged to himself he was prejudiced in her favour, Shukor because he took his lead from the inspector from Singapore and Mohammad because he could not face arresting the same woman twice. But they all acknowledged that having favourites was utterly irrelevant because they did not have any compelling evidence against any of them. The only suspect against whom they previously had a cut and dried case on the evidence of his confession — Jasper — was a free man. Motives abounded, but evidence was thin on the ground.

Mohammad even wondered out loud if the murderer could have been the proverbial stranger — perhaps scared off before he had robbed the body. Singh was dismissive of the possibility. For a man with as many enemies as Alan Lee to be finally bumped off by a stranger would require a divine providence with a sense of irony and that was not a possibility that Singh was prepared to give credence to — not even if it got Chelsea off the hook for good.

The police were not being idle. They had launched an appeal for witnesses again. The foot soldiers were sent to comb a wider area for the murder weapon. The Lee family home was searched once more as well as Marcus's locker at school and the library. Sharifah's flat was ransacked — although no one really thought she had anything to do with it. Their friends and acquaintances were questioned. Mohammad especially was convinced that Marcus, the wealthy son of a timber magnate, might be able to buy himself a gun but would lack the experience to cover his tracks adequately and they might be able to track down his supplier.

But so far he had not been able to find even a whiff of evidence, perhaps, as Singh had suggested snidely, because there was none to find. Even Kian Min's offices and bachelor flat in Ampang were searched. Shukor had reported back that the apartment was modern, stylish and soulless, a perfect habitat for the man. But there was no physical evidence tying him to the murder.

'The thing is, the only really useful evidence would be the gun,' said Mohammad impatiently. 'And with a bit of time and a cool head it could be almost anywhere.'

Singh rubbed his eyes with his knuckles like a child. 'And hardly anyone with a television would throw the gun away within the vicinity of the crime scene — let alone with something useful on it like fingerprints.'

'Not even Marcus . . .'

'No, he probably watches all the CSIs,' said Singh with disgust.

'None of the possibilities — Chelsea, Marcus, Kian Min — would be stupid enough to be caught with the weapon. It was an audacious murder but, having got away with it, I don't think they're going to screw up now.' Mohammad sounded thoroughly fed up. It was the highest profile case of his career and he was clean out of clues. He brightened up. 'Unless Marcus wakes up and confesses, of course.'

Singh grimaced. 'If he recovers full use of his mental facilities. I don't think the doctors are that optimistic. Anyway, I still don't think he did it.'

Mohammad snapped at Shukor, 'Have they got the car up?'

'Just, sir — and they're going through it — but so far there's been nothing in it. No gun, no farewell note, no confession — nothing!'

'Why should I suddenly get lucky?' asked the Malaysian inspector rhetorically, running his thin fingers through his grey hair until he looked like an Asian Einstein.

Jasper asked her hesitantly, 'Would it be so awful to convert to Islam and keep the children?'

'Jasper, I don't believe in God. My husband became a Moslem in name only to spite me. Can the solution really be for me to fake a religious awakening in order to mislead a court of law into giving me custody over the children I have brought up, loved and who are mine by any sensible measure of parenthood?'

'When you put it like that . . .' said Jasper humorously and Chelsea smiled — a thin, tired but genuinely amused curve of her pale lips.

'Besides, if I convert to Islam it means that Alan is still dictating the way I live my life. But don't worry, I'm not going to allow anyone to separate me from my kids — and that's final.'

'What about that?' Jasper nodded in the direction of Sharifah, who had fallen asleep in a chair with her head resting against the side of Marcus's hospital bed.

'If Marcus comes out of this all right and that girl can give him a reason to live, do you think I would stand in their way?'

'If he wanted to marry her, he'd have to become a Moslem,' Jasper pointed out diffidently.

'That would be his decision and I would support it. It is just not going to be mine. Not if I can help it, anyway.'

'You need to have an escape plan.'

She looked at him and decided after a careful scrutiny of his honest, open, ugly face that she could trust him, really trust him. 'I have made plans,' she said cryptically. She looked around the ward. 'If it wasn't for this . . .' She didn't finish the sentence and Jasper did not inquire further. He was not sure he wanted to hear what she was going to do.

Chelsea stood up. 'I've got to get back to the boys.'

Jasper stood to walk her out and they both turned to look at Marcus. Chelsea always told Marcus when she was leaving and explained that she would be back as soon as she could, she just needed to make sure his brothers were all right. The doctors had told her bluntly that he would not be able to hear her but she was determined not to risk his waking up and wondering where she was.

Chelsea walked around the bed, leaned over, whispered her farewell to Marcus and saw his eyelids flutter. It was not the first time there had been some movement. The doctors had warned her that they were very, very gradually reducing the anaesthetic. But this time, his eyes flickered open, closed again and then opened once more.

Chelsea gasped and said, 'Marcus?'

Sharifah woke up and looked around bleary eyed, remembered where she was with difficulty and then saw Chelsea leaning over Marcus and leapt to her feet. Jasper stayed at the foot of the bed, ready to go to Chelsea's assistance but knowing it was not his place to take the three steps to the bedside.

Marcus's eyes were unfocused, his pupils

dilated, his corneas intricately patterned in red lines. One of his hands was in splints and bandaged, his right, where he had shattered all his fingers against the steering wheel on impact with the water. But his other hand, swollen, with the intravenous needle attached, jerked convulsively and then closed into a fist. His lids closed once more, like the measured descent of theatre curtains. When they opened again, his eyes were wide. His pupils narrowed to a black pin-point in the bright, cold room. He looked at his mother and she willed him, with the entire physical and mental energy that she had at her disposal, to be all right.

Marcus said, 'Mum?'

Chelsea did not cry or fall down on her knees. Bubbles of hysteria floated around and popped against her insides — it felt like champagne in a flute. But she smiled at her son calmly, reassuringly and said, 'I'm here, son. Everything's going to be all right.'

Marcus turned his head slightly and saw Sharifah standing diffidently by his bed, nervous of her reception, and a tiny, pained, stiff smile creased his dry lips.

Sharifah said quietly, taking her cue from Chelsea, 'Your mum's right, everything is going to be fine.'

His smile widened slightly and he nodded, the tiniest of movements, almost imperceptible — but enough.

Chelsea felt a pang that her son should find reassurance not from her, but from Sharifah. But she put the thought aside gamely and let the tears of joy, quivering in her eyes like morning dew on grass, roll silently down her cheeks.

His appointment was at two and he arrived ten minutes late. As a representative of powerful government interests, he did not want to appear needy or anxious. He needed Kian Min on the defensive. Rupert walked in unhurriedly and shook hands with his host. He was dressed well with that hint of extra style that comes with wearing good clothes with confidence. His shades, for the bright Malaysian sun, were resting on his hair and his briefcase was leather, new and discreetly embossed with an expensive designer logo. He wore an old school tie, diagonal stripes in cheery colours. Kian Min recognised it for what it was, an indication that his guest had pedigree.

Rupert said in his plummiest tones, 'Thank you for seeing me at such short notice.'

Kian Min was not to be outdone in a battle for politeness awards. 'It is my pleasure. We at Lee Timber are always happy to welcome people to our business.'

Rupert said solemnly, 'But I understand that I should offer you my condolences . . .'

Kian Min looked puzzled.

'Didn't your brother, the previous head of the company, die recently?'

'Oh, yes, yes. Thank you. We are all very shocked and miss Alan very much,' said Kian Min, recovering quickly.

Rupert allowed himself to look mildly sceptical but said, 'I am sure we are all glad that Lee Timber is in good hands. But perhaps we could get down to business?'

'Can also! What do you want from Lee Timber?'

'Bio-fuel,' said Rupert bluntly. 'Lots of bio-fuel.'

'Well, you come to the right place. We are shifting from logging to oil palm to enter bio-fuels business.'

Rupert said, 'Your brother was a visionary to spot this opportunity so early.'

Lines appeared around Kian Min's mouth, the expression of someone who had bitten into something very sour, but he said, 'Yes, we are proud of him.'

'The European Union would be interested in your crops as soon as they become available. Have you contracted with anyone else?'

'No,' said Kian Min solidly, ignoring the claims of Douglas Wee as well as the expectations of his Hong Kong clients.

'That is good news,' said Rupert, showing off shiny, white teeth in his darkly tanned face. 'But there is a problem,' he continued.

'What is that?'

'The European Union has strict rules about bio-fuels. We cannot have any sourced from protected virgin rainforest or at the expense of indigenous cultures.'

'We only clear secondary forest and farm land,' said Kian Min with an air of great frankness.

'That is not your reputation,' said Rupert, his tone lightly accusing.

'We cannot help all these tree-huggers who always accuse us of doing the wrong thing. But the police never find anything wrong with Lee Timber.'

'Isn't that because you bribe them?'

Kian Min looked irritated. Only his desire to land a really big long-term contract kept him from evicting his visitor. He said stiffly, 'We no do that.'

Rupert patted his briefcase suggestively. 'I have testimony here from the Penan group that you are clearing them off their land. It was passed to me by wildlife activists . . .'

'They are all liars, the Penan,' interrupted

Kian Min angrily. 'You should not believe what they tell you. Lee Timber never does anything illegal.'

'It is not a pretty story. A woman was killed. She was pregnant. You can see why my bosses might be worried.'

'Why they not go to the police?'

'They are a nomadic tribe scattered around Borneo. They may not feel they can trust the police!'

The two men looked at each other.

Rupert changed tactics. He leaned forward in his chair, put both hands on the table, and said, 'Look, Kian Min, we both know you can't make an omelette without breaking some eggs. I need bio-fuels. I have targets to meet, quotas to fill. There isn't any source in the world which would meet our policy guidelines. That's what you get when the rules are written by bureaucrats sitting in small offices in Brussels. I just need to know — can you keep this stuff under wraps?'

'What do you mean?' asked Kian Min cautiously.

'I know you have the officials and police in your pocket. What about the Penan? Can you stop stories like this getting out?'

'Of course,' said Kian Min, growing in confidence. 'A few Penan in loincloths cannot stop Lee Timber!'

'What about this story about the pregnant woman. Is it true?'

Kian Min nodded. 'It was an accident. But a good thing. They will know we mean business. It will be easier next time to chase them out.'

'There will be a next time?'

'Yes — until your bio-fuels are safe.'

'Good, then we only have one more thing to discuss. Is it possible to send your secretary away? This is private.'

'She will not listen.'

'Please, I would feel more comfortable.'

Kian Min recognised the drill. This was the bit where the upstanding representative of a major governmental organisation asked for a kickback.

He pressed the buzzer on his desk and said, 'Mrs Lim, you can go home now.'

'Yes, Mr Lee. Are you sure?'

'Yes.'

Rupert waited for a few moments and then went to the main door, slightly ajar, and peeked out. She was gone.

He came back in and Kian Min said jovially, 'So, how much?'

'Oh, I don't want money,' said Rupert. 'I just wanted to tell you that my real name is Rupert Winfield and the pregnant Penan woman who died was my wife. Her unborn child was my son.'

TWENTY-ONE

Chelsea was at the hospital when she got the news.

'The civil courts have decided, as a matter of law, that they have no choice but to follow the latest precedents on apostasy. Questions of whether an individual is or is not a Moslem are a matter for the Syariah courts under the Federal Constitution.' Subhas Chandra delivered the news in a sober tone.

She said, 'But they didn't ask to see me!'

'It wasn't necessary. They are not deciding as a matter of fact, but of law. They only needed or wanted submissions on law. And the recent precedents, although dealing with apostasy — the right of an individual to renounce Islam as his or her religion — were found to have great importance.'

'All right, I guess I was not expecting much else. So now we wait for the Syariah court?'

'Yes, but apparently they are convening

already . . .'

'And they don't want to see me either?'

'They will only hear testimony if they decide that they are going to examine the authenticity of the conversion to Islam. If they decide as a matter of law that they will not . . .' He was unable to continue. How was he to explain to this woman that all the courts in the land could achieve such a result in an individual case without even hearing from the mother of the children?

As she sat by Marcus's bed, listening to him and Sharifah chat about trivial things, finding pleasure in conversation for its own sake and the sound of each other's voices, her Syariah lawyer called. The Syariah court had decided. Alan Lee, having gone through the official form of conversion to Islam, had been a Moslem and died a Moslem and the children were Moslem too. 'In the circumstances,' he warned heavily, 'they might send court officers to take the children into care.'

'Is there anything else I can do?'

'Appeal — but they might take the kids while you do that.'

'All right,' she said calmly. 'Thank you for trying.'

Chelsea moved quickly. She told Marcus

and Sharifah what she was going to do. They nodded and agreed. Marcus was in hospital, overage and recovering. She would leave him. She did not like it but she had no choice and he understood. Jasper and Sharifah would look after him. She was sure of that.

She picked up the younger boys from school. They were surprised but once re-assured that it was not bad news in any way — the last time they were pulled out early was when their father was killed — they treated the whole thing like an unexpected holiday and were excited and cheerful. Chelsea swung by the house and picked up the pre-packed suitcases, passports, cash and travellers' cheques. She had been preparing for this moment for a while.

They got to the airport without mishap. It was at the check-in for the flight to Australia that there was the first sign of trouble. They were early for the next flight to Sydney and queued up in the carpeted First Class aisle. The clerk was well dressed, well made up, polite and then suddenly worried. Chelsea saw the furrows on her brow appear as she stared at the screen in front of her. Chelsea gripped the hand of her youngest son so tight he protested. She loosened her hold and waited, polite, patient and, inside, a wreck. Was she too late?

The check-in girl got up suddenly, said, 'Excuse me,' and scurried away in her high heels, balancing expertly on the baggage conveyor belt, until she got to a counter a few rows down and had a whispered conversation with a man in a suit. Chelsea leaned on the counter and tried to look bored and slightly impatient. The typical reaction of a rich woman held up by officialdom as opposed to the abductor of her own children desperately trying to flee the country.

The man in the suit came over, accompanied by the clerk, looked at her screen and glanced surreptitiously at the woman and children in front of him. Perhaps he recognised them, or their names, although he showed no sign of it. In any event, he spent a bit of time fiddling with the computer while the boys fidgeted and Chelsea asked in an irritated tone, 'Is there a problem?'

He looked up at this and said heavily, 'Yes, ma'am. For some reason, and I'm sure it must be some mistake, your details, and that of your children, appear on a police list. You are not allowed to leave the country.'

'It's a mistake!' said Chelsea firmly.

'Yes, ma'am, but my hands are tied. I cannot check you in until and unless your name is removed from this list.'

Chelsea thought hard. She would have lost her temper there and then and demanded to be checked in if she thought it might work, but she knew it would be useless.

She leaned forward and said in a low tone, 'I'm sure you recognise me and know my story. They're trying to take my children away from me. Can you please help me?'

He dropped the pretence and said, 'I think the situation is very unfair but if I don't stop you here, immigration will stop you in there.' He nodded towards the departure gates. 'And you might be arrested.'

Chelsea bit her bottom lip to keep it from trembling. What was she going to do?

The Chinese man said softly, 'Your best bet is Johor.'

She didn't understand him. The sound of her heart thumping was muffling his words.

'The border with Singapore — there is so much traffic there, quite often they don't check everything as carefully. That might be your best chance of getting out.'

She looked at him and made up her mind. 'I'll try that,' she said.

Jasper was on the way to the hospital when his phone rang. He picked it up but did not recognise the voice, it was high-pitched and breathless, speaking quickly — not making sense.

Jasper interrupted the caller, 'Who is this? Can you tell me who this is please?'

There was a surprised silence and then Rupert said clearly and slowly, as if Jasper had caused him to climb off some mental treadmill, 'It's me, Rupert Winfield. I just wanted to tell you . . . I've killed your brother.'

'What?' Jasper ejaculated. 'Rupert, are you all right? What are you saying?'

'I'm in Kian Min's office. He's dead. I stabbed him with a Penan blowpipe needle. I dipped the end in one of their poisons.'

'My God, Rupert! Why? What have you done?'

Rupert's voice broke. He had his ending and his revenge and suddenly the terror and pretence of the last few weeks overwhelmed him. He said, 'I told you they killed a pregnant woman?'

Jasper said automatically, 'Yes.' His mind was racing, trying to come to terms with what Rupert had said. Not even sure whether to believe him.

'That woman — she was my wife.'

Inspector Mohammad decided, without telling the others, that he was going to arrest

Lee Kian Min for perjury. He doubted he would be charged, not one of the leading businessmen in the country, but he had enough evidence for an arrest. After all, he had heard it from Kian Min himself, as well as Douglas Wee, that Kian Min had lied in court about his brother's good character in exchange for agreement on the bio-fuels expansion.

Inspector Mohammad firmly believed that he needed a breakthrough in the case. He needed to shake some trees and see what fell out. He had been to see Marcus and Sharifah, trying to break their alibi for the Alan Lee murder, which he knew full well to be false. But they had improved their stories in consultation and he had not pressed as hard as he could have. Marcus was still recovering slowly. He would wait a while before applying more pressure. Chelsea had enough public sympathy without stories about how the brutal Malaysian police force had caused a relapse in the slow recovery of her son. But later, he would turn the screws. Perhaps threaten to charge the boy with attempted suicide. It was still a crime on the statute books, albeit not very often prosecuted.

That left Kian Min and Chelsea. As he was not about to let the other two policemen on the case near Kian Min, he decided to go on his own. It was unlikely that he would resist arrest but Mohammad left a couple of uniformed men downstairs just in case. Probably Kian Min would behave in the customary way of the business élite when confronted with a policeman. He would go quietly and call his expensive lawyers and influential friends *en route.*

Shukor and Singh were instructed to question Chelsea again. Mohammad had told them to and they were willing, not because either of them thought there was any chance she was guilty, but because they were tired of sitting around achieving nothing. Singh knew that he would have to get on a plane in the next couple of days. His leave was almost over, he was not getting anywhere with the investigation and Inspector Mohammad's hospitality was wearing thin, as was his sister's. It was time to be on his way. He would not object to seeing Chelsea one last time. Convey his pleasure that her son looked like surviving his attempted suicide. Perhaps give her a heads-up that the police had nothing and, if she kept her cool, she would ride the murder investigation out. That would not be very professional, but professionalism had not been the hallmark of his conduct in the case to date. Perhaps he was getting old.

The two policemen were disappointed to see her limousine pull out of the house with Chelsea and the boys in the back just as they got there. They were not to know it but Chelsea had stopped at the house to repack. If she was going to try Johor, she needed to travel light.

Singh said idly to Shukor, 'Follow them. They must be going to the hospital. We can talk to her there.'

They drove in silence for a few minutes and then Shukor said, 'She's not going to the hospital, sir.'

'What do you mean?' asked Singh.

'We're heading out of town. This is the road to Seremban.'

'Hmmm, well, do you have anything on this afternoon?'

'No, sir.'

'Let's see where she's going then. Maybe she has a rendezvous with Ravi.'

They drove on, each lost in his own thoughts. The highway was busy but flowing smoothly. Three lanes led to the satellite town of Seremban, packed every morning and every evening with commuters heading to and from the big city of Kuala Lumpur. But in the middle of the afternoon, traffic was bearable. Shukor had no difficulty maintaining a discreet distance from their quarry, a silver S-Class Mercedes with a woman and her two children in the back.

'We're passing Seremban, sir. She's going further south.'

Singh was genuinely taken aback. 'I wouldn't have thought she'd leave Marcus to go for a drive in the country,' he said thoughtfully. He continued abruptly, 'Call in. Find out if there's something we don't know.'

Rupert's revelations had almost destroyed Jasper's ability to think coherently. But he knew he had to if he was to save his friend.

He said to Rupert authoritatively, 'Stay there, don't move. I'm on my way.'

Rupert had protested incoherently, 'No, no . . . stay away. I just called, I'm not sure why I called. I wanted someone to understand why . . .'

Jasper just said, 'Don't worry, Rupert. I know what to do. For God's sake, just wait there. Where's the secretary?'

'Gone home. Kian Min sent her home.'

'All right, sit tight. Lock the door if you can. I'll be there in twenty minutes.'

Jasper drove fast but not recklessly. He didn't want to be stopped by the police. He most certainly didn't want to get involved in some minor fender-bender and have to spend ten precious minutes having an altercation on the streets. He made one stop on his way and recovered a carefully wrapped package tied up in string from a locker at the railway station. It was a strange detour for a man in a hurry but Jasper had his reasons.

He parked his car in the Lee building. There was a security desk where visitors had to sign in but Jasper walked past like someone who belonged and no one stopped him. He knew the way, of course, although he hadn't been back there for years. He was heading for his father's office, where he had played in the corner as a small boy — to Alan's office, where he had exchanged so many harsh words over the years. And now it was Kian Min's office except, if Rupert was to be believed, Kian Min was dead.

The layout worked for him. On other floors the worker bees of Lee Timber went about their cubicle business. They visited the pantry for coffee, stopped at the water coolers for a chat, read the newspapers on the toilet and attended interminable meetings in small windowless rooms. But Kian Min had a big office on a separate floor, with an empty boardroom on one side and his secretary, long gone, protecting the entrance.

Jasper walked in and tried the door. It was unlocked. Rupert had not done as he had suggested. That did not surprise him — he had sounded incoherent. He put a hand on the doorknob and hesitated, afraid of what he might find. Taking a deep breath — he felt he was trying to suck actual courage out of the dry, air-conditioned atmosphere — Jasper turned the knob and pushed. The heavy door turned quietly on its hinges.

It was a very peaceful scene. Kian Min was slumped over his desk. He might have been catching forty winks. Rupert was sitting on the sofa in the reception area tucked away in one corner of the office. His hair was tousled, his tie loosened and his suit jacket flung across a chair. But he smiled at Jasper as if he was perfectly comfortable welcoming people to the scene of his crime.

Jasper walked in, went across to his brother and felt for a pulse. Kian Min was quite dead. It was not some sort of elaborate, highly unfunny joke. He came over and sat across from Rupert in an armchair. He looked at his friend. 'She was your wife?' he asked gently.

A single teardrop followed the laugh lines

on Rupert's face down to the corner of his mouth. He tasted the salt on the tip of his tongue, astonished that his sorrow had such an intense flavour.

He said in a tired voice, 'I came to Kuala Lumpur to confront Alan, but he was dead. I would have gone back to my jungle and my people, maybe died trying to blockade a logging company — I didn't really care what happened to me.' He looked up accusingly at Jasper. 'But then you told me that he' — he nodded in the direction of the slumped figure — 'he was the boss. He would have ordered the clearing of the land — and the killing.'

Jasper nodded but said, 'I had no idea what you had in mind.'

His friend shrugged off the regret. 'How could you?'

Jasper asked, 'How did he die?'

Rupert leaned down over the arm of his chair and picked up a slim, wooden blowpipe. 'I wanted to kill him with a weapon of the Penan. They would never consider taking a life but it seemed fitting somehow. I stabbed him with the poisoned needle.' He smiled suddenly. 'I didn't quite trust myself to use the blowpipe, I'm not that good a shot!'

'What did you use?'

'Tajem latex.'

Jasper nodded. He was familiar with the poison the Penan put on the end of their blowpipe needles to hunt wild boar and mouse deer in the forest. It affected the heart and would kill a small animal instantly and a large animal in minutes. He looked doubtfully at Rupert. 'It was strong enough to kill a grown man?'

'I distilled it a few times. He died almost immediately.'

Jasper nodded. An ancient knowledge with a modern touch — it was a pity Kian Min had no sense of humour.

Rupert continued conversationally, 'He admitted it, you know. He thought it would be what a buyer of his new bio-fuels might want to hear.'

'I'm not surprised,' said Jasper.

He unwrapped the bundle he had brought with him.

Rupert looked at the revealed contents in astonishment. He said, 'Why did you bring a gun?' And then, a trace of resignation in his voice, he said, 'Are you going to kill me?'

'It's not good,' said Shukor, eyeing his superior warily.

'Just tell me — don't try and drip-feed me bad news,' grumbled Singh. He was in a bad mood. He needed a piss but he didn't dare tell Shukor to pull over at a petrol station in case they lost their quarry. What was the matter with the people in the car in front? They must have cast-iron bladders, he thought tetchily.

'I spoke to HQ,' said Shukor. 'The Syariah court has issued a custody order in favour of a Moslem children's home.'

'What? They are taking the kids away from Chelsea and putting them in a *home?*'

'It's the law, sir. There are no family members entitled to custody. None of them are Moslem.'

'But what about Marcus? I can't believe she left him.'

'He's eighteen. The court order did not include him.'

Singh nodded in understanding. He said, 'She's trying to get to Singapore. I'd bet my pension on it.'

'But she's bound to be stopped at the border,' protested Shukor.

'Yes, but she probably thinks she has a better chance there than at the airport.'

'Will Singapore keep her?'

'Probably not, but I'm sure she's just passing through on the way to Australia or somewhere like that.'

Shukor said, 'Well, she's not going to get

through immigration in the first place.'

'Let's go and watch,' was Singh's only response.

'If you're not planning to kill me and he is dead, why have you brought a gun to this party? Celebratory gunfire?'

In the midst of their truly bizarre encounter in an empty office with a dead man nearby, Rupert was showing resilience. It convinced Jasper that he was doing the right thing.

He said, 'Kian Min is dead. I don't want you to hang for it.'

'I don't care,' said Rupert. 'You might notice that I don't have a careful escape route planned? I have no reason to live.'

It was a dramatic sentence delivered calmly. Jasper had no doubt Rupert meant it. But he said, 'I know you feel that way, but there is important work still to be done amongst the Penan. You should honour her memory by trying to preserve her way of life.'

'It's a nice idea,' said Rupert. 'But I just killed a man.'

'That's why I'm here,' said Jasper, picking up the gun carefully with his handkerchief.

'Where did you get that gun anyway?'

'I bought it from some bent copper in Sarawak once. Not sure what I had in mind — defending myself if the cops or the loggers turned nasty, I suppose. It has been very useful.'

'What do you mean?'

'I used it to kill my brother Alan.'

TWENTY-TWO

On reaching the Lee building, Inspector Mohammad nosed around looking for parking. He could have just abandoned the car by the side of the road and left his police ID in the window for any passing traffic warden but he didn't like to do that. He was a conscientious man who preferred to save police privileges for when they were needed, not when they were convenient. He finally found a spot and reversed in carefully. He uncurled his long legs, swung them out of the car and walked towards the building with a spring in his long stride. He was pleased to be doing something. Making Kian Min's life miserable was an added attraction. He was such a slimy bastard. It would be fun to make him squirm in that big office of his. He had tried to be too cunning, sending them after Douglas Wee, another desperately unattractive character — but hardly a murderer. He, Mohammad, had enough evidence to arrest Kian Min for perjury. It was a crime Mohammad took seriously. As a man who did not even tell half-truths, let alone lies, he knew the importance of honest dealings in everyday life. How much more so in the administration of justice? He smiled, self-deprecatory, attractive. A gaggle of secretaries stole a second look. How naïve was he, Mohammad thought, that even after thirty years in the force he was still muttering platitudes about justice to himself?

Inspector Mohammad stopped at the security desk and showed the overweight Indian guard who was dressed in a uniform with an excessive amount of braid and gold bars — private security guards were largely for show — his police ID. It merited a quick glance but that was all. He was waved on without any further curiosity or inquiry.

There were two crossing points into Singapore. The Causeway in Johor Bahru was crowded, old and narrow. It had a parallel train crossing and pedestrian lanes for the thousands of day labourers who worked in Singapore but lived in Johor. Tourist buses lined up in fleets, dropping off passengers and picking them up on the other side. Goods vehicles were stopped and searched and hundreds of cars; shoppers, visitors, business people and relatives — all crossing international borders in their everyday business — clogged the Causeway up further. It was a mess. The Second Link, the other way of getting across, was new, ultra-modern, efficient and attractive. But the tolls to cross over to the other side were also too expensive for most of the flood of travellers to and from the two countries. And it was out of town, not as convenient for residents. Singh saw with approval that Chelsea intended to make for the Causeway. She was thinking — betting her chances were higher with tired officials and a crowded crossing.

As they got closer to the border, Chelsea surprised him. The limousine pulled over. She got out with the kids, tied up her hair and slipped on a pair of sunglasses. The chauffeur opened the boot. He seemed to be remonstrating with her but she was not paying him any attention. She took out a wheelie bag and passed the boys a rucksack each. She shook hands with the driver, slipped him something in an envelope and set off at a brisk, determined pace, the boys trailing in her wake.

Singh watched from the car in admiration. He said, 'She's going in on foot. It's the most crowded bit.'

He gestured for Shukor to pull over. The two men got out of the car and followed the escaping Lee family.

'You killed Alan? Why?'

'For Chelsea . . . his wife. I've always loved her. I thought I was just going to waylay him, talk to him, threaten him to let her keep the kids — that's why I took the gun. But maybe I always knew I wanted him dead.'

'But you changed your mind about the confession . . .'

'Yes, I found out Chelsea had a boyfriend on the side. I was just destroyed by that. I decided that, even though I had killed for her, I didn't need to die for her as well.'

Rupert was stunned by the revelations. For a short while, he had almost forgotten his own despair. He was sitting up, looking intently at Jasper, his sapphire eyes flashing with interest.

Jasper continued, 'It turned out the boyfriend was nothing serious. The cops just lied to me about it. But I was out. And they didn't seem to be keen on rearresting Chelsea or anyone else. Too embarrassed by the cock-ups, I suppose, so I thought maybe I was going to get away with it.'

'But why did you keep the gun? It might

have been found!'

'In case I ever had to prove I did it . . . I never planned to let anyone else hang for my crime.'

'Does Chelsea know?'

'Of course not!'

Rupert asked gently, 'Are you hoping for a happy ending?'

Jasper looked at him and for the first time there was stark, exposed emotion in his voice and eyes. 'I don't know. She depends on me now. That might have to be enough.'

Rupert dragged him back to the present. 'So what do you plan to do now?'

'Where did you stab him?'

'In the neck . . .'

'Well then, that's precisely where I plan to put a bullet. With luck the police will assume that Kian Min killed Alan and then himself in a fit of uncharacteristic remorse.'

'Do you really think we can get away with it?' asked Rupert sceptically.

Jasper sighed. He said at last, 'Look, I don't know. But I do know I don't want you to hang. He' — he nodded in the direction of Kian Min's body — 'deserved what he got. I don't have any better ideas. But you need to get back to Borneo and your people.'

Rupert asked, 'And what about you?'

'I? I would like, more than anything, to have a second chance — to be there for Chelsea if she needs me. This is my best hope too.'

Inspector Singh was growing steadily more irritable. He was a short, fat man in a sweaty turban. The stench of petrol fumes from the cars, buses and lorries, all with their engines running as they waited to cross over into Singapore, was making him light-headed. He slipped on a black patch of oil and would have fallen if Shukor had not grabbed his arm. There was not a dry patch on his shirt, he was perspiring so heavily in the heat. His trousers chafed his thighs and groin. He glared at Shukor, who was still managing to look fresh and neat.

The queue they were in wound back and forth, along the temporary aisles created by bollards. Chelsea and the children were about ten people ahead. He was dreading her turning around and spotting them. But he need not have worried. All her attention was focused on the distant booth with its tired female officer sitting in a small air-conditioned box behind tinted sliding windows, stamping passports with a cursory glance at their owners.

■ ■ ■ ■

Mohammad heard the gunshot in the lift, muffled but distinct. The elevator doors opened with their loud 'ping'. He stepped out into the corridor and looked up and down. Had it been a shot? How could it be? Was it on this floor or had it echoed through the elevator shaft from some other part of the building? He drew his own gun from the holster tucked into the back of his trousers. He was not taking any chances. He walked along slowly, whirling around from time to time. He turned corners abruptly and kept low. He was behaving like a television cop. On the other hand, he had heard a shot, he was sure of that. What was the use of experience if he did not recognise the sharp report of a gun? And television cops, or at least their producers, read the same manuals on how to behave in a potentially hostile situation as did real policemen.

There was no sign of anyone. Not a sound could be heard except for his own heavy breathing. Mohammad straightened up. He had reached Kian Min's office. There was no one at his secretary's desk. The tycoon was probably inside dictating his unpleasant business plans to her, he thought. Nevertheless, he approached cautiously. When he got to the door, he readied his gun, turned the knob slowly, pushed it in and whirled in low, his eyes and his gun following a two hundred and seventy degree trajectory around the room. The only soundtrack accompanying his action film sequence was the thumping of his heart.

There were just two people ahead of her — an old, stooped Chinese man dragging his bag along with difficulty and a young Malay man with a wispy beard and brawny shoulders. And then they were at the counter.

Chelsea slipped the three passports through the slot in the Perspex window and told the boys, for whom the adventure had long since turned into a chore, not to fidget. The immigration official, a woman with bad skin from sitting in traffic fumes and grime all day, a dark blue head scarf pinned neatly under her chin with an official Immigration Department pin, and the most tired, blank eyes Chelsea had ever seen, picked up the passports, typed in the numbers quickly, did not bother to glance back at the screen, picked up her big stamp, opened Chelsea's passport to a blank page, raised her hand to stamp it — and her attention was caught by her screen. Chelsea could see the lights reflected in the woman's name badge. Her heart sank. The official retyped the numbers to check that there was no mistake.

She turned to Chelsea, looking at her for the first time. 'You are not allowed to pass.'

Jasper Lee stood there, gun in hand. Inspector Mohammad's finger tightened a fraction on the trigger of his weapon. Jasper dropped the gun he was holding at his feet and put his hands in the air. He said conversationally, 'Just in time, Inspector Mohammad.'

There was a man slumped over his desk. Inspector Mohammad went closer. He raised a limp wrist, there was no pulse, not even the briefest flutter of life. There was a gaping artery-severing wound on his neck but not a lot of blood. Much less than Mohammad would have expected. The man was well and truly dead. The body seemed cold for someone who had presumably died within the last few minutes, when Mohammad had heard the gunshot. On the other hand, the policeman thought, the room was cold too. It felt like the air-conditioning was turned up high. He raised the dead man slightly, he needed to confirm his identity. He saw that Jasper Lee was now an only child — both his brothers were dead.

Inspector Mohammad called for back-up.

■ ■ ■ ■

'They've stopped her,' said Singh urgently. He hurried forward, ignoring the angry commuters who thought he was trying to cut the queue. Shukor hurried in his wake, saying apologetically, 'Sorry, police. *Lalu. Lalu!* Make way.'

They got to the counter just as Chelsea was turning away. She looked at them in surprise and then said ruefully, 'You had to hound me to the border? Don't worry. Your minions here are up to the job of separating me from my children.'

She had forgotten the boys in that bitter comment. The younger one looked at her, panic in his eyes, tears springing forth. 'Mum, what do you mean? Are you going to leave us again?'

The older child grabbed her arm with both his hands and hung on as if she was a piece of wood on a stormy sea. Their tears came in noisy, angry sobs.

Chelsea looked at the two policemen; her disgust was palpable. She asked, and each word was flung at them like a knife, 'How can this be right?'

Singh made up his mind. He had been sent to protect this woman and he would do it. He leaned towards the immigration official and said, 'Let them go.'

She said, 'I cannot.'

'I'm with the police. She's wanted in Singapore. This is a joint operation. Let them through!'

'ID?'

Singh pulled out his wallet and slid his police ID through. She looked at it and said, 'Singapore police. No authority here. I cannot let them pass.'

Singh was desperate. The crowd behind them was getting impatient, muttering with annoyance at being held up. They formed a phalanx at the counter, preventing people going about their business. They were beginning to attract attention. A moustachioed officer, standing some distance away, was looking at the rumpus, trying to decide whether he should intervene. Singh knew that once someone senior arrived, the game was up.

Shukor stepped in. He held up his ID to the window. He said authoritatively, 'I'm Malaysian police. This is a joint operation. Let them go.'

She visibly wavered and Shukor smiled at her charmingly. 'Don't worry, lah. If there is a problem you can blame me.'

She made up her mind. The young policeman's shoulders were broad enough for her to hide behind if there was trouble.

She picked up her stamp and quickly did all three passports. She passed them to Chelsea, who picked them up with numb, cold fingers. She did not say anything to the policemen. She did not dare — in case it made the immigration official suspicious again. Chelsea looked at them with gratitude in her eyes and hoped they understood. Then she grabbed the boys and hurried towards Singapore.

It took them four hours to drive back to the police headquarters in Kuala Lumpur. Neither man said much. They were not sure what they had done or why they had done it — but it felt right.

Mohammad was waiting for them impatiently. He snapped when they came in looking tired and dishevelled, 'Where have you been?'

'Following Chelsea Liew and the two younger kids,' said Singh wearily. 'But she got away, across the Johor border into Singapore.'

Mohammad looked at them suspiciously. 'You couldn't stop her?'

'No, we just missed her . . .'

Mohammad said, 'Well, she's probably on

her way to Australia by now. Still, it might be for the best.'

Shukor asked, 'You don't suspect her of the murder any more?'

Mohammad said with elaborate casualness, 'Oh, did I not mention? It's case closed on the Alan Lee murder.'

'What? How?' It was Singh who exclaimed.

'Jasper Lee killed his brother.'

'Jasper? How do you know? Did he confess again?'

'Yes, but that's not all,' said Mohammad and proceeded to tell them about his day. About hearing a shot and finding Jasper Lee standing over the body of Kian Min with a gun in his hand.

'You're sure it was the gun that killed Alan?' asked Singh, still trying to take the whole thing in.

'Yes, the ballistics report is back. There's no doubt.'

'And it was that same gun he used on Kian Min?'

'Something a bit odd about that,' confessed Inspector Mohammad. 'Kian Min had a load of poison in his system as well. And the forensics team almost suggests that he was dead *before* the bullet, although it's close. There just wasn't enough blood. In any event, there was a hole in Kian Min's neck that matched the gun in his brother's hand.'

Singh said hesitantly, 'But why did Jasper kill his brothers?'

'We're back to saving the rainforests, I'm afraid.'

Singh scratched his beard thoughtfully. 'I would never have put Jasper down as the type to commit multiple murders . . .'

Mohammad stood up and stuck a hand out. 'Thank you for your assistance in this matter, Inspector Singh. We look forward to greater cooperation between the Malaysian and Singapore police in the future as well. I won't fail to mention your contribution at my press conference.'

Singh's eyes twinkled as he remembered their numerous run-ins. 'Just don't get into the details,' he chortled. He shook the other man's hand and said, 'I have a plane to catch.'

Rupert Winfield could barely understand what had happened.

Jasper had carefully shot Kian Min at close range in the neck, aiming for the point of entry of the blowpipe needle. They had been heading for the lift to get away from the scene when they saw the elevator doors slide open. Only Jasper's quick thinking saved them. He, Rupert, was rooted to the spot. Jasper grabbed his arm, turned the corner sharply and dragged him down the corridor, their footsteps muffled in the thick, pile carpet. They were cornered and desperate until Jasper saw the fire escape door. He hurried them towards it. Flung it open. Shoved Rupert through. Jasper had taken a step forward to follow him but then hesitated. He looked back down the corridor and at Rupert. He said, 'Go back to Borneo. Honour her memory. I will handle things here.'

Rupert had started to protest but Jasper had put a hand up to stop him, put a finger to his lips to demand silence and closed the door firmly on his dumbstruck friend. Rupert stood there on the wrong side of the door for a few long moments. He made up his mind. Rupert ran down eighteen flights of stairs, walked out into the open and hailed a taxi.

And now he was on his way back to Borneo and the Penan people. He would work to save them — do everything in his power to preserve a disappearing people. In memory of his wife, his unborn child and the friend who had given him a second chance.

EPILOGUE

Inspector Mohammad was in a cell with Jasper, recording his confession to the murder of his two brothers. At last they were done and the two men sat looking at each other.

Mohammad said, 'That's your story and you're sticking to it?'

Jasper smiled. 'This time I am, yes.'

The policeman nodded thoughtfully. He seemed to be making up his mind about something but at last he asked, 'How do you explain this then?' He slid an envelope, its seal broken and a letter sticking out of it, towards Jasper.

Jasper stared at it, puzzled. He had a horrid feeling of *déjà vu*. He was not going to be fooled into retracting his confession this time though. Besides, he had produced the murder weapon.

He picked up the letter and read it slowly. At last he looked up and said in an even voice, 'Where did you get this?'

'Your apartment.'

Jasper nodded in acknowledgement. 'I'd completely forgotten about Rupert's letter. Otherwise I would have destroyed it, of course.'

'Why?'

'Kian Min deserved to die.'

'But you didn't kill him.'

Jasper shrugged. 'I killed Alan.'

'Why would you take the blame for what this Rupert Winfield did?'

Jasper picked up the letter between two fingers. He said, 'You've read it. He gave it to me just before he went to see Kian Min. I didn't know what he was planning . . . but he obviously wanted someone to understand why he was going to do . . . what he was going to do.'

'They killed his wife?'

Jasper nodded. 'Yes. She was pregnant. Kian Min was boasting about it just before he died.'

Both men fell silent. Rupert's letter to Jasper lay on the table between them. The plea of a brokenhearted man for some understanding.

'It explains why the body was cold even though I heard the gunshot just a few minutes before and why Kian Min was full of poison,' remarked Mohammad. 'In fact, if you shot him after he was dead — that explains the lack of blood as well.'

Jasper asked, 'What are you going to do?'

Mohammad looked at him. 'You're sure you know what you're doing?'

'They can only hang me once.'

Mohammad fished in a pocket and brought out a clear plastic cigarette lighter. He had found it under his desk — a remnant from the visit of the inspector from Singapore. He ran his thumb over it and a blue and yellow flame flared. Inspector Mohammad picked up Rupert Winfield's letter and held the flame to a corner. He dropped the burning sheet of paper onto the concrete floor and the two men watched it burn, curling and dissolving into ashes.

Jasper said, 'Thank you.'

Mohammad nodded and put the lighter back in his pocket. He suspected that Inspector Singh would have been proud of the use to which it had just been put.

ABOUT THE AUTHOR

Shamini Flint is a Cambridge graduate and was a lawyer with the UK firm Linklaters for ten years, traveling extensively in Asia during that period, before giving up her practice to concentrate on writing. She is the author of several children's books.

The employees of Thorndike Press hope you have enjoyed this Large Print book. All our Thorndike, Wheeler, and Kennebec Large Print titles are designed for easy reading, and all our books are made to last. Other Thorndike Press Large Print books are available at your library, through selected bookstores, or directly from us.

For information about titles, please call:
  (800) 223-1244

or visit our Web site at:
  http://gale.cengage.com/thorndike

To share your comments, please write:
  Publisher
  Thorndike Press
  295 Kennedy Memorial Drive
  Waterville, ME 04901